Christmas at Thrush Green

* * *

Miss Read
with Jenny Dereham

An Orion paperback

First published in Great Britain in 2009
by Orion
This paperback edition published in 2010
by Orion Books Ltd
Orion House, 5 Upper St Martin's Lane,
London WC2H 9EA

An Hachette UK company

7 9 10 8 6

A CIP catalogue record for this book
is available from the British Library.

ISBN 978-1-4091-0254-0

Typeset at the Spartan Press Ltd,
Lymington, Hants

Printed and in Great Britain by Clays Ltd,
St Ives plc

www.orionbooks.co.uk

Miss Read, or in real life Dora Saint, was a teacher by profession who started writing after the Second World War, beginning with light essays written for *Punch* and other journals. She then wrote on educational and country matters and worked as a scriptwriter for the BBC. She has collaborated with her long-time editor, Jenny Dereham, for this new book. Miss Read was married to a schoolmaster for sixty-four years until his death in 2004, and they have one daughter.

In the 1998 New Year Honours list Miss Read was awarded an MBE for her services to literature. She is the author of many immensely popular books, including two autobiographical works, but it is her novels of English rural life for which she is best known. The first of these, *Village School*, was published in 1955, and Miss Read continued to write about the fictitious villages of Fairacre and Thrush Green for many years. She lives in Berkshire.

Books by Miss Read

To Jill
with our love

ACKNOWLEDGEMENTS

I would like to thank my long-time editor, Jenny Dereham, for all the work she has done on this book. We discussed the initial idea, developed the unfolding story-line and then I left her to put that into words, based on my original Thrush Green characters. I am more than happy with the result and hope those people who enjoyed all the other Thrush Green books will enjoy this as much.

Miss Read

I would like to thank a wonderful author for teaching me so much over the past thirty years. This book has been a perfect partnership.

I would also like to thank the following for their help: Mr Ben Cobb, Ophthalmologist; the Macular Disease Society; and the performers of the Nativity in St Laurence's church, West Woodhay, for such brilliant inspiration.

Jenny Dereham

CONTENTS

* * *

CHAPTER ONE

Albert Piggott Makes a Decision

'I know there's a saying that "if March comes in like a lion, it will go out like a lamb",' said Winnie Bailey, gazing out of the kitchen window, 'but is there a saying about this dreadful December wind?'

Jenny, her housekeeper and friend, paused from slicing the carrots she was preparing for lunch and looked through the window, too. The branches of the sturdy chestnut trees on the green – all their leaves gone by now, of course – were being vigorously blown about. Rooks made slow progress across the sky, using their big black wings to balance themselves against the sudden gusts.

'My mother,' Jenny said, resting her knife on the chopping board, 'always used to say that there's no such thing as *bad* weather. Whatever the weather, it is bound to suit someone.'

'Well, I'm not sure who's going to benefit from this

gale. Look, the litter bin on the green has blown over and the contents are scattering all over the place.'

Winnie turned away from the window and watched as Jenny resumed her chopping. There was going to be a nice Irish stew for lunch, with crusty herb dumplings and carrots. She was devoted to Jenny, and the feeling was mutual. It was not that Winnie disliked cooking – in fact, she prided herself on her cherry cake, which invariably won a prize at the village's summer fête – but Jenny had a passion for cooking and Winnie was more than happy to indulge her.

Jenny had come to live with Winnie Bailey after Winnie's husband, Donald, had died some years before. Winnie had found she was a little nervous of living alone in the house which, she had to admit, was really much too big for her. She had thought briefly – but very briefly – of moving somewhere smaller but she loved the house, which stood well back from the road in a pretty garden, and could not bear to leave it. She had lived here for over fifty years with Donald, and there were memories everywhere of him.

There was the little mirror in the hall that they had bought in Swaffham when on holiday in Norfolk one year; they had collected most of the pictures together; and every time Winnie took a safety pin out of the little china bowl on her dressing-table, she remembered Donald buying it for her as a joke. The lettering round the inside of the bowl, 'Greetings from Torquay', was a little faded now, but the memories were still as sharp as if it had been yesterday.

It was not long after Donald's death that Jenny had arrived at work one morning with the news that her elderly parents had at last got a place in an old people's home. It was just in time, too, because their crumbling terrace cottage was scheduled to be pulled down: the whole row had been condemned. She lived there with her parents, looking after them, and Winnie was initially concerned about where Jenny would now live. Then the pieces of the jigsaw fell into place: Jenny needed somewhere to live, and Winnie needed companionship. And so it was that Jenny came to live in the rooms on the top floor of Winnie Bailey's house, an arrangement that suited them both.

' "The north wind doth blow and we shall have snow," ' began Jenny, as she swept the chopped carrots into a saucepan.

' "And what will poor robin do then, poor thing?" ' they both said together, and laughed. They were very content in each other's company.

'I wonder if it'll snow this Christmas?' mused Jenny, lifting the lid of the casserole that she had just taken from the oven. With the pointed end of a knife, she gently tested a piece of lamb to see if it was cooked.

'It would certainly please the children if it does snow,' replied Winnie, looking out of the window again, 'but I have to admit I'd be perfectly happy if it didn't. It makes such a mess of the church we shall no doubt have spent hours cleaning when everyone tramps in with snowy boots.' She turned from the window and sniffed the air

appreciatively. 'My goodness, that does smell good, Jenny! What a treasure you are.'

Jenny beamed. She had been a little worried about Winnie a few weeks ago when the old lady had had to spend several days in bed with a nasty bronchial chest, but that seemed to have gone now and it was comforting to see her in such good spirits.

Winnie Bailey's house was the tallest on the green, standing on the east side of the large expanse of grass which was the hub of the village. Next door lived Frank and Phyllida Hurst in a cottage called Tullivers. Phil Prior, as she had been then, had bought it for herself and her young son Jeremy. To ensure that she could give as much time as possible to the boy – she was estranged from her husband at the time – Phil was anxious to have a job she could do from home. She had always had a good ear for words and so tried her hand at writing short stories. She had been delighted when first one, and then more stories were accepted by a London magazine.

She was a most attractive woman, and her solitary state caused not only a good deal of sympathy from the residents of Thrush Green, but also a few male hearts to flutter.

Phil's settled life was suddenly shattered when news came through that her absent husband had been killed in a car crash. Everyone in Thrush Green rallied round and Phil was always grateful to them for their kindness. But it was not a local man who won Phil's heart, but Frank Hurst, the editor of the magazine that was publishing her stories. When they married, the whole village wished them the happiness they deserved.

Frank and Phil were now in their sitting-room, each with a diary open on their knees. A fire burned in the little hearth and occasionally a gust of the strong wind outside would rattle down the chimney and make the flames dance.

'The problem with giving a drinks party,' said Phil, flicking through the pages of her diary, 'is that one has to find a day when no one else is.'

'At least,' Frank replied, looking up at his pretty wife, 'no one who is going to invite the same people as us.'

Phil giggled. 'Yes, I don't expect we'll clash with any parties that take place in the Woodstock Road.'

'Now, now!' reproved her husband, but he was smiling, too.

The lane down the east side of Thrush Green, past Winnie Bailey's house and Tullivers, ran into the Woodstock Road, in due course reaching that attractive little town and, further on, interesting places such as Stratford-upon-Avon. As with all Cotswold villages, planning regulations were very strict within the designated conservation areas. However, the authorities were less demanding further out and, as everyone grudgingly accepted, new homes had to be built. The houses in the Woodstock Road nearest the green were mostly ones built between the wars but further out, they were newer. An occasional turning would lead off the Woodstock Road into a modern close. Where once there had been fields with contented cows chewing the cud, wildflowers for children to pick, and butterflies to chase with nets, now there was just a spread of look-alike houses. It wasn't that the people who lived here weren't friendly; it's just that they didn't really involve themselves in Thrush Green activities.

'We haven't received any invitations yet,' said Phil, looking at the mantelpiece. 'At least, nothing that would clash with a drinks party. If we are going to go to that charity concert in Lulling, we should do something about the tickets now.'

'You go if you want,' said her husband, 'but personally I'm not too good on string quartets. It's the wrong time of year for that sort of music. I think good, rousing Christmas oratorios are the right kind of music for the festive season.'

'I agree,' said Phil, and she got to her feet, removed the invitation from the mantelpiece and put it on the fire. 'There might be a performance of *The Messiah* on in Oxford. I'll check the local paper on Friday. But let's make a note of going to the carol service at Lulling. I see from the parish magazine that they are having that on the Sunday before Christmas.'

'Agreed!' and they both wrote in their diaries.

'But we are no further forward about the date for our party,' sighed Phil.

There was silence for a minute or two, broken only by the gentle tick of the clock on the mantelpiece, and the occasional crackle from the fire. 'Do you think,' mused Phil, her pencil in her mouth, 'that we might have it on the 20th, *after* the Nativity service?'

'No, we'll be whacked,' said Frank, shaking his head.

'Nonsense! Our contribution will be done and dusted by then,' countered his wife.

Frank and Phil had combined to write the text for the Nativity play that was going to be performed in St Andrew's church the Saturday before Christmas.

'Don't you think everyone will want to get off home? And what about the people who come to the service who we wouldn't ask to the party? Won't they be offended?'

'I don't think they need know. And, anyway,'

continued Phil, 'the people we'd be asking are those involved in the play, so we could call it a post-Nativity party for the workers.'

'Ah, that would be all right. Also, it's unlikely that anyone else is planning a party on the evening of the Nativity play. Yes, my dear, I think that's an excellent day.'

Once more pencils were applied to the diaries.

Frank looked up at Phil. 'That's the easy part. We must now get down to the invitation list, and get them sent out as soon as possible before anyone else has the same bright idea.'

'I need to pop down into Lulling this afternoon, so I'll pick up some invitation cards at Smith's.' Phil looked at her watch. 'And now I must get us some lunch. Will cold lamb and salad do you?'

'Indeed it will, especially if I can have some of that delicious chutney to go with it.'

'Of course!' said Phil, and lightly kissed the top of her husband's head as she made her way to the kitchen.

Although Frank was much older than Phil – in fact, one of his grandchildren was about the same age as Jeremy – the marriage was a very happy one. The inhabitants of Thrush Green thoroughly approved of the Hursts, who played their part in village life to the full.

Harold Shoosmith, a handsome man in his late sixties, was returning home after a morning spent in Lulling. The little market town was half a mile down a steep hill from Thrush Green, and what goes down must come up so

Harold was puffing a bit. His wife Isobel had suggested he should take the car since it was blowing such a gale but Harold was determined to stick to his resolution to walk to Lulling and back whenever possible.

This had been his New Year's resolution the previous January. He hadn't expected to keep going all year, but well-meant teasing from some of his friends had made him all the more determined. He had taken great pleasure in reporting that Dr Lovell had told him at his medical check-up during the summer that he had the blood pressure of an eighteen-year-old.

Today was rather different, he thought, stopping a moment on the green. The wind had been against him on the hill, and it had been hard work. He would take the car, of course, when he had a quantity of shopping to bring back, but today's visit had just been to collect his new spectacles.

As he set off for the last fifty yards across the green to his house, he saw the familiar hunched figure of Albert Piggott, the sexton of St Andrew's, coming out through the churchyard gate. I bet he's off to The Two Pheasants, Harold thought and then smiled as Albert predictably turned left to walk the few yards to the village pub. The day that Albert *didn't* go to the pub would indicate something was very wrong with the old man. In fact, looking at Albert now as the man disappeared inside, he seemed to be more bent than ever, and limping.

I wonder if the time has finally come for him to retire, Harold mused. Perhaps it's something to bring up at the PCC meeting on Wednesday.

The strong wind swirled dead leaves around the green, and Harold put out a hand to catch one as it flew past at head height – and laughed at himself when he missed. He righted the litter bin that had blown over, extracted a soggy plastic bag that had been caught underneath it and placed it inside.

As he approached the end of the green, Harold paused in front of the statue that stood there. It was some years now since he had been involved in erecting the memorial to Thrush Green's most famous son, and he felt very responsible for it. In fact, he noticed that there were some rather unseemly bird droppings down the side of the missionary's face, and he made a mental note to bring his step-ladder over with a bucket and sponge.

'Wretched pigeons,' he muttered.

Nathaniel Patten had been a Thrush Green boy, born when Queen Victoria was on the throne. As a young man, he had gone to Africa as a missionary and had set up a church, a mission hall, a school and the beginnings of a medical centre. Thrush Green still kept in close touch with the African village, and it was Harold who annually organized a fund-raising function of some kind, and ensured that the proceeds were sent to the current administrators of the little hospital.

When he had worked in Africa, he had lived near the small community and admired their hard work and constant cheerfulness. On his return on England and looking for somewhere to retire, he thought where better than the village where Nathaniel Patten had been born? He was delighted that a house on the green, next to the school, had been for sale and quickly bought it. The house had been built at the turn of the nineteenth century for a retired colonel from the Indian Army, and Harold felt that the building would now feel at home with a retired businessman from Africa.

The garden had been a jungle when he arrived and he set to with billhook and shears and soon discovered there was immense satisfaction in clearing the rampant under-growth. He found childish pleasure in the subsequent bonfires and, ever since, looked forward to the autumn chores of cutting down the garden plants and raking up the leaves in order to have a deliciously pungent burn. The evenings would be drawing in, and he would often pull back the sitting-room curtains to see the soft glow of the day's bonfire at the far end of the garden.

'Hello, darling!' he called now as he shut the front door behind him. 'What's for lunch? I'm starving!'

His wife, Isobel, came out of the kitchen to greet him, and helped him off with his overcoat. 'I thought you might have had something in Lulling when you were down there. You're a bit later than you said you'd be.'

'It's so windy it took much longer than usual to get up the hill,' Harold replied. 'It was almost a case of two steps forward and one step back! Are you saying there's no lunch?'

'Of course not!' replied Isobel. 'I'll rustle something up in a jiffy. You go and sit down and have ten minutes with the paper.'

Harold went into the sitting-room, and sank gratefully into his favourite chair. He was indeed a most fortunate man to have found Isobel to be his wife so late in life. They had met when Isobel, recently widowed, had come to stay with an old college friend, Agnes Fogerty, who at the time was one of the teachers at Thrush Green School. When Harold learned that Isobel was planning to return to the Cotswolds where she had lived as a child, he offered to drive her round to look at the various houses for which the estate agents had sent particulars – most of them totally unsuitable, they both agreed. However, Isobel returned to Sussex without finding what she wanted.

After she had gone, Harold realized how much he missed her and the weeks went by very slowly until Isobel returned the following summer to start house-hunting again. Harold was determined not to let the grass grow under his feet a second time and without delay he asked Isobel to marry him. Although her friend Agnes Fogerty had retired, moving to Barton-on-Sea where she shared a house with the school's old head-mistress, Dorothy Watson, Isobel had made friends quickly with many of the Thrush Green residents.

Harold was brought out of his reverie by his wife calling, 'Lunch is ready!' He put his newspaper aside – the crossword would have to wait – and went eagerly to the kitchen.

Harold had been right about Albert Piggott. He was definitely feeling his age, and grunted loudly as he pulled himself up onto his regular bar stool.

'What's all that noise about, then?' asked Mr Jones, the

landlord of The Two Pheasants, reaching for the tankard that Albert particularly favoured.

'It's that dratted wind,' grumbled Albert. 'Gets right into me bones.'

'As does the rain, you're always tellin' us,' said Percy Hodge, the local farmer who was sitting further along the bar.

'And you don't much like it when it's very hot, neither,' added another regular, putting down his paper where he'd been studying the form for the afternoon's racing.

'In fact,' said Mr Jones, pushing the tankard brimming with dark ale across the counter towards Albert, 'you aren't happy unless you're grumbling about something.'

Albert Piggott was an arch-moaner, and was the regular butt of well-meant cracks from his drinking cronies.

'Is there anythin',' took up Percy Hodge, 'that would make you happy, and put a smile on that grumpy ol' face of yours?'

Albert didn't answer, but drank deeply from his tankard. Then he wiped a grubby sleeve across the froth that had lodged itself on his unattractive upper lip, and turned to face his companions.

'There's one easy answer to that! Retire! I've 'ad enough of diggin' and cuttin' and mowin'. And I've certainly 'ad quite enough of clearin' up after folks what dumps their litter in the churchyard. You should've seen it this mornin'! Plastic bags, paper, heaven knows what else. And I only cleared it right through last Friday.'

'I think you'll find that the wind had something to do with it,' said Mr Jones, looking out of the leaded windows of the pub. 'I saw one of the bins had been knocked over, and there was litter flying all over the place. With the wind in this direction, it's bound to end up in the church-yard. Stands to reason.'

'Well, reason or not, I've 'ad enough,' mumbled Albert, and took another huge gulp of beer.

'Are you serious?' asked Percy Hodge. Percy was a respected member of the Thrush Green community. He was a churchwarden and a member of the Parochial Church Council. 'You moan so much, it's hard to tell when you actually mean it.'

'Well, this time I'm serious,' replied Albert. 'After all, I don't need to work at all cos Nelly is doing awright – good girl,' he added somewhat surprisingly. He didn't often praise his wife.

'When I passed the caff the other day,' said the third person drinking at the bar, 'it looked fit to burstin'. Must be doin' well.'

'Hey, less of the caff, Joe,' said Albert rather crossly. 'It's The Fuchsia Bush to you, and it's no caff. It's a tea-shop!'

'Sorry, I'm sure,' replied Joe, turning away so Albert shouldn't see his grin. It was very unusual to hear the old moaner being so supportive of his wife. 'Want 'alf a pint in there, then?'

Albert pushed the tankard across the counter. 'Thanks, Joe, don't mind if I do. Got young Cooke coming over this afternoon so I can take it easy while 'e does all the work.' Albert laughed, which was a mistake since it set off a spasm of coughing. He'd always had a troublesome chest that, together with peptic ulcers, had put him into hospital more times than he cared to remember.

'You needs to watch your bronichals,' remarked Joe, leaning back to avoid any germs that might be heading in his direction.

'They'll be awright,' replied Albert when he'd caught his breath. 'They'll be just fine when I retires.'

CHAPTER TWO

The Fuchsia Bush Blooms

The person who Albert Piggott was expecting to provide for his old age after he retired, his long-suffering wife Nelly, had her hands covered with flour as she was in the process of making scones. At this time of year, these were always a great favourite, served warm with a thick spread of butter and a choice of jam that she bought from the Women's Institute stall at Lulling's Wednesday market. She knew she could get cheaper jam but good jam made all the difference and people appreciated that she supported the local WI branch.

'Home-made Scones' said the little printed notice propped up against the large plateful on the counter, 'served with *locally made* jam'.

During the summer, when it was sunny and hot, she would serve the scones with whipped cream (made by Percy Hodge who had a fine herd of dairy cows) with strawberry jam. The notice then read: 'Home-made

Scones, served with *locally made* cream and strawberry jam'.

As she rubbed the butter into the flour, she let her gaze wander across her pristine kitchen. Never let it be said that there was a speck of dirt in Nelly Piggott's kitchen at The Fuchsia Bush. There was a large hatchway in the middle of the far wall, and through it she could see Gloria was hard at work. Goodness how things had changed over the last couple of years!

Nelly had had a somewhat chequered life, but that was all in the past. Suffice to say she set her cap at Albert Piggott at a time when he seemed to be at a particularly low ebb. Despite his protestations, she scrubbed and polished his little cottage next to The Two Pheasants until it was gleaming, and cooked him the most mouth-watering dinners. When therefore she suggested she make her presence a permanent arrangement, he found himself agreeing and they were married in the church on the green. The marriage had had its up and downs for both of them but Albert had to admit that when she returned to him after a liaison away with Charlie the oilman, he was thankful to see the untidy and dirty cottage put to rights, and his nose wrinkled with pleasure at the smell of her steak and kidney pie coming out of the oven.

After a few unsatisfactory jobs, Nelly was taken on as a cook at The Fuchsia Bush by Mrs Peters who had been the tea-shop's proprietor for many years. Mrs Peters soon recognized that Nelly was a great asset and acted quickly to ensure that she was not prised away by any other establishment in the High Street. She made Nelly a non-financial partner, leaving her to produce all the food while she herself concentrated on the business side of things. 'That suits me,' Nelly said. 'I might be able to cook but I be hopeless at sums.'

It had come as a great shock when, just over two years earlier, Mrs Peters's health had suddenly deteriorated and, after a distressing illness, she had died. For once, Nelly's usual brash cheerfulness let her down: what would happen to the business now? The people who bought it would probably bring their own staff or, worse, they would close down the tea-shop and turn the premises into yet another hairdressing salon. The Fuchsia Bush was in a prime position in Lulling's High Street.

But Nelly underestimated the high opinion her employer had of her. Having no direct relatives of her own, Mrs Peters left the whole business, lock, stock and cake plates, to a completely stunned Nelly.

Mr Venables, the more-or-less retired Lulling solicitor who had always looked after Mrs Peters's affairs, told Nelly that she was not to worry at all about the business side of The Fuchsia Bush; perhaps Mrs Peters had told him about Nelly's protestations that she 'be no good at sums'. In due course, Mrs Border was appointed to look after the ordering and the accounts. This efficient woman in her early thirties wanted a part-time job so she could spend more time with her young children. Nelly and Clare Border got on well together, neither interfering with the other's side of the business.

During the heyday of Mrs Peters's and Nelly's

partnership, they had expanded the business to handle some outside catering. To begin with, this was local catering – small wedding breakfasts and birthday celebrations – but that section of the business had grown fast as word got round that The Fuchsia Bush provided excellent food at reasonable prices. Not very long before Mrs Peters was taken ill, they had separated the catering business from The Fuchsia Bush and had brought in a highly competent manageress to run the catering side. When Nelly inherited her legacy from Mrs Peters, she was thankful that she didn't have that to look after as well.

Nelly had now finished gently kneading the dough for the scones and concentrated while she cut out 2½-inch rounds and placed them on a huge baking tray. She had some time to spare while they cooked so she made herself a mug of coffee and gave herself the luxury of taking her not inconsiderable weight off her feet. Sipping her coffee, she continued to think back to the events that took place after she had become sole owner of The Fuchsia Bush.

It was the following July that Nelly heard that the lease of the ground floor of the premises on one side of the tea-shop was for sale. She was secretly pleased that the shop that had been selling what she considered to be less than useful or even pretty knick-knacks was closing down.

'I can't understand why they thought they could make a go of it in the first place,' Nelly said to her friend, Mrs Jenner. They still managed to meet once a week for a game of Bingo in one of Lulling's community halls. 'Apart from anything, why would anyone even go into a shop

with such a silly name as "Little Pressies"!' She snorted, her bosom heaving in indignation.

Mrs Jenner agreed that she would not. 'Are you worried what might replace it, though?' she asked. 'The devil you know and all that.'

The two women were walking back up the steep hill to Thrush Green, and Nelly used her friend's question as an excuse to stop for a breather while she pondered the answer.

'It seems to me,' she said, 'that most folk are like a flock of sheep. They just follow on aimlessly, not botherin' to ask why the gift shop that was there before wasn't a success. Little Pressies seems to have a sale most of the year, and even now is using the Christmas rush as an excuse to get rid of its stock.'

Nelly set off up the hill again, the overhead lights throwing her large shadow onto the pavement.

'You ought to buy it, and expand,' said Mrs Jenner behind her.

This stopped Nelly in her tracks again, and she turned so suddenly that Mrs Jenner bumped right into her.

'You must be mad!' Nelly said to her friend. 'I've more than I can cope with as it is.' And with that, she turned on her heel and marched on up the road.

Nelly was reminded of this conversation the following day. Standing on the pavement opposite The Fuchsia Bush, waiting to cross the High Street, she looked at the two premises across the road with fresh eyes, and suddenly saw how well they looked next to each other. On the left of The Fuchsia Bush was a handsome Georgian house, its fine front door – albeit in need of a coat of paint – approached by three steps and two elegantly curved iron handrails. This is where the ancient Misses Lovelock lived. The house was one of the few remnants of old Lulling High Street. Many years ago, the houses on either side of the road had been converted into shops, modern windows and fascias being inserted into the fronts of the ground-floor premises, with only a vestige of the glories of the Georgian architecture remaining above. However, both The Fuchsia Bush and the three shops next to it in the row had retained the steps up, although none sported such fine handrails as the Love-locks' house.

Yes, thought Nelly, if they were decorated in the same style as each other they would look pretty good. She knew that Little Pressies only occupied the ground floor – a good-sized room in the front, and a couple of smaller back rooms that held the shop's stock.

'Hmm . . .' she said to herself. 'I wonder . . .'

At eleven o'clock that July morning, Clare Border ar-rived, and settled down in the little office to look after the order books.

Nelly took her a cup of coffee but instead of just putting it down on the desk and returning to the kitchen as usual, she sat down somewhat heavily on the spare chair. 'Do you have a moment, Clare? I've something I wants to ask you.' And she proceeded to tell Clare of her half-formed plan for the premises next door.

'I've been a bit concerned recently,' she said, 'that we don't – that we can't – give enough room to the sand-wiches and rolls for the office workers' lunches. What we prepare is gone in a flash. I've tried to make more but, to be honest, they get in the way when we're serving lunches.'

Although The Fuchsia Bush was officially a tea-shop and its busiest time was generally in the afternoon, it had always served light lunches as well.

Nelly proceeded to tell Clare about the lease of Little Pressies being for sale and asked whether they could afford to buy it, and turn it into a sandwich bar. There was no doubt that sandwiches were a growing market.

Office staff no longer made their own sandwiches to take to work, and few of the workers seemed to come in for a proper lunch. The Fuchsia Bush's clientele was mostly shoppers and visitors to the little town.

It was agreed that Nelly would enquire from the commercial agent who was selling the lease what price was being asked, and then Clare would see whether, with a mortgage, Nelly could afford to buy it.

In due course, Clare reported back to her employer. The long and the short of it was that Nelly couldn't. The mortgage would put an impossible burden on the business.

'Oh,' said Nelly, feeling deflated when Clare told her, 'that's a real disappointment. I'd begun to think how I would plan it. I'd even started to think of names. Foolish of me, I know, to have pipe dreams.'

'Well, there is one way you could afford it,' Clare said.

Nelly's heart did a little jump. 'Yes?'

'You could sell the catering side, and expand into the sandwich business instead.' Clare looked at some figures she had written on a piece of paper. 'You should be able to sell the catering business as a going concern, staff and everything, and have enough to buy the lease of next door and what it would need to convert and decorate the place. And, if you did need a bit more, then you could get a small bank loan.'

Nelly stared at her, and then her big face broke into a smile. 'That sounds just the biscuit!' she exclaimed. 'I don't have any great affection for the catering side. I'm so remote from it now. The kitchen here shares a wall with the back room of next door. Do you think we would get planning permission to knock the two together?'

The two women's faces shone with excitement.

And so it came about that a new sandwich shop opened in Lulling High Street. Nelly had originally thought she would call it Peter's Sandwich Parlour, with a nod to her benefactor's memory, but no one seemed very keen on the name.

Clare Border, who was never backward about coming forward, robustly disagreed with her employer. 'I don't think that's a very good name. People will endlessly ask who Peter is. Unless, of course, you have a Peter in mind to run it for you?'

Nelly explained her thinking behind the name. 'Mustn't have anything too twee,' she said firmly. 'Nothing like Little Pressies.'

'Well, if not the last owner of The Fuchsia Bush,' said Clare, 'what about the present owner?'

Nelly looked at her in surprise. 'What? Piggott's Sandwich Parlour?'

Clare laughed. 'No, I don't think that sounds right. But what about Nelly's Sandwich Shop? That has a really good ring to it.'

'Well!' exclaimed Nelly, going rather pink in the face. 'Nelly's Sandwich Shop, indeed! Yes, I have to agree. It does sound good, doesn't it?' She repeated the words slowly. 'Nelly's Sandwich Shop. Yes, I think that will do just dandy.'

One of the last jobs that the solicitor, Justin Venables,

had done before he retired for good was to look after the acquisition of the lease, having ascertained from the proper authorities that it would be in order for the nature of the business to change from gift shop to catering. There seemed to be no problem over this at the county council offices: Mrs Peters had ensured that The Fuchsia Bush had built up a very good reputation, and Nelly had proved herself a worthy successor. The planning department had, however, baulked at the request for two kitchens to be made into one, and Nelly had to accept that the best she could have was the large hatch and a connecting door.

Before Nelly had had time to think about who was going to be in charge of the new sandwich bar, Gloria Williams, the senior waitress, had presented herself one morning in the little office and asked if she could be considered for the job.

'You see, you've always admired my sandwiches, and liked some of the fillings that I've suggested. You'll need a manageress next door and I just don't see why it can't be me!' Then she shut her mouth firmly and gazed at Nelly in an almost challenging way.

Nelly was taken by surprise. Now, there's a thought!

She leaned forward across the desk. 'Well, Gloria, that's certainly an idea. I will, of course, need a supervisor for next door. I hadn't given it any great thought yet because we shan't need anyone till the building works are done and the kitchen installed. But, yes, when the time comes, I'll certainly consider your application.'

Over the next few months, Gloria blossomed. When Nelly had first started working at The Fuchsia Bush, the girl had been uninterested and would rather file her nails than see to the customers. But Nelly had encouraged both her and Rosa, the other waitress, to be more a part of the establishment, and it now seemed that they actually enjoyed working there rather than enduring it. Gloria certainly worked hard, and the sandwiches in particular were very popular. The office workers seemed to come in earlier and earlier to buy their lunches before the sandwiches ran out. It was when one of the most regular customers – her bank manager – complimented her on 'the superb sandwiches you provide for us' that Nelly decided to put Gloria out of her suspense and appoint her manageress of the new shop.

'Oh, Mrs Piggott, oh dearie me!' Gloria looked as if she were about to burst into tears.

'Now, now, Gloria!' Nelly soothed. 'Am I to take it that you accept?'

Gloria looked at her employer with shining eyes, and nodded vigorously, quite unable to speak.

'Good, that's good. Now, could you ask Rosa to come in and see me?'

Rosa had joined the staff of The Fuchsia Bush a few years after Gloria and the pair of them had set up a good partnership. They needed to be watched, of course, in order that they weren't so busy chatting about what they had seen on the television the evening before that customers were kept waiting, but they were efficient enough.

Nelly now told Rosa that as she was promoting Gloria to be in charge of the sandwich bar, she wanted Rosa to take over as No. 1 in the tea-room – after herself, of course. Although Nelly spent much of her time in the kitchen making the scones and cakes, and preparing the lunches, she would often pop out front to see that everything was going smoothly and perhaps to have a few words with any regular customers who might have come in. Rosa was as thrilled as Gloria had been, and tentatively said that she had a younger sister just about to leave school, and might she be considered as the second waitress?

'Poppy's a good girl, Mrs Piggott. And she's good at sums so won't have no trouble with the bills.'

Nelly admired anyone good at sums, and promised she would consider Poppy in due course. Rosa and Poppy – it sounded as though they were made for The Fuchsia Bush!

A head now appeared in the hatchway between the two kitchens. 'Is that burning I can smell, Nelly?' called Gloria.

'Great Scot!' cried Nelly, leaping up. 'My scones! I've been dreaming and quite forgot the time. Oh dear, oh dear, I'm going to have to start all over again. Thank goodness it was the second batch, and there's enough to be going on with for the moment.'

Gloria came through from the sandwich shop's kitchen. She was very neat and tidy, and wearing a clean white apron with the word 'Nelly's' printed across the bib section. That had been her idea, but she had quite properly asked her employer's permission first. And Nelly was more than happy to give her approval.

She would never be 'best friends' with Gloria – they

were many years apart in age – but they worked well together. When she had invited Gloria to stop calling her 'Mrs Piggott' and to call her Nelly, it had taken a bit of time for Gloria to get used to the familiarity but that was in the past.

'Since it was King Alfred wot burnt the cakes, we shall have to call you Queen Nelly now!' Gloria laughed, but sensibly returned quickly to her kitchen before Nelly could think of a riposte.

Nelly opened a window to let out the smell of burning, and tipped the scorched offering into the huge waste bin that stood near the back door.

A moment later, the swing door from the tea-room opened. 'We'll be needin' more scones soon, please,' called Rosa.

'Well, you'll have to wait about twenty minutes. I regret to say that Management has slipped up,' said Nelly, pulling the huge container of flour towards her, 'but I'm back on the case.'

CHAPTER THREE

A Wash Behind the Ears

'We've had a lovely invitation to drinks with Phil and Frank after the Nativity play,' said Joan Young a few days later. She and her husband Edward were having breakfast, and Willie Bond the postman had just delivered the morning post.

'Are we going to the Nativity play?' Edward muttered from behind his newspaper.

'Of course we are!' Joan replied, adding marmalade to her toast.

'If you think we must,' said the voice behind the newspaper.

Joan was not to be put off. She was used to her husband being a little unforthcoming early in the morning. 'We usually go and, anyway, we *must* go this year because the Curdles are so involved and we should support them.' She looked across the table at Edward who was still intent on his newspaper. 'Don't you agree?' she said, raising her voice just a little.

Edward sighed, and laid down the paper. He knew when he was beaten. He would have to finish the article when he had some peace and quiet in his office later that morning.

'Did I know about the Curdles being involved?' he asked patiently.

'Of course you did! Ben came round a month ago to make sure that Paul would be home in time.'

Paul was their son and away at boarding school.

'Isn't fourteen a bit old to be in a Nativity play?' Edward asked. 'I thought they were for little children? I'm not sure he'll be best pleased. Have you broken the news to him?'

'Don't worry,' laughed Joan. 'I wouldn't let him be landed with being a shepherd, with a silly headdress and a toy sheep tucked under his arm. Phil and Frank are organizing this year's Nativity and Phil is particularly keen that Paul should be one of the narrators. I understand Jeremy is going to be the other one.'

'Ah,' said Edward, re-filling his cup with coffee. 'That should be all right, then. Actually, Paul has turned into a good out-loud reader. I heard him reading something to Jeremy when he was here over half-term – something incomprehensible to do with currents in the Antarctic Ocean.'

Paul and Jeremy Prior had been good friends from the day that Jeremy had arrived with his mother Phyllida to live at Tullivers. Because the garden there was quite small,

Jeremy tended to cross the corner of the green to the Youngs' house. This had a fine garden with plenty of trees for the boys to climb, and their own complicated version of 'hide and seek', which appeared to consist of one or other of them spending hours crawling through the undergrowth.

Their pride and joy, however, was old Mrs Curdle's gypsy caravan which, after much pleading, Paul had been allowed to turn into a den. When Mrs Curdle had died a number of years earlier, the beautiful traditional caravan had been given a final resting place in the Youngs' orchard. It proved to be an ideal lair, and Paul was more than happy to let Jeremy share it with him. There had been the odd spat between the two boys, of course, but nothing that hadn't been quickly patched up. Phil Hurst marvelled at how tidy they kept the caravan, since she wore herself out asking Jeremy to clear up his bedroom. She assumed it must be Paul's good influence.

The Youngs' house was the finest on the green and, with its garden, it occupied a prominent position looking south towards St Andrew's church at the other end of the green. The handsome building was of the honey-coloured stone that is so much admired throughout the Cotswolds.

Next to the church had been a hideous Victorian rectory that had vexed Edward, who was a fine architect, every time he looked at it – which had been several times a day. The ugly building, heavy with porticos and window surrounds, upset him deeply. He was therefore the first to rejoice when, one May night, the house burned nearly to the ground. The good vicar and his wife, Charles and

Dimity Henstock, were fortunately away on holiday at the time. The villagers had turned out to form a human chain to try to rescue as many of the Henstocks' belongings as possible.

There was no question of the rectory being rebuilt. In fact, the diocese took advantage of the situation to make some big changes. Anthony Bull, the much loved vicar at Lulling, went to London to take on a fashionable parish there. Charles Henstock moved to Lulling to be in charge of the town's lovely St John's church, and three other parishes – Thrush Green and the nearby hamlets of Lulling Woods and Nidden. He and Dimity relished living in the elegant, comfortable and warm Queen Anne vicarage that overlooked Lulling's extensive green.

In place of the Thrush Green rectory, a row of apartments for elderly people was built. Since the architect chosen for this new development, called Rectory Cottages, was none other than Edward Young, he ensured that what he now looked at across the green was pleasing to the eye.

As Edward sat at the kitchen table reflecting on Rectory Cottages with some pride, the back door burst open, and Molly Curdle came in, shaking her hair and sending a few drops of rain into the air.

'Morning,' she called across to the Youngs at the breakfast table. 'It's still pretty wild out there.'

Joan Young looked out of the window. The trees and shrubs in the garden were blowing about, but nothing as bad as it had been a few days ago when a branch of their magnolia tree had broken off.

'There!' Edward had cried in some distress. 'I told you that those boys would weaken the branches and damage that lovely tree.'

Joan had laughed. 'Go on with you! The boys haven't been climbing trees for years now.'

Edward had harrumphed. He liked to have someone to blame.

'Now, is there anything what needs doing special this morning?' asked Molly, putting on her gingham-patterned overall.

Joan considered the matter, looking round the big kitchen as though for inspiration. 'No, I don't think so, thank you, Molly. But there's rather a lot of ironing in the basket. Just do what you can.'

'I'll take any I can't manage back across, and do it with my lot this afternoon.'

'Back across' referred to where Molly lived with her husband Ben and their three children. Ten or more years earlier, Edward Young had converted some old out-buildings – a range of stone-built stables, a coach house and tack-room – into a cottage for Joan's elderly parents when they moved down from London.

Molly Piggott, as she was then, had been employed to look after Paul Young and the boy had always adored her. In fact, she was still the first person he rushed to greet when he returned home for the holidays. Ben Curdle, the dark-haired, handsome grandson of old Mrs Curdle, had married Molly who was thankful to get away from her curmudgeonly father, Albert.

After old Mrs Curdle had died, Ben took charge of the travelling fair that she had founded and, it has to be said, controlled with a rod of iron. The fair on Thrush Green every May Day was a red-letter day for the village. Two days before the first of May, the fair was set up. There were swingboats, switchbacks, dodgem cars and a big tall helter-skelter. Then there were the stalls – the coconut shy, the shooting range and the wheel of fortune. Over each stall dangled prizes on hooks, prizes that made the children's eyes wide with excitement and longing. There were stalls selling jewellery and stalls that sold hot dogs and candy-floss.

But times changed, and Ben had found it increasingly difficult to make ends meet. New health and safety regulations were introduced, requiring a great deal of money being spent, money Ben didn't have. When he was made a good offer for the fair, it was with a heavy heart that he finally decided to sell.

The Curdle family was popular with the Thrush Green residents but especially with the Youngs. After Ben had sold the fair, not only did the Youngs offer the Curdles the flat at the top of their house, but Edward was responsible for finding Ben a job. The young man, who had always been good with engines, secured a decent job as a mechanic with a family firm of agricultural engineers in Lulling.

When Joan Young's father died of the old people's disease, pneumonia, one February, his widow went to live with her other daughter, Ruth Lovell. Stable Cottage had therefore become vacant. Initially, the Youngs had discussed renting it out but neither was very keen on having what they called 'strangers' living on top of them. It was Joan who had the bright idea of offering Ben and Molly the cottage, which was a good deal more spacious than the flat at the top of the house. The two Curdle children, George and Anne, were growing fast and Stable Cottage gave them all much more room.

Although the rent they paid the Youngs was low because Molly worked in the house three mornings a week, while Ben did odd jobs round the house at the weekend, they were finding it difficult to save money to put down for a house. However, Ben was promoted to chief mechanic and the considerable increase in salary was very welcome. At last, they thought, they would be able to start saving for a house of their own.

Ben and Molly had reckoned that two children were enough for their circumstances. Therefore, it came as a great shock to both of them when Dr Lovell pronounced that the reason that Molly wasn't feeling well was not a stomach bug but because she was pregnant.

'What *are* we going to do?' Molly wailed when Ben got home that evening and she told him the news.

Ben loved children and, once he had got over the initial surprise, he was delighted. As for George and Anne, they were thrilled. George wanted a brother to play football with on the green, and Anne wanted a sister she could play nurses with.

'Yes, but . . .' continued Molly, 'where is everyone going to sleep? The cottage is fine for the four of us – but five . . .' and her voice trailed away in despair.

'We'll cross that bridge when it comes,' replied the ever pragmatic Ben.

Seven and a half months later, a healthy boy was born. He had a mass of dark hair, as dark as Ben's, and gurgled prettily in his carry-cot on the day they brought him home from the hospital.

They had both been so certain that the baby was going to be a girl that they had only discussed girls' names, and had decided on Josie.

'Pah!' Albert had spat out when his daughter told him. 'What sort of name do you call that?'

He didn't have to worry when a boy arrived, but Ben and Molly had to start thinking of names all over again. George was named after Ben's father who had been killed in the Second World War, just three weeks before the end of the conflict. How cruel can life – and death – be. Anne was named after her redoubtable great-grandmother, Mrs Curdle.

'Since George is called after your father,' said Molly, 'I would like the baby to be called Albert after mine.'

Ben stared at her in horror. Molly tolerated her old dad – who, she had to admit, had improved since her step-mother Nelly had taken control – but there was little love between the two of them.

Then Molly burst out laughing. 'I was only joking! You should have seen your face.' She ducked the cushion that Ben playfully threw at her.

'Seriously, though, I would like a name from my side of the family. After all, you've had both George and Anne from your side.'

'You've got an Aunt Anne, too,' Ben pointed out.

'That's as maybe, but we all know that our Annie was named after your beloved grandma.'

'All right, then. What names are there on your side?' Ben asked.

Molly wrinkled up her nose, and concentrated. 'Well, Dad has his sister Anne and a brother – that was Uncle Percy.'

'No thanks!' said Ben, then added, 'Without wishing to hurt Farmer Hodge's feelings, of course.'

'Grandpa on my mum's side was called Herbert, and I can't remember what Dad's father was called. I'll ask him when I go over tomorrow.'

'Cedric, probably,' said Ben. 'The problem with all these family names is that they are so old-fashioned. We want something more modern.'

In the end, they settled on William – which was what Albert's father turned out to have been called – but they soon began calling their new son Billy, and Billy he remained.

On the other side of the green, the Shoosmiths were delighted to receive the Hursts' invitation to drinks.

'What fun!' exclaimed Isobel. 'I love Christmas and all the parties. I'll ring Phil this morning to say that we'd love to go.'

'I'll be seeing Frank at the PCC meeting this evening,' her husband replied. 'I'll tell him then.'

'Good idea. I'd forgotten it was the meeting tonight. Is

it going to be a long one, or shall I have supper ready at the usual time?'

'I can't think of anything that will delay us,' her husband replied. 'We'll be finalizing arrangements for the Christmas services, but that shouldn't take long.' Harold got up from the kitchen table where they'd had breakfast. 'Now, if you don't need me this morning, I'm going to attend to poor old Nathaniel – some wretched pigeon has been sitting on his head again with inevitable consequences. If I do it this morning, I'll be out of Betty's way.'

Betty Bell was their cleaner, and although she was undoubtedly a good source of gossip, she drove Harold mad with her chattering.

'Take care when you climb up,' Isobel called after her husband's retreating back.

Harold whistled to himself as he collected the step-ladder from the garage and filled a bucket with water, but he stopped when a thrush began to sing its exquisite melody from a nearby roof-top. The thrush's winter song, he thought, was always so beautiful because it stood out. In the spring and early summer, it was often drowned by the cacophony of the other garden birds.

As he walked across the green to the statue of Nathanial Patten, Harold looked up at the sky. The clouds were scudding across, still being pushed by the wind. He'd listened to the weather forecast before the eight o'clock news and was glad they were reckoning it would blow through by midday.

Harold set the step-ladder down on the side of the

statue where the offending white splodge of pigeon dropping was scarring the missionary's face. He tested the
ladder's balance. Not quite right. He saw there was a
small twig under one of the ladder's feet, and bent down
to remove it. 'That's better,' he said out loud, wiggling the
ladder again.

Carrying the bucket in one hand, he carefully climbed
up a few rungs, then, sensing it was holding steady, he
climbed up another three steps so his own head was just
above the statue's. He carefully balanced the bucket on
the statue's plinth. Now he was up here, he could see that
Nathaniel's head and upper torso were a bit muckier than
could be seen from the ground. He got rid of the pigeon
droppings first of all, and then gave Nathaniel's face a
good wash.

As Harold carefully cleaned all round the statue's head,
he chatted to the missionary. He and Nathaniel Patten
had never met, of course, but Harold felt he knew the
man well enough to administer such personal ablutions.
'Now for the back of your neck,' he said, 'and I mustn't
miss out on your ears!'

'You've missed a bit round 'ere,' said a voice behind
him from the ground.

Harold started violently, and the step-ladder rocked a
bit but held firm.

He looked round, and saw Albert Piggott standing
there. 'Goodness, man, you gave me a fright! You almost
made me fall off.'

' 'Ave you got a moment, then?' said Albert. 'I needs to
talk to you, an' it's important like.'

Harold made his way down to the ground. 'Yes, I can stop because I need some clean water anyway,' he said. 'What can I do for you, Albert?'

Albert took his old cap off his head, and stood looking somewhat uneasy. 'Well, see, I thinks it's time I was retired. I've done me best for the place but the wind gets in me ol' bones an', as you knows, me chest ain't good.

No, not good at all.' And, as if to press home his point, Albert went off into one of his gut-wrenching spasms of coughing.

Harold took the opportunity to consider quickly what his response should be. He wasn't surprised, of course, because Albert's health had had its ups and downs – rather more downs than was comfortable for anyone – but if Albert retired, who on earth would they get to take over his duties?

He clapped Albert on the back, which seemed to help and Albert's coughing stuttered to a halt.

'Also,' he said, shoving his cap back on his head, as though the important business had been said, 'I bin drawin' my pension for over five year now, an' it's time I put me feet up and took things easy.'

Put his feet up on the bar stool of The Two Pheasants, more like, thought Harold.

'It's the PCC meeting tonight.'

Albert nodded. 'Yes, I knows. That's why I thought I'd say summat now.'

'Yes, sensible. Er, did you have any thoughts of when you might want to go?' Harold asked, thinking of all the Christmas services that would soon be upon them.

'The end of the year seems as good a time as any,' Albert replied. 'Once them Christmas festivities is over, it's usually a quiet time. Unless, of course,' he added, 'folks start dyin' and then there's all that diggin' what needs doin'.'

'Yes, of course.' Harold picked up the bucket, and shot the remains of its dirty water across the grass. 'Any thoughts of who might take over? I know Bobby Cooke's been giving you a hand with the heavy work. Would he have enough time to take over?'

'Ah! Well, now, I did 'ave a word with him earlier this week. 'E's doin' a bit o' this an' a bit o' that. Bin doin' some hedgin' and ditchin' for Perce Hodge. An' 'e does some time in the Lovells' garden but that's more of summer work.'

'Did he say he would be interested in your job?' Harold asked.

' 'E said 'e'd be willin' to give it a try.'

'Well, thank you, Albert. We'll discuss it at this evening's meeting.'

Albert set off across the green towards St Andrew's, and as Harold made his way back to get some clean water, he saw that the old man's gait was very unsteady, and reckoned his feet were giving him as much trouble as the famed 'bronichals'.

That evening at the Parochial Church Council meeting, when the main business was concluded, with all details for the Christmas services agreed, Harold, who was chairman of the PCC, asked round the table if anyone had Any Other Business.

'Yes, please, Mr Chairman,' said a weaselly-looking chap, staring at Harold over his rimless spectacles.

Harold sighed inwardly. This was Derek Burwell and when he got going it was difficult to stop him. The Burwells were relative newcomers to the area, but they had managed to inveigle their way onto a number of committees. It had to be admitted that they were good church-goers, attending St Andrew's regularly. When Mr Gibbons – who Harold had rather naughtily dubbed 'Gauleiter Gibbons' owing to his bossiness during meetings – had died of a sudden heart attack the year before, and no one else had rushed forward to fill his place on the council, it was difficult to refuse Derek Burwell's application.

His wife, Jean, had pushed her way onto the church flower arranging rota, and Harold felt it wouldn't be long before she targeted the WI Committee. Since they weren't real country people, having moved here when Derek had retired from being some sort of civil servant in London, Isobel Shoosmith was determined not to let Jean Burwell come onto the WI Committee yet. She had to earn her colours.

The Burwells had bought one of the houses that had been built between the wars on the Woodstock Road leading north out of Thrush Green. They had spent the first year 'doing it up', they called it, but 'doing it down' according to the ever critical Edward Young.

'That house is of the period,' he said to Joan. 'Do it up, modernize it inside, if you must, but leave the outside as it was meant to be.' He snorted. 'For heaven's sake, why put on that neo-Georgian front porch! It's terrible, it shouldn't have been allowed.'

'That's what happens outside the conservation area,' pointed out his wife soothingly.

But Edward found fault with everything. He criticized the modern windows that were put in and loathed the strident yellow paint on the front door. He took to driving past the house with his eyes shut.

'Edward,' cautioned his wife, 'that is taking things too far! You'll have an accident.'

Edward had to agree and resorted to closing just one eye.

When the Burwells started on the garden, Edward's good taste was tested even further. A little pool was dug in the centre of the lawn – 'makes it so difficult to mow' Edward had muttered – and although they didn't go as far as putting a gnome with a fishing rod on the little wall surrounding the pond, they produced a large and rather ugly plastic heron that stood uncomfortably on one leg in the water.

Even Joan agreed that the borders down the edge of the short tarmac drive were a disaster. 'Those colours just don't go together. It's what the worst of municipal plantings look like,' she said.

Harold now looked at his watch. 'I hope you can be fairly speedy, Derek,' he said. 'I've got some Other Business of my own, which is going to take about ten minutes, and none of us wants to be late tonight.'

'Thank you, Mr Chairman,' Derek said, and then proceeded to ask whether it would be possible to change the night of the PCC meetings in future since Wednesdays clashed with his bridge evening in Lulling.

Harold stood firm. 'No, I'm sorry, Derek, that is not possible. We've always had the PCC meetings on a Wednesday, and on Wednesday they shall remain. I'm afraid you'll have to miss your bridge evenings four times a year. Now,' he said briskly, 'to my own Other Business. It's about Albert Piggott.'

There was a general groan. Albert Piggott usually

cropped up at some point during the meetings and had, indeed, been the subject of some comment already when the decoration of the church for Christmas had been discussed. He was always asked to provide the holly and ivy.

'Albert is going to retire, and definitely this time,' Harold announced, and proceeded to tell the meeting about his conversation with Albert that morning.

There was a flurry of exclamation from round the table, and Percy Hodge said, 'I thought as much. Albert said summat about it in the pub the other morning. He's not been that well.'

'I'm not at all surprised,' said John Lovell, Thrush Green's doctor. 'How his tubes have lasted this long, I don't know. He should really have retired years ago.'

'I think he continued for so long in order to fund his beer money,' said Harold.

'Yes, well,' cut in Percy quickly, 'he reckons his Nelly will provide that now. The caff is doing that well, I hear.'

'It's time the old curmudgeon retired,' said Frank Hurst.

'I agree,' said Derek. 'He's no good at his job anyway.'

Percy came to his drinking colleague's defence. 'He does all right, does Albert. Considering his infirmities.'

'Exactly!' retorted Derek.

Harold went on quickly. 'Albert thinks young Bobby Cooke might be willing to take over—'

'Oh lor'!' cut in Percy, who once had had a dalliance with young Cooke's flighty sister. 'Is that a good idea? Them Cookes is no good.'

'It may be a question of beggars can't be choosers,' said Harold, folding up his spectacles and putting them in their case, which was his way of indicating the meeting was at a close. 'He doesn't live as close to St Andrew's as Albert, but the Cooke family aren't that far up the Nidden Road. I shall see young Bobby over the weekend, and report back. Albert wants to go at the end of the month.'

'What?' Derek exclaimed. 'That's less than a month's notice. He should give at least three months.'

Harold sighed. 'Here in Thrush Green,' he said quietly, 'we don't always do things like the civil service. If Bobby Cooke can take over, then we can let Albert go when he wants. If Bobby won't or can't, then we may have to think again, but I'm sure Albert wouldn't leave us in the lurch.'

Harold looked round at the assembled meeting. Derek Burwell had pursed his mouth together but his face still registered disapproval.

'Now,' concluded Harold, after the date for the next meeting had been set, 'I think that's all, ladies and gentlemen. Thank you for coming out tonight. We are sure to see plenty of each other over the weeks leading up to Christmas.'

And after the customary final prayer, the members of the Thrush Green PCC dispersed into the night.

As Harold walked back across the green, soft moonlight was shining down on Nathaniel Patten's now well-scrubbed head and face.

'Good night, my friend,' he said, putting a hand out to touch the plinth on which the statue stood, and then he hurried home to a nice warming pheasant casserole that had been promised for supper.

Chapter Four

A Lion and a Unicorn

Friday, two days later, provided joy and anguish in equal parts for several people in Thrush Green and Lulling. During the morning, the weather seemed to match the mood – it was like April: rain one moment and soft sunshine the next. The bare branches of the lime trees round St Andrew's church had hardly stopped dripping when they were once more drenched.

Nelly Piggott knew it was going to be another busy day in The Fuchsia Bush, and had arrived especially early to make the cakes and scones that would be needed. The High Street was bursting at the seams with people who looked increasingly harassed the closer it got to Christmas. By mid-morning, the tea-room would be full of exhausted shoppers who had decided they couldn't face another moment without a restorative cup of coffee and a piece of lemon drizzle cake or a warm scone and butter.

Then there would be the lunches. The Fuchsia Bush

didn't have a large menu. There was always the 'soup of the day', something wholesome at this time of year, served with home-baked crusty bread. Nelly had prepared some creamed fish today as one of the two main courses – it was funny how 'fish on Fridays' was still an accepted ritual – and there was also steak and ale pie, which was always a great favourite with the men.

Shoppers would come in for tea throughout the afternoon, their parcels and overflowing carrier bags littering the floor.

'Do be careful of them bags when you're carrying the trays across,' Nelly would exhort Rosa and Poppy daily. 'We can't be doing with any accidents. Try to get the customers to put them under their chairs.'

Nelly was hard at work rolling out the puff pastry for the steak and ale pies when Poppy came into the kitchen with the morning post.

Poppy had worked here for nearly a year now. She was a pretty girl with long fair hair pulled back in a loose pony tail. When she had left school, she had tossed her head at her sister Rosa's suggestion that she should join her working at The Fuchsia Bush. She had her sights set on the music industry and thought that working in a shop that sold guitars and recorders, drum kits and music in all shapes and sizes, would be a good stepping-stone. But a few months working in a rather dingy shop at the far end of the High Street had decided her that perhaps, after all, the music business was not for her.

A brief spell as an assistant in a chemist's shop had followed, but Poppy didn't like the ogling eyes of the pharmacist, and had left before he got any funny ideas. Her next job was in one of the High Street shoe shops, but she complained about having to handle customers' often smelly and grubby feet, and didn't last more than a few months there.

Rosa was beginning to despair that her little sister would ever settle down, so when a vacancy occurred at The Fuchsia Bush, she again suggested Poppy should go along for an interview. Rosa herself was enjoying being in charge of the tea-room (after Mrs Piggott, of course) now that Gloria was next door running the sandwich shop, and had smartened herself up. When Poppy arrived for her appointment with Nelly after the tea-room had closed for the day, Rosa checked her over to ensure that she was clean and tidy.

'Go on, then,' she said, dusting down the shoulders of Poppy's coat, 'and mind you're polite.'

Poppy did as she was told, and said 'Yes, ma'am' or 'No, ma'am' to every question Nelly put to her. When asked whether she could add up quickly and accurately, Poppy replied, 'Oh yes, ma'am. I came top of my class for arithmetic at school.'

That settled it as far as Nelly was concerned. Anyone who was good at sums earned her admiration. She agreed to take Poppy on a month's trial and now, a year later, was satisfied in every way. The two sisters made a good team and were careful to keep their chatter for either before customers arrived or when they were in the kitchen.

'Morning post for you, Mrs Piggott,' Poppy sang out, brandishing a wodge of envelopes.

Nelly looked up from where she was working. 'Could you sort through them for me? My hands are covered with flour. Anything that is obviously a bill can go straight through to the office for Mrs Border, along with anything that has a trade address on the front.'

Poppy hummed as she sorted the post into two piles. 'It looks as though you've got quite a few Christmas cards, Mrs Piggott. From satisfied customers, I expect. Gosh, that smells great,' she said as Nelly pulled a tray of individual steak and kidney pie dishes towards her, the meat steaming gently from inside.

'We'll add the cards to the others out front later,' Nelly said. 'It's good to show off what folk think about us.'

Poppy held up the last of the envelopes, which was slightly larger than the rest. 'I'm not sure which pile to put this into. I don't think it's a Christmas card because the envelope's been typed.' She turned it over. At the bottom of the gummed flap was a symbol printed in gold. She ran her thumb over it.

'Look,' she said, holding the back of the envelope out towards Nelly, 'that's embossed, that is. Very posh!'

Nelly leaned back a bit and squinted at the envelope that Poppy had thrust in front of her. A symbol of a teapot! She knew what that meant.

'Aha!' she exclaimed, pushing away the envelope with a forearm. 'I know who that's from. That'll be from the Guild of Tea Shops. Put it on my pile. Then take the rest through to Mrs Border.'

'Ooh, do you think we've got the certuficate again?' asked the girl, examining the envelope. 'I see now, that teapot thing is the same as on the certuficate out front.'

'We'll soon find out,' said Nelly. 'Now, get on with you.'

Poppy did as she was told and disappeared. The kitchen was quiet again, with just the murmurings of chatter coming through from the pantry where the two kitchen girls were working.

Nelly cut a strip of pastry and carefully lined the edge of the first pie dish with it. Then she dipped her pastry brush into the bowl of beaten egg beside her on the work table, and painted the strip. Next she cut a circular piece of pastry for the lid, and carefully placed it over the meat. Using her forefinger, she pressed the lid on firmly all the way round before trimming it.

As she prepared the nineteen other little pies, she thought about the Guild of Tea Shops. It was an organization Mrs Peters had applied to join a year or two before she had died, and Nelly had been so pleased for her when, after an inspection that had been carried out incognito, The Fuchsia Bush had been awarded membership of the Guild.

Now as the sole proprietor of the tea-room, Nelly had strived to keep up the standards that had meant so much to Mrs Peters. She knew that at some time during July or August an inspection would be made and towards the end of the year she would receive a letter with the results of the inspection – and, hopefully, a Certificate of Excellence. For the first couple of years, there had been no certificate, just a gentle letter of criticism yet also of encouragement. One year, the Guild had said the inspector had reported there was a stain on the tablecloth and Mrs Peters had reprimanded Rosa who should have changed the cloth. Another year, it had been stones in the cherry jam.

'That was bad luck,' Nelly had said to her friend, Mrs Jenner, shortly after the letter had been received. 'Whoever the inspector was must have had the only cherry stone in the place. We are always careful to buy jams without stones. Stands to reason, doesn't it?'

Nelly had half considered giving up the membership of the Guild but she changed her mind when Mrs Jenner told her about a Guild certificate she had seen, framed, in a tea-shop she'd visited in Chichester.

'It's ever so nice,' Mrs Jenner said, reporting back to Nelly. 'It's all in scrolly sort of writing, red and gold, and has the date big in the middle. You know, the year. Like those awards you see in B&B places.'

Nelly knew what Mrs Jenner meant, not that she had any occasion to stay in that sort of establishment. She had heard from Albert, however, that The Two Pheasants had a certificate saying the inn provided good beer.

Two summers ago, she had introduced more varieties of tea – leaf tea always, never a bag! – and was pleased that some of her regular customers appeared to enjoy choosing a different variety each time they came in. And at the end of that year, The Fuchsia Bush had been awarded a Certificate of Excellence, one of just thirty or so awards the Guild told Nelly they handed out each year. Nelly was thrilled to bits, and rewarded her hard-working staff with a few extra pounds in their Christmas pay packet. She bought a pretty photograph frame to put the handsome certificate into, and it now hung close to the till in the tea-room. She wasn't sure how many of her customers noticed it, but it made her and the staff feel good.

She hoped that this big envelope contained a Certificate of Excellence for the coming year. Once more, there hadn't been a customer who had been definitely identified as a Guild inspector, although Gloria thought that one particular woman was a possibility.

Telling Nelly about it at the end of the day, she said, 'She were sitting at table 2 in the window, and writing in a little notebook, and kept looking round her. I had just taken a tray to table 1, and instead of coming back to the counter, I turned to her table very quick, hoping to catch sight of what she were writing.'

'And did you?' asked Nelly.

'Yeah, but it were just a shopping list. I could see the name of the supermarket at the top.'

'I'm told it's likely to be more than one person when the inspector comes,' said Nelly. 'A couple isn't so obvious.'

When her tray of twenty steak and ale pies were all topped, and waiting to go into the oven in batches a little later, Nelly washed her hands and then turned to the small pile of cards that Poppy had left on the edge of the work table – with the bigger envelope on the top. She wiped her hands down her apron before picking it up.

She slit the envelope with one of the kitchen knives and

carefully extracted the contents. Yes, hooray! There was
the Certificate of Excellence with next year's date glitter-
ing in gold in the middle. There was also a letter, which
Nelly now read:

> Dear Mrs Piggott,
> We are delighted to enclose the Certificate of
> Excellence for the forthcoming year, and would like
> to congratulate The Fuchsia Bush on another good
> performance. Our inspector commented especially on
> the wide range of teas that you provide, but also asked
> me to mention that he was totally bowled over by your
> coffee cake.
> I am also very pleased to tell you that the Guild has
> decided to award The Fuchsia Bush first place in the
> regional awards, in your case the Cotswolds area.

Nelly gasped with delight, and sat down heavily on the
kitchen chair. First place in the regional awards! Oh
lordy-pips – this was totally unexpected. In fact, she
wasn't even sure she knew anything about regional
awards. She read on. The Guild explained that the regional awards were made following a second inspection,
incognito of course, to a select number of tea-shops that
had most pleased the inspectors after the first round. Both
the inspectors, the letter continued, had been fulsome in
their praise for The Fuchsia Bush which would now
receive the Guild's Gold Award for the Cotswolds.

The final paragraph said that the president of the Guild
would come in person to present the award, and they

hoped four o'clock on Thursday 18th would be convenient. The award, Nelly read, was sponsored by *Cotswold Highlights* – a local glossy magazine – which would arrange for the local media to be present.

'Oh crikey!' Nelly exclaimed. 'What on earth shall I wear?'

Nelly's heart beat even faster, and she fanned herself with the letter. She would have to take some time off to go shopping. But now, she thought, pulling herself together, she must get on with the lunches.

That afternoon, Ella Bembridge – spinster of this parish, and in her late sixties – had arranged to visit her friend Dotty Harmer. The sun that had occasionally struggled out during the morning had seemingly given up the effort, and was well hidden behind heavy clouds from which rain of the most depressing kind persistently fell. There were puddles lying on the green, and garden birds huddled miserably in the shelter of shrubs and bushes.

Ella, who was swathed in a mackintosh that resembled something between a cyclist's cape and a Scout tent, left her cottage and took the narrow alleyway that ran down the side of Albert Piggott's cottage. This led to a path through the meadows lying between Thrush Green and Lulling Woods and it was here, in a thatched cottage, that Dotty lived with her ever-patient niece, Connie, and Connie's husband, Kit.

Dotty was one of the local institutions. She was now in her mid-eighties and, despite being stick-thin, she had remarkable resilience and was often to be found outside, tending her beloved ducks, chickens and goats, in all sorts of weather and rarely dressed adequately. Some years previously Connie had come to live with her ancient aunt and, not long afterwards, the inhabitants of Thrush Green had been delighted when Kit Armitage returned to the area and had wooed and won Connie. They were a pair of mature love-birds, it has to be said, but the marriage worked exceedingly well. It had meant that Dotty could continue to live in the cottage that had been her home for so many years, with her animals round her. They had extended the cottage to make room for the three of them, and despite Dotty's protestations had installed central heating which was a great comfort to old bones.

Dotty continued to concoct alarming potions from the herbs she grew in the garden, or gathered in the spring and summer from the hedgerows, and these she pressed upon anyone who called to see her. Her friends from Thrush Green and Lulling would think up any of a dozen reasons for not partaking of a glass of nettle beer or sweet cicely cordial that would undoubtedly lead to a go of what was known as 'Dotty's Collywobbles', a complaint with which Dr Lovell was well acquainted.

Connie had long stopped trying to persuade her aunt from making these concoctions. She knew it made her aunt happy and she reckoned that their friends were well aware of the risks they took if they accepted a glass of 'a little something' from Dotty. One of the blessings, if you could call it that, of Dotty's old age was that she didn't seem to miss the bottles and jars that Connie would quietly take from the pantry, disposing of the contents down the sink or onto the compost heap.

Ella was stomping along at a fair pace, her mind turning over which excuse she had given Dotty on her last visit, and which excuse she might use this time. She had only recently had a lunchtime snack so perhaps she could—

And at that moment, Ella went flying. She was a substantially built woman and there was no way she could save herself. She landed in a heap in a particularly muddy part of the path.

For a moment she lay there, breathing heavily and uttering little curses under her breath. When she struggled to her knees, she decided nothing had been damaged other than her pride. With some difficulty she heaved herself to her feet. Her voluminous mackintosh was covered in

mud, and was not improved when Ella found a cleanish bit round the back on which she wiped her hands. She peered down at her skirt. 'Drat!' she muttered. There was a tear near the hem.

Ella turned round to see why she had fallen. There was a small but stout branch lying across the path, obviously brought down in the wind earlier that week. But why hadn't she seen it? she thought. She would normally sidestep such a hazard automatically.

Since she was so close to Dotty's cottage, Ella decided to continue on her way. The old girl would be disappointed if she didn't turn up as promised. As she plodded on, she thought back to what the eye specialist had told her some eighteen months earlier, information that she had pushed to the back of her mind and refused to think about. She had blamed her fall on the muddy and slippery path, but she couldn't ignore the fact that she hadn't seen the small branch.

A few minutes later, it was a very bedraggled Ella who presented herself at the cottage.

'Hello, Dotty!' she called, letting herself into the kitchen.

'Through here, Ella. Come along in,' sang out Dotty from her sitting-room.

Dotty, sitting on the sofa with a favourite tartan rug over her legs, was looking expectantly at the door to greet her old friend. When Ella's muddied bulk loomed in the doorway, she squawked in dismay.

'Good gracious, Ella! What on earth has happened to

you? You look as if you've been competing in an obstacle race – through hedges, over ditches, that sort of thing.'

'I had a close encounter with the path coming down here. A branch I swear wasn't there one moment suddenly tangled itself round my legs and I went a purler.'

'Sit down, sit down,' ordered Dotty. 'Connie will be back in a moment, and she can make us both a nice cup of tea. That is unless you would like a little of my crab apple brandy?'

Ella shook her head firmly. 'No, thank you, Dotty. Tea will do nicely but first I must wash off some of this dirt, so I'll put the kettle on at the same time.'

She disappeared back into the kitchen and from the huffing and puffing noise Dotty surmised correctly that Ella was taking off her mackintosh. There followed a few bangs and crashes, then the tap was turned on and the kettle filled.

Ella came back into the sitting-room, pushing her now-clean hands through her short-cropped and wet hair. She had large hands for someone who was a most accomplished needlewoman.

'What I need now most of all is a ciggy. Do you mind, Dotty?'

'No, of course not – except I thought you were trying to give up.'

'And so I am but I'm not succeeding very well,' replied Ella, extracting from a pocket a battered old tin which contained her cigarette-making equipment.

There was silence in the room for a moment, then from

among a billow of blue smoke came a great contented sigh and 'That's much better!'

At that moment, they heard the sound of Connie and Kit's car returning, and soon Connie was clucking round Ella to make sure she was all right.

'I expect I'll have a bruise or two in the morning, but nothing to worry about,' said Ella robustly, accepting a mug of sweet tea. 'It worries me that I didn't see the wretched branch.' She took a sip of tea then continued: 'I've got an appointment with the eye man next week so will find out more then. I know I'm not seeing as well as I did because it takes ages to thread a needle, even with my specs on.'

A little later, kind Kit drove Ella home and as she heaved herself out of the car, clutching her dirty mackintosh to her ample frontage, he called after her. 'I hope the appointment with the optician sorts things out, Ella.'

He wasn't sure she'd heard him since she shut the car door with a bang and stomped up the path to her front door without a backward glance.

Edward and Joan Young had decided to go to The Bear in Woodstock for dinner that evening. Their son Paul was due home from boarding school any day now, and this was an opportunity to give Joan a treat before she had to cook endless meals to satisfy the fast-growing boy, let alone the festive food for Christmas itself.

Edward had just got to the stage when he found he was able to drive past the Burwells' house in the Woodstock Road without turning his head to see what latest ghastliness had been perpetrated, but from the corner of his eye this evening he saw something that made him apoplectic. He pressed the brake so hard that Joan's seat belt locked automatically.

'What on earth—' she spluttered. 'Edward! What's the matter? Are you ill?'

'I am most definitely ill,' stormed Edward, and got out of the car, slamming the door behind him so hard that the car rocked.

Joan released the seat belt and swivelled round to see what had made her husband so angry. Edward was standing on the pavement, looking across at the Burwells' house. By the glow of a nearby street light, she saw immediately what the problem was. The perfectly ordinary wooden gate that used to stand permanently open had gone, together with its metal gateposts. In their place were two large new stone pillars and on the top of each – even Joan shuddered – there was a lion and a unicorn, turned slightly inwards. It was one thing to have such resplendent statues on the gateposts of a stately home, but not a house built between the last two wars!

But her eye was drawn not so much to the statues but to something much worse and, knowing her husband as she did, she knew it would further enrage him. At the foot of each pillar was a light which shone up the stonework, and seemed to end under the chins of the two stone statues. 'Floodlighting's for places of beauty, and nowhere else!' Edward had said to her not long ago when they had passed a Victorian pile that had been converted into a hotel, and had been garishly illuminated.

Edward returned to the car, again slamming the door shut. 'I simply can't believe it. How *could* anyone be so vulgar! And do you know what else they've done?' He turned almost accusingly towards Joan.

'No, dear, but I'm sure you're going to tell me.'

'Did you see those shield things set in front of each of the statues?'

Joan hadn't and it was too late now since Edward re-started the car, letting the clutch out so quickly that the car kangaroo-jumped forward and stalled. She shook her head.

'They've gone and put the name of the house on the shields. And do you know what they've called the place?'

'No. I didn't think it had a specific name. I thought the houses along here were just numbers.'

'Hah!' snorted Edward, re-starting the car. 'Mr and Mrs Hoity-Toity Burwell have gone and called it Blenheim Lodge. Blenheim Lodge! Can you beat it! I can't think why they didn't call it Blenheim Palace while they were at it.'

It wasn't surprising that dinner that evening at The Bear was not a very happy one. Once Edward's architectural taste had been slighted, he was a difficult man to calm down. As they drove home, past Blenheim Lodge, Joan was horrified to see that both her husband's eyes were tightly shut.

CHAPTER FIVE

New Clothes and Old

The Fuchsia Bush was increasingly busy as Christmas approached and Nelly Piggott was dog-tired when she got home each evening, but even so her thoughts often turned to the forthcoming award ceremony.

Clothes also were very much on her mind but there was nothing she could do about it until her day off the following Sunday. As soon as Albert had left the house to go and open up the church for the ten o'clock service, Nelly lumbered up the cottage's steep stairs to her bedroom and went through her entire wardrobe to see what she could wear for the ceremony.

She tried on several dresses and, to her shame, had to set two aside to take down to the charity shop in Lulling. 'Must've shrunk,' she muttered to herself, knowing perfectly well that wasn't true. One dress was possible but, having a rather low neckline, it was more suitable for the evening. She had bought it when Charlie the oilman had taken her to a dinner dance when they lived in Brighton, and that had been the only time she'd worn it.

There was nothing for it, she decided, surveying the pile of discarded dresses on the bed, she'd have to buy a new one. And why not? She rarely spent any money on herself, and had Mrs Peters been alive, she'd have insisted.

Next she checked on her pair of good black shoes. They were several years old, but were still in decent shape. She rubbed her sleeve across the toe, and planned to ask Albert to give them a polish. It was one of the few things her husband did without complaining.

As she made her way downstairs to prepare the Sunday dinner, she felt a flutter of excitement about both the shopping trip and the ceremony.

It was a few days later that Harold Shoosmith decided it was time to have a word with Bobby Cooke. He walked the short way down his garden path and leaned over the gate. Yes, he could see the lad's figure over the churchyard wall. A sullen plume of smoke rose from somewhere close by, which meant that at last the leaves had been raked up and were now being burned. Harold looked at his watch: twelve-thirty so Albert would be out of the way in The Two Pheasants.

The previously unsettled weather had changed and a weak winter sun shone in a sky that was streaked with soft clouds. However, the sun belied the temperature and Harold popped back into the house to collect his sheep-skin jacket. He walked down the green to the churchyard and, as he usually did, detoured slightly to the statue of

Nathaniel Patten. As he approached, a blackbird that had been perching on the figure's shiny head flew off with a squawk of alarm. Harold inspected the statue for any telltale white markings, but the good missionary was pristine.

The lime trees round the churchyard were now quite bare of leaves, of course, but Harold noted there were plenty of leaves still to be swept up this side of the church wall. There was always something of a dispute as to who was responsible for clearing them up – the sexton of St Andrew's or the street-cleaner.

He found Bobby Cooke, a scrawny lad, desultorily sweeping up the twigs that had come down in the previous week's gale. He was whistling a Christmas carol so totally out of tune it was difficult to know which one it was. A bit of everything, Harold decided.

'Ah, Bobby,' Harold said as he approached him.

Bobby stopped what he was doing and leaned on his broom, just like Albert did, Harold noted.

'Af'noon, sir.'

'Now then, Bobby, has Albert talked to you about his decision to retire?'

The boy shifted from one scuffed boot to the other. 'Yeah, well, he did mention somethink about it. Christmas, I thinks he said.'

'Well, the end of the year probably. Neater, don't you think?' Harold asked.

Bobby wasn't sure whether he was meant to reply to that, so just grunted.

'I know you do some gardening work for various

67

people in the village, but I – at least, the PCC – was thinking that you would be the ideal person to take over Albert's job full-time. How does that appeal to you?'

Bobby pushed his less than clean cap to the back of his head, and scratched at his mop of untidy hair.

'Well, I don't rightly know. What's it involve, then?'

Harold pulled an old envelope out of his jacket pocket on which he had scribbled a few headings and peered at it.

'To be honest, I think it'll be just what you've been doing ever since you started helping Albert. Is there anything you don't do?'

'I don't get all dressed up when there's a funeral. I don't 'ave a dark suit, see.'

'But you do everything else?'

'Yeah, and more besides. I do most of the diggin' and liftin' heavy things due to Albert's rheumatics, like.' A crafty look suddenly crossed his face. 'What'll be in it for me, then? I ain't doing no extra work for the same wages. I'd need more, wouldn't I, lots more.'

Harold had anticipated this, and had already cleared the details with the PCC treasurer.

'Yes, we can certainly increase your wages. I suggest that I get a formal letter drawn up by the PCC with details of your duties and the wages we will pay you. Does that sound all right?'

Bobby shifted the broom from one hand to another. 'Yeah, OK, but I'm not committin' to nothink till I've seen that letter.'

'Of course not, I quite understand. Equally, you will

need to decide how much gardening you can do for other people. This job will come first.'

Bobby nodded.

'Very well. I'll have the letter ready for you tomorrow. Goodbye for now.'

Harold turned to leave but Bobby stopped him. 'What about a suit, then? I won't be able to afford a suit out of what I gets now.'

'I'll discuss it with the treasurer. We must be having you neat and tidy for any funeral.'

As he made his way home across the green, Harold wondered if that would ever be possible. The Cooke family were a tearaway lot, and Bobby was one of the worst. He hoped that these new responsibilities would settle the lad. He also wondered if there might be a dark suit among the piles of old clothes that Isobel endlessly collected from friends and neighbours, and then sorted through, setting aside garments that could go to the next village fund-raising jumble sale. He must remember to ask her, he thought, as he pushed open the gate.

'Can I go and play with Toddy this morning?' asked George Curdle at breakfast in Stable Cottage the following Saturday.

'No,' replied his mother, trying to persuade Billy, her youngest, to put the spoonful of cereal into his mouth rather than his ear.

'Oh, why not?' grumbled George.

'Because,' said Molly, looking up at the clock on the

kitchen dresser, 'you and Annie are due over at the school—'

'But it's Sat-tur-day!' broke in George.

'Because you and Annie,' repeated his patient mother, 'are due over at the school for a rehearsal of the Nativity.'

Little fair-haired Annie looked up, a bit of jam-covered toast hovering in mid-air. 'Oh, Mum,' she whined, 'do we have to? We know the story and I'm right bored with them carols.'

Molly wasn't surprised at her daughter's reaction. She only had a small part as an angel. Like every little girl, she'd hankered after being the Virgin Mary, but Louise – a year older and a quiet, sensible girl – had been given the starring role.

George, on the other hand, brightened. 'It's not really boring, not when you've got things to do, like me,' he said importantly. He was playing Joseph. 'I just hopes I remembers me words.'

'I think Mrs Lester is going to be trying on the costumes first thing,' said Molly, giving up with Billy, and wiping his face. 'We ought to leave here just before ten so, if you've finished, go and play quietly till then.'

George and Annie scrambled down from the table, leaving Molly to clear away the breakfast things.

'High time them kids learned to clear the table,' muttered Ben who was sitting in his armchair near the Rayburn. He was reading a magazine to do with cars.

'It's not worth the hassle, Ben,' replied his wife. 'More gets broke than washed up. They're not bad at laying the table.'

'I'm not needed at this rehearsal, am I?' Ben asked.

'Mrs Lester thought we'd need an hour to sort out the costumes. Can you come up about eleven?' asked Molly, raising her voice a little above the noise of the tap filling the sink.

'Fine,' said Ben, getting to his feet. 'I'll just go and have a look at the car. It's rattlin' somewhere.'

Molly smiled. The car was her husband's pride and joy, and a rattle was an insult to his considerable engineering skills.

'See you then,' she said, and waved a soapy hand at Ben's departing back.

Up at Thrush Green School, Alan Lester, the headmaster, had pushed the desks back against the walls in the largest classroom to make space for the rehearsal. In the adjoining classroom, his wife was pulling some work tables together so the costumes could be laid out on them when they arrived. They were boxed up after each year's Nativity and stored by Edward Young who had space in his attic.

'Ah, I see I've arrived at the right time,' said a voice from the doorway.

Margaret Lester turned, and then put a hand to her mouth to stifle a laugh. 'Oh my! You do look funny!'

Edward was submerged under a chaos of angels' cardboard wings and halos stuck on the end of thin pieces of wire.

'Where do you want this lot?' he asked.

'On this table, please,' replied Margaret, and helped Edward lay down his armful as gently as possible.

'Hello,' said Alan Lester, coming to join them. 'Let me give you a hand in with the boxes.'

The thing about the school Nativity was that as long as the same good people of the village helped, the easier things were. They knew the ropes. And Edward was one of these. He didn't have to be reminded that the Saturday before the Nativity was held would be 'costume morning'.

This year, however, the Nativity was going to be a little different. The story – the greatest story of all time – would be the same, of course, but Phil and Frank Hurst had devised some changes to the production. Phil had suggested they become involved when, the previous year, her son Jeremy had declared he wasn't ever, not never, going to do that boring play again.

No one was to know, that mid-December morning, quite how different it was going to be.

In various houses, big and small, parents – or more usually the mothers – were cajoling their youngsters to get ready for the rehearsal up at the school.

Little Louise, due to play the Virgin Mary, was going through her lines with her granny, who lived with them. Not that she had many lines; all she had to do really was sit quietly and look pretty.

'I'm so tired, Joseph,' she said.

'That don't sound as if you're tired,' said her gran.

'But I ain't. I've only just gotten up.'

'You must *pretend* to feel tired. That's what actin's all about. Now, the words again.'

'I'm *so so* ti-erd,' said Louise through a great big yawn.

Her grandmother laughed. 'That's better, but it'd be better if you said the words and then yawned, rather than try to do both at the same time.'

In a large house on one of the roads leading north out of the village towards Woodstock, Mrs Gibbons was similarly instructing her twin boys in the parts they were to play – two of the Three Kings. Since Mrs Gibbons was chairman of the PTA, Alan Lester had thought it sensible to give the lads big roles. However, James and Anthony Gibbons were reluctant thespians. They reckoned the Nativity play was for the younger children, and had only agreed when they heard Paul Young and Jeremy Prior were going to take part. When the twins had been in the bottom class of the school, they had looked up to Paul and Jeremy, then at the top of the little village school.

'We are the Three Kings come from afar,' intoned James, who had slightly darker hair than his brother.

'Just two at the moment,' quipped Anthony. 'The other will be along in a moment.'

'Anthony, behave!' said his mother sharply.

'Come to see the baby,' continued James.

'Spin out the word "baby",' commanded Mrs Gibbons. 'It's what the whole play is about. Baaaaby.'

'Ba-aa-by,' giggled Anthony, baa-ing like a sheep.

'I wish we could be sheep, just lying in the corner, and not having to be decked out in stupid robes,' James grumbled.

'Sheep are unimportant parts,' said Mrs Gibbons sharply. 'Now, once more, and then we must be off.'

'Do you think we'll ever get this play off the ground?' Frank Hurst asked his wife anxiously over the breakfast table.

'I don't see why not,' replied Phil. 'Anything must be better than the Nativity being done in the same old way. I'm sure that having Paul and Jeremy in different parts of the church, with their voices coming from unexpected places, will keep people awake. I just hope the parents have coached the main parts properly. I know it's difficult to do this during school because the children without parts tend to interrupt the whole time. Let's hope this morning's rehearsal, without the unwanted extras, will go better. Now, have you had enough coffee? We ought to leave in a moment – or at least I do because I said I would help Margaret with the costumes. You could come up later.'

'I'll do that.'

Phil bent down and gave her husband a little peck on the cheek. 'I'll see you at about eleven then.'

When Phil arrived at the school on the other side of the green, she found a hive of activity. In one classroom, eight or ten young children were practising 'Away in a Manger' to the accompaniment of Miss Robinson at the piano.

No, not Miss Robinson any more, remembered Phil. The young woman who taught the infants had got married that summer and was now Mrs Hope. Although the children had become quickly accustomed to her new name, some of the parents still found it difficult to remember so she was often called 'Miss Robin-I-mean-Hope'.

Phil went into the other classroom which had been turned into the temporary dressing-room. She stood in the doorway and surveyed the scene in front of her.

Little Louise was sitting on a desk, her legs swinging in front of her. Behind her, the young probationary teacher was stitching something on the shoulder of the child's long blue dress.

'Oh bother!' she exclaimed. 'I've gone and sewn through to your vest, and will have to unpick it.'

Margaret Lester had dressed Anthony Gibbons without too much trouble, and had gone off to see to the shepherds. Mrs Gibbons was left to deal with James, who was wriggling inside a bright red robe that had been dropped over his head.

'Can't find the armholes,' came a muffled cry from inside.

'Shall I shine a torch down the front, Jimmy?' called his brother.

'His name is James,' snapped Mrs Gibbons, who was trying to sort out the muddle from underneath. 'Now stop struggling,' she commanded. 'You're like a ten-armed octopus inside there.'

Finally, James's head, hair all sticking up, emerged from the top of the robe, a rather pink face following. 'Phew! Hot in there.'

His mother tied a length of coloured cord round the boy's waist. She straightened the robe on the shoulders, pulled the hem down a bit at the back, then stood back to check on the overall effect.

'You'll do,' she announced. 'Or, at least, you will once everything is ironed. Now, off you go to Mrs Hurst to sort out your headdresses.'

Phil pulled a box marked 'Headgear but not halos' towards her. 'Hello, you two, how're things going?'

'Awright, I suppose,' mumbled James. He still wished he could be a sheep.

'Now, which is which? I never can tell,' asked Phil.

'I'm Anthony,' said James automatically. 'And I'm James,' replied his brother Anthony.

The boys grinned as Phil turned back to the box to rummage inside for the crowns that were set aside for the kings.

She put three crowns on the table and then looked at

each of them in turn. 'I think we might jettison that one,' she said. 'It's got a bad tear in it. I'll make a new one in time for next week.'

Mrs Gibbons, who had stopped to have a chat with one of the other mothers, now arrived. 'I'll do it, if you like,' she said to Phil. 'You'll be busy with other things. I'll get some gold card on Monday.'

Phil thanked her. Mrs Gibbons wasn't so bad – her bark was much worse than her bite. And she had changed a bit since her husband had suddenly died the previous year. It almost seemed that she'd had to compete with her husband's bossiness. Phil had gone out of her way to be friendly with the woman; after all, she'd known what it was like to be a single mother.

At the far end of the room, Alan Lester clapped his hands together. 'Is everyone ready? It's past eleven o'clock and we should be getting on with the rehearsal.'

Although this was not the official dress rehearsal, it was felt the children would perform better if they kept on the costumes they had been allocated, creased as they were. The angels, with neither wings nor halos yet attached, were a drab group.

There was a cry from one corner of the room. 'I've gone an' lost me crook. 'As anyone seen me crook?'

Margaret Lester unearthed a two-foot-high crook from under a pile of discarded jeans and jumpers, and waved it in the air. 'Here you are, Patrick. Come along now, all next door.'

'Do you need us?' called Ben Curdle, who had arrived

and was sorting through bits of scenery with another parent.

'No, I think you're more useful there,' replied Phil. 'We'll run through your part next Saturday morning when the costume arrives.'

The next hour was, to put it mildly, something more akin to a Whitehall farce than a Nativity play. Alan Lester and Frank Hurst took the narrators' parts – Paul and Jeremy would just have the final rehearsal the following Saturday morning to learn what they were supposed to do and where – and Phil encouraged the youngsters as the play hiccupped from one little scene to the next.

One of the angels had a little 'accident' in the middle of the scene with Archangel Gabriel's pronouncement that Mary was to have a baby, and everything had to stop while she was mopped up.

'But now I ain't got no knickers on,' she wailed.

The shepherds and kings smirked.

'It doesn't matter, darling,' soothed Phil. 'No one can see.'

Finally, it was the turn of the Three Kings to make their entrance. When the little entourage stopped in front of the crib, James and Anthony remembered their lines perfectly – making Mrs Gibbons feel a trifle smug – but the third king, a slightly smaller lad called Davey Biddle, was very lacklustre.

'I am – er – number – er . . . What number am I, miss? I can't remember.' The child wiped a finger under his nose.

'Three, Davey, number three.'

The child stood and looked at Phil dumbly.

'Go on,' called Mrs Gibbons who was sitting on a chair to one side. 'Number Three King.'

Little Davey took a deep breath and started again. 'I am Number – er – Three King and – um – I bring you gold.'

'No, not gold! My James has just brought the gold,' Mrs Gibbons cried.

'Thank you, Mrs Gibbons. Perhaps you could leave this to me,' called Phil across the room. 'In fact, I think the children would do better without any parents in the room. It's been a long rehearsal. Could I ask you all to wait in the other classroom?'

Mrs Gibbons looked affronted, but moved next door with a handful of other parents.

'Now, Davey, will you try again?' asked Phil gently. 'You are bringing myrrh.'

'Can't I bring gold?' the boy pleaded. 'I knows what that is.'

'We're bigger than you,' said Anthony Gibbons, giving the smaller boy a little push. 'And we get to bring the frankincense and gold.'

Phil intervened. 'Now then, lads, go easy. The kings mustn't be seen to be having fisticuffs.' She turned to young Davey. 'Myrrh isn't difficult to say, Davey. It might be spelt in a funny way, but it's pronounced "mer" – just like "her" but with an "m".'

To her horror, the boy dissolved into tears. 'I want to go home.'

Mrs Hope, who was sitting at the piano and in whose class the child was, came across the room. 'This is very unlike you, Davey,' she said. 'We chose you because we felt you would do it so well.'

But the child wasn't to be comforted. 'I want to go home to my mum.'

Phil nodded in resignation. 'We'll go and see if we can find someone to take you home. Did he come with a parent?' she asked Mrs Hope.

'Yes, he's next door with the scenery.'

Phil took the sobbing child by the hand. 'Come along then. When I get back, Mrs Hope, we'll have another run-through of "Silent Night". It's much too dirge-like at the moment.'

Phil took Davey into the other classroom and reunited him with his father who was holding a papier-mâché palm tree while Ben plugged a hole near the bottom of its trunk.

Phil explained the situation and suggested Mr Biddle should take the over-wrought child back to his mother.

'Come along, then, son,' he said. 'We'll get you home. All been a bit much for you, has it?' He turned to Phil. 'I don't know what the matter can be. He's usually fine at things like this.'

'Never mind,' said Phil. 'Just so long as you're all right for next weekend.'

If she had been a superstitious person, she might not have said that.

After the rehearsal, and once the classrooms had been restored to order, Frank suggested he and Phil should go along the road to The Two Pheasants. There was often a gathering of their friends in the pub before lunch at weekends, and both felt they deserved a drink for their efforts.

They found Harold in there, with Edward Young and his brother-in-law, John Lovell.

Harold hailed them with pleasure. 'You've survived! Well done. Now, what can I get you?'

The small group sat at a table in the window, and Phil told them about the rehearsal, and the small drama with the reluctant King Number Three.

'I remember going to a Nativity play when I was out in Africa,' said Harold, 'and they had a real live baby in the crib, and Mary rode up the aisle on a real donkey.'

'Now there's a thought,' mused Phil, putting down her glass of cider. 'Are there any new babies in the village, John?' she asked.

'Not in my care,' he replied. 'Anyway, I'm not sure many parents would want their newborn baby in a draughty church.'

'St Andrew's isn't draughty,' protested Harold. 'At least, not once the south door is shut.'

'But what about a donkey?' asked Phil. 'Does anyone have a donkey?'

'You could ask Dotty,' suggested Edward. 'It's the sort of thing she'd know.'

'Good idea. I'll pop over and see her tomorrow. I owe her a visit anyway,' said Phil.

'Mind you don't eat or drink anything that will give you a go of the collywobbles,' warned John Lovell. 'The Nativity play will need you at full strength next week.'

The group laughed. It was good to be among friends in Thrush Green.

In a cottage set beside the lane to Lulling Woods, Mrs Biddle clucked over young Davey like a mother hen.

'Poor lamb, you not feelin' well, then?'

'Me head aches,' said the boy, running a hand through his tousled mousy mop.

'We'll have some dinner. That will make you feel better. Probably all the excitement were too much for you.'

This roused Davey who said more forcefully, 'No, it weren't that. Nothing much to get excited about. I just didn't feel like joinin' in.' Then he added, 'An' I'm not hungry.'

Mrs Biddle wiped her hands down her flowered pinny, and then felt the boy's forehead. 'You feels all right. If you don't want no dinner, just you sit there, quiet like. Dad,' she said, turning to Mr Biddle, who was washing his hands at the sink, 'go and call them other two. They're out the back somewhere. No doubt they'll eat what Davey don't want.'

But not even the thought of his elder brother and sister eating his dinner stirred young Davey from his apathy.

CHAPTER SIX

In Search of a Donkey

The following morning, which turned out to be another dull overcast day, Phil went to see Dotty. Because the low clouds threatened rain, she took the car and was glad of her decision since it began to pour shortly after she had left Thrush Green. As she drove down the narrow lane that led to Dotty's cottage, puddles had already formed on the pitted surface and the car sent up a spray of water on either side, soaking the already bedraggled grass verges.

'High time this lane was resurfaced,' she muttered, swerving to avoid another pothole.

'Come in quickly out of the rain,' cried Kit, opening the back door as Phil arrived. 'Here, let me take your mac. I'll find a hanger for it.'

'Oh heavens, don't worry about that old thing,' laughed Phil. 'It's my gardening mac. The one I throw on when it's raining but the rubbish must be put out, or some herbs gathered in.'

'Herbs?' rang out a frail voice from the sitting-room. 'Have you come for some of my herbs?'

'You go on through,' said Kit, 'and I'll put the kettle on. Connie will be back soon.'

Phil went into the next room, and kissed the wrinkled and paper-thin cheek that was offered to her. Dotty was lying on the sofa as usual, the tartan rug wrapped round her legs. A small earthquake appeared to take place under the rug then a hairy white head appeared.

'Hello, Bruce,' said Phil, ruffling the Westie's head.

'Go back under the rug, there's a good boy,' commanded Dotty. 'He's my hot-water bottle, you see.'

'It's nice and warm in here,' said Phil, stretching out her hands to the fire. 'It's pretty miserable outside. Definitely a day to stay indoors.'

'Yes, maybe, but I'll still have to go out and shut up the chickens and ducks this afternoon,' said Dotty, rearranging the rug back over the bump beside her on the sofa.

'We'll see about that,' said Kit, bringing in a tray of mugs. 'Coffee for you, Phil, and here's your tea, Dot.'

'Coffee! Pah!' spat out Dotty inelegantly. 'Can't think why you drink the stuff. Now a good cup of herbal tea does you the world of good. And this is a particularly good batch – blackberry and elderflower!'

'Good gracious!' said Phil. 'I thought you made elderflower cordial and blackberry wine, but I've never heard of blackberry and elderflower tea before. Which does it taste of?'

Dotty proffered her mug towards Phil.

'I don't think I'll taste it, but I will smell it, if I may.' She sniffed at the steam that arose from the mug. 'Hmm . . . I think I can smell the elderflower, but the blackberry eludes me.'

'The blackberry gives the colour and the sweetness, the elderflower the flavour,' said Dotty, taking a sip and sighing with deep contentment. 'Now then, tell me all the gossip.'

Considering that Dotty very rarely left her cottage or garden nowadays, it was amazing how much she knew about what was going on in Thrush Green and Lulling. Phil wasn't one for gossip so Dotty had to be content with hearing all about the Nativity play.

'Which is why I'm here really,' Phil said finally. 'I'm looking for a donkey.'

'A donkey?' said Connie, coming into the room. 'Hello, Phil. Nice to see you. Sorry I wasn't here when you arrived. It was Matins at Lulling Woods this morning, and I thought someone from this house should go.'

'Many people?' Phil asked.

'Oh, the usual crowd – eight of us, I think. I feel so sorry for Charles Henstock, coming all the way out here for so few people. But tell me about the donkey. I trust one hasn't been found in the porch of St Andrew's and is looking for a home?'

This was where Bruce, the West Highland terrier, had been found several years previously.

Phil laughed. 'No, don't worry. I'm actually looking to borrow one, for the Nativity play next Saturday. I thought you, Dotty, might know where I could find one.'

Connie sounded surprised. 'A donkey – in church? What would the good rector think of that?'

'He won't actually be there,' replied Phil. 'St John's have got their own Christingle service that evening, so Harold as senior churchwarden will be in overall charge. But Charles has given permission. So long as we clean up behind it.'

Dotty was deep in thought. Then she said, 'The Hughes in Nidd had a donkey but they passed it on when the children grew up.'

'That must have been at least twenty years ago, Aunt Dot,' murmured Connie, but Dotty wasn't listening.

'There used to be one in a field on the outskirts of

Lulling, but I seem to remember hearing that it had fallen into the Pleshey and drowned.'

'Poor thing,' said Phil.

'I believe it was very old,' said Dotty. Then she brightened. 'I know! What about contacting the Blue Cross at Burford? They often have donkeys and might be prepared to lend one for the play.'

'That's a good idea. Thanks, Dotty. I was sure you'd come up with a solution.'

'Good place that, the Blue Cross. We ought to give the proceeds of one of our jumbles to it, instead of endlessly to church thingies.'

Dotty was always trying to persuade the village committees to give money to one of the animal causes dear to her heart, but the church roof or the African appeal usually won.

'I'll ring the Blue Cross tomorrow and let you know what happens. Now, I must get home and give Frank his lunch.' As Phil rose, she suddenly remembered there was a bit of news they might not yet have heard. 'Did you know that Albert Piggott is retiring?'

'What, again?' asked Connie. 'He must have retired three times since I've been living here with Aunt Dot.'

'Apparently, it's for real this time. Or so Harold says. Been approved by the PCC, and young Bobby Cooke is taking over.'

'Well, he's a waste of space if ever there was,' snorted Dotty. 'Albert's bone idle most of the time, but he's good with animals. He and I have always got on.'

'He'll probably drink his pension away at the pub,'

remarked Kit, going with Phil through to the kitchen and helping her on with her mac. 'Thanks so much for coming down. It does the old girl a world of good to see people other than us. I hope the Nativity goes well. I'm sorry I won't be there, but I'll be at your party afterwards. One of us must be here with Dotty so I'm doing first shift, and Connie will do the second.'

'It will be nice to see you at whatever time,' said Phil, pulling a headscarf out of her pocket and covering her head. The rain was still lashing against the kitchen window.

Kit held the door open. 'It's getting a bit of a problem, I'm afraid, but there'll be plenty of time to enjoy ourselves when old Dot has gone.'

Phil wasn't sure how to reply to that, so she ran through the rain to her car. 'Goodbye,' she shouted over her shoulder.

Phil's call to the Blue Cross the following morning was to no avail. They would have liked to help, they said, but policy deemed otherwise. They hoped Mrs Hurst understood. Phil didn't really and Frank tried to allay her disappointment.

'It's probably just as well. A donkey might bite one of the children, kick a doting granny or, heaven forfend, infest the entire cast with fleas.'

Phil laughed but her good humour didn't last long. The telephone rang; it was Alan Lester calling to tell her that Davey Biddle had chickenpox.

'Poor mite,' she said. 'No wonder he was feeling so rotten on Saturday. Can you find me a replacement king?'

Alan told her that he had drafted in Bill Hooper, saying he'd had to do a bit of persuading because Bill, being the tallest boy in the school, definitely considered himself too big for the Nativity play. However, when the headmaster had casually mentioned that he thought Bill would make a good Playground Captain the next term – the child responsible for seeing that the lines of children were straight before going back into school from the play-ground after the various breaks – Bill had been won over.

But the finger in the dam didn't last long. On Wednesday morning, Alan telephoned Phil with the news that both James and Anthony Gibbons were smitten with spots.

'Now what do we do?' Phil cried. 'If three have got it, then surely all the rest will?'

'Not necessarily,' replied Alan. 'We had an outbreak a couple of years ago and a number of children got it then. I've asked Mrs Hope to check the register to see if we can track down who was absent at that time. I'll ring you during the dinner break.'

Phil went to Frank's study where he was working to tell him the news. As usual, he was quite calm.

'Don't worry about it, Phil. There is nothing we can do for the moment.'

'But if more go down with it . . .' Phil's voice faded away.

'Then we'll have to cancel, and resurrect it for next year.'

'I suppose so. But it's all the hard work that we've put into it so far. And should we stop the mothers ironing and mending the costumes? It will be a waste of time if they're just going to be packed away in boxes again.'

'Do you need to make a final decision now? Can't we wait another day to see whether any more catch it?'

'Yes, I suppose so,' said Phil again. 'Thank you, dear, you're so sensible.' She looked at her watch. 'You should've left for Sussex by now. Jeremy will never forgive you if you're late collecting him.'

Frank took off his spectacles and put them in their case. 'I'm going now and we'll be back for a late lunch.'

Phil waved him off and then returned to the house. She'd woken that morning in good spirits, only for them to be dashed when the headmaster had rung about the Gibbons twins. She was sitting at the kitchen table, idly looking at the newspaper, when the telephone rang again, making her jump.

'Hello, Phil, it's Alan Lester again. I've got some more bad news, I'm afraid,' and as Phil gasped, he added quickly, 'and some better news. I'll give you the bad news first. You've lost the Virgin Mary now. Louise has caught the wretched pox.'

'Oh, Alan!' cried Phil. 'We'll definitely have to cancel.'

'I don't think it'll be necessary. Not yet, anyway. Mrs Hope has checked the register and our various medical records and, apart from one angel, all the rest of the cast has had chickenpox. But what about Jeremy and Paul?'

'Jeremy had it a few years ago, and I've rung Joan who's confirmed Paul has had it. So we should be all right with our narrators. But what about our kings and a Mary? We can't go on without those.'

'I've had a think,' said Alan. 'In fact, I have been doing little else.' He laughed. 'What about Annie Curdle? She's a self-assured little thing, and I'm sure she could cope. Especially since George will be there beside her as Joseph. More importantly, they've both had chickenpox.'

'It's a good idea. Have you asked her parents?'

'Not yet. I wanted to run it past you first. I'm tied up here at the moment. Could you ring Molly?'

'Better still, I'll walk across now,' responded Phil. 'But what about our kings, and aren't we going to be a bit short of angels?'

'Leave it with me,' said Alan. 'I'm going to have a word with Mrs Todd to see if she will let Jimmy join us.' Then by way of explanation, he added, 'They're Plymouth Brethren, you see, so Jimmy doesn't go to St Andrew's. Or we might have to do with just two shepherds instead of three, and I'll think of someone for the third king. As for angels, Mrs Hope is sure she can get a few more of the older infants. In fact, it's not the infants that we have to persuade but their parents. It seems that the whole of Thrush Green goes shopping on Saturdays. I must rush now. Ring me, will you, after school, to let me know about Annie Curdle.'

After the headmaster had rung off, Phil stood for a moment gathering her thoughts. Was it really worth all this trouble? Yes, she told herself sternly. Even if the younger generation of parents didn't want to go to the

Nativity service, there were plenty of older residents of Thrush Green who would certainly attend.

She looked at her watch. There was time to pop across to see Molly Curdle, and be back by the time Jeremy arrived home. She peered out of the window. The trees on the green were being buffeted by the wind, but it didn't appear to be raining, so she put on an old jacket, pulled on a woolly hat and set out.

Winnie Bailey was in her garden next door, replenishing the bird-nut feeder, and Phil walked down the pavement a short way so she could talk to her over the fence.

'Well done, Winnie. You are good. I keep forgetting to fill my container but I'll give the chore to Jeremy as a holiday job.'

'I wouldn't ever forget the birds. They give me so much pleasure. Also' – she paused a moment to secure the top of the container and re-hook it to a slender branch of the apple tree – 'it always reminds me of dear Donald. He used to love having his second cup of breakfast coffee sitting at the study window, so he could watch the birds. Nuthatches were his favourite.'

'You fill me with good intentions,' said Phil. 'I will put bird nuts on my shopping list as soon as I get home.' She waved goodbye to Winnie and then walked across the corner of the green to Stable Cottage.

It proved to be a successful visit. Molly was sure that Annie would be thrilled to be the Virgin Mary and confirmed that both her children had had chickenpox. She also agreed to go down to the cottage where spotty Louise lived and collect the blue robe. It would need to be short-ened, but Molly was good with her needle and said it would be an easy job.

Having thanked her profusely, Phil walked back to-wards Tullivers. There was a glimmer of sun in the sky – the first they'd had for some days – and Phil tipped her face up towards it. She was sure she could feel the faintest of warm rays on her cheeks. A robin celebrated from a nearby chimneypot, fluting its melody sweetly, and Phil stopped to listen to it, her eyes closed.

Peep – peep! Peep – peep – peeeeeep!

Phil opened her eyes, and saw her husband's car draw up outside the house. From out of the car flew her beloved son, Jeremy.

'Hi, Mum, I'm home! Oh, happy, happy Christmas!' And, reaching her, he gave his mother a great big hug.

'Jeremy's home,' remarked Harold Shoosmith, who was standing at his sitting-room window that overlooked the green.

'Phil'll be pleased,' replied Isobel, looking up from a pair of socks she was darning. 'She loves that boy.'

'He still seems to be a nice lad. It's sad how adolescence makes such a mess of the young nowadays, the boys especially.'

'And you would know,' Isobel responded, smiling. 'So much experience.'

Harold turned from the window to look at her. The remark had rather wounded him. 'All right, I know I haven't had children, but I like to think I'm broad-minded. I read the newspaper every day and—'

'And listen to the news twice a day,' Isobel continued. It was a well-worn theme.

'Mock me if you must,' Harold said ruefully, 'but I consider myself up to date with the present day.'

'Of course you are, dearest. Now, what are you going to do this afternoon? You've finished the newspaper, including the crossword, and there's another four hours until the six o'clock news.'

'If you don't mind, I thought I would pop over and see Ella, make sure she's quite recovered from that fall she had.' The village grapevine had ensured the news of Ella's fall on the way to see Dotty was common knowledge in less than twenty-four hours. 'I think she sometimes gets lonely over there on her own,' Harold continued.

'I don't, for a moment, think Ella is lonely. From what everyone tells me, she and Dimity got on well together when they both lived there, but I think Ella is someone who appreciates her own company. Think how often she leaves some gathering or other and goes off home, long before the party has broken up.'

'That's true,' Harold conceded. 'It's almost as though she gets bored with the small talk. Anyway, if it's all right with you, I'll go over and chat with her for a bit.'

'Fine by me,' replied his wife. 'I could pretend I'm quite happy darning these socks but, I'm warning you, my New Year's resolution is to darn no more socks. Life's too short both to stuff mushrooms and to darn socks. You must learn to wear socks that are a mixture of wool and nylon, or whatever. Something that doesn't go into holes.'

'But those are my favourite yellow cashmere socks,' protested Harold. 'And it was only a tiny hole.'

'Tiny holes turn into bigger ones,' replied Isobel. 'But I know you love these socks and since I love you, I'm darning them.'

Harold bent over the back of Isobel's chair and kissed the top of her head. 'I won't be long.'

The pale sun that Phil Hurst had turned her face towards was still shining as Harold left the house. He hesitated whether to go via the green, which was the shortest way, or go round by the road. How wet was it? He went and stood on the edge of the green: it looked dry enough so he set off across it.

'Good afternoon, Nathaniel,' he said as he strode past the statue of the missionary on its plinth. Harold was gratified to see that it was still gleaming clean from his ministrations earlier in the month.

A large black bird flapped lazily across the sky ahead of him. 'Lots of crows is rooks, one rook is a crow,' he murmured. It was one of his favourite adages. 'And good afternoon to you, Mr Crow.'

He was shortly pushing open the gate leading to Ella's house. He saw the formidable bulk of his friend standing in her sitting-room window, and waved to her. But she didn't wave back. She was peering at something in her hand, and obviously hadn't seen him so Harold hailed her.

'Ella, hello–o!'

Ella looked up then, and raised her hand in greeting. A second later the front door opened and she ushered him in.

'How lovely to see you. It means I can put this wretched piece of needlework aside and have a ciggy. You don't mind, do you?'

'It's your house so of course I don't mind. Any chance of a cup of coffee?'

Ella shoved her cigarette-making equipment back into the side pocket of her capacious trousers. 'Of course. Let's go into the kitchen. Warmer there.'

Harold followed the large figure through into the kitchen at the back, and settled himself at the table. Ella put some water in the kettle and turned it on. She then plumped herself down in a chair opposite Harold. 'Well, then, what's new?' she asked.

This was a typical Ella Bembridge opening. She might as well have said: 'I've got a good bit of gossip, but you go first.'

'I don't think I've got any news. Jeremy Prior has just got home for the holidays. And I hear Frank and Phil are having a bit of trouble with the Nativity service. A number of children going down with chickenpox.'

'Joan told me that Molly had told her that Phil had told her that they were hanging in there for as long as possible. But they may have to cancel if any more children fall out.'

After a moment, the kettle boiled and Ella pulled herself to her feet and went to attend to the coffee. She made it straight into a mug, added a bit of milk, and put it in front of Harold.

'Not having any yourself?' he asked.

'No, I had some earlier. Actually,' she said, leaning across the table to peer at Harold's mug, 'is it all right? Mine tasted most odd.'

Harold took a tentative sip and immediately spluttered. 'This isn't coffee, Ella! I'm not sure what it is, but it's certainly not coffee.'

'Oh dear!' cried Ella. 'I hope I haven't poisoned you.'

Harold got up to fetch a spoon from the draining-board and he stirred the brown mixture in his mug. 'It's got bits floating in it. It's not one of Dotty's concoctions, is it?'

'Heavens, no! I know when to leave well alone.'

Ella turned to the shelf above the stove, took down a jar and peered at it. 'That's coffee in there, isn't it?'

Harold looked at the glass canister. 'Well, if it is, it's the funniest-looking coffee I've ever seen.' He took the lid off the canister and cautiously sniffed inside. 'Don't know what it is. It doesn't have much of a smell. But it's certainly not coffee.'

Ella took the container from him, and tipped a little of its contents into the palm of her hand. She tilted her head on one side and peered at it. Then she stuck out a pink tongue and licked at the pile.

'Do be careful,' Harold cautioned. 'It might be poisonous.'

'If it's on that shelf, it's certainly not poisonous. I keep everything like that in the garden shed.' She had another lick, a bit bigger than the first.

Harold looked at the shelf she'd pointed out, and took down a jar of instant coffee. 'Here's the coffee,' he said and took off the lid to check inside. 'Yes, that's coffee all right. But what's in your jar?'

'I know!' said Ella triumphantly. 'It's bran! I heard a piece about it on the wireless the other day, about how it's good for you, fibre and all that. Thought I'd have a try. Didn't like it much. Got in the teeth.' And with that, she tipped the contents into the pedal bin beside the sink.

'I could have used that for my slug traps,' said Harold. 'Now sit down, Ella, and I'll make us both some coffee with this.' And he held up the jar of instant coffee.

Over the mugs of perfectly decent coffee, Harold talked to Ella about her eyesight. He knew Ella was a very proud, independent person, but they'd always got on well and Ella appreciated Harold's good sense.

'I went to see the eye man a week ago, and he wants me to go back to the specialist in Oxford. He reckons the macular degeneration has got worse . . .' Her voice trailed away, then she added very quietly, 'Much worse.'

'Oh, my dear, I'm so sorry,' said Harold, with immense sympathy for Ella. 'I knew you were having problems with your eyes, but I didn't know quite what. Tell me about it.'

Ella gave a great sigh and she didn't speak for a moment.

'Ella,' prompted Harold, 'a problem shared is a problem halved.'

Ella shifted in her chair, and looked at Harold. 'It developed quite slowly to start with. About eighteen months ago, the optician thought there'd been degenerative changes to the back of both eyes, and sent me to Mr

Cobbold, the specialist in Oxford. He confirmed the onset of macular degeneration, which was worse in the left eye. Both eyes are affected but because the right eye wasn't as bad as the left, I've been managing.' Ella stopped to cough, a wheezing chesty cough. 'But now the right eye is in trouble. If I look at you head on' – and Ella turned her head so she was staring straight at Harold – 'then I can hardly make you out at all. But if I turn my head, and look at you sort of sideways, I can see you a little better but your face is still blurred.'

'Can anything be done to stop the degeneration?' Harold asked.

'Apparently not. The chap told me they're throwing a great deal of money into research but it won't be in time to help me.'

'And what of the future?'

Ella sighed. 'I don't know. He wants me to go back to see Mr Cobbold. He said the disease can progress at different speeds. I won't go completely blind and will always retain a little peripheral vision but the central vision of the right eye is damaged, which is why I've recently been having such difficulty with the things I love most – my handiwork, my sewing and knitting. And reading. Soon I may not be able to do them at all.' She swallowed hard and looked away.

Harold sat quietly and waited for her to get her emotions under control.

Then Ella got up and walked through to the sitting-room. She returned with the piece of needlework that she had been inspecting when he had arrived.

'Look at that,' she said, tossing it onto the table in front of him.

Harold picked it up, and then turned it so the design was the right way up. He recognized the rabbit and the unicorn from the famous tapestries he had seen in the Musée de Cluny in France. He didn't know anything about tapestry or needlepoint, but he had always admired the way Ella's chubby fingers were able to produce such tiny stitches.

'Just look at it! Stitches all over the place.'

Even Harold, who seldom had the need to hold a needle, was able to see there were a great many false stitches and, in several places, the coloured thread seemed to be in quite the wrong place. The unicorn's horn, for instance, definitely had a kink in it.

'More than anything,' Ella said, 'is my worry about what I shall do when I can't do my needlework or handiwork any more.'

'What did the optician say?' asked Harold, handing the needlework back to Ella. 'What about using a magnifier? I've seen advertisements for those.'

'But it won't work if my central vision goes completely. At the moment, it comes and goes, but I'm finding it much more difficult. It's fine at one moment, then the lines go all distorted and squiggly. That's why I am putting the stitches in the wrong place.'

Ella heaved a great sigh, and then in what Harold realized was an act of great frustration, she hurled the piece of needlework across the kitchen.

'To be honest, Harold, life just won't be worth living.'

And with that, she turned her back on Harold and stared out of the kitchen window.

'Ella, I'm so sorry—' began Harold.

'Don't,' said Ella fiercely. 'I can't be doing with sympathy. Just go, will you?'

Harold put out his hand and touched Ella's shoulder. 'Chin up, old girl. We'll think of something. Bye now.'

When Harold looked back as he left the kitchen, she was in the same position. But as he put his hand on the front door knob to let himself out, he thought he heard a faint, 'Thanks for coming.'

When Harold got home, he found Isobel in the kitchen icing the Christmas cake, and told her of his worries about Ella.

'It's not that I think she's a danger to herself. It's not like someone beginning to lose their mind. You know, like putting the electric kettle onto the gas ring to boil. But she seems so utterly depressed.'

Harold pulled out a chair and sat down. He dipped a finger into the bowl of icing, like a child might do. And Isobel, equally as she might with a child, gently admonished him. 'Don't pick! You can have the bowl to lick out when I've finished – although too much sugar isn't good for you.' She dipped her palette knife into a jug of hot water standing on the table beside her, and continued to smooth down the icing.

'Don't make it too level,' said Harold. 'I like the top to look a bit like snow. It makes it more fun for the little sledges.'

'Honestly!' laughed Isobel. 'Grown men turn into little boys when it comes to Christmas. But talking of sledges, can you fetch the box of cake decorations for me. They're in the spare-room cupboard.'

When Isobel had married Harold, she had left most of her old life behind but she had brought the old Clarks shoebox that contained the Christmas cake decorations her mother had used when Isobel was a child. There was a little snowman, his once-red scarf now very faded; a couple of sledges; and a reindeer with only three legs. Isobel now craftily set it against a little crest of icing to compensate for its lost limb. The final decoration, which was always placed in the middle of the cake, was a robin on a log – and the robin was on a tiny spring so it wobbled.

After Isobel had carefully placed this on the cake, she stood back to admire her work. 'That'll do, I think,' she said, wiping her hands on her apron.

Harold leaned across the table, and tapped the robin so it rocked back and forth. 'Hello, robin. Happy Christmas!'

Isobel smiled indulgently at her husband. 'Now, once I've cleared all this up, what about a cup of tea? You can tell me more about Ella, and we can have a think about what we can do to help.'

CHAPTER SEVEN

A Very Special Teapot

On the Monday morning of the award week, Nelly Piggott at last found time to take an hour off to go shopping. Her plan to look for a new dress had suffered a set-back when Rosa had called in sick the previous Monday, which meant they were one assistant short in the tea-room and Nelly had had to help out. But the girl had sent a message with her sister on Friday to say she was better and would be back to work the following week. It was always quiet first thing on a Monday and Nelly had gone in early to get the lunch preparations under way.

'Just poppin' out,' she said to Rosa as she walked through the tea-room. 'Won't be a tick.'

After her large bulk had gone down the handsome steps in front of The Fuchsia Bush and turned left down the High Street, Poppy turned to Rosa. 'Want a bet that she comes back with a bag from one of them designer clothes shops?'

'And why not,' her sister responded, sticking up for their boss. 'Wouldn't you if you'd won an award? We'll have to be extra neat an' tidy on Thursday, too.'

Nelly was away a little longer than she had intended. She found just the dress she wanted – hyacinth blue with a white collar – but, after turning this way and that in front of the changing-room mirror, she had to admit that she really needed one size larger and the assistant said they were sold out of that size.

Typical, thought Nelly, as she struggled out of the dress. Why don't they order more of the most popular sizes? She seemed quite oblivious of the fact that the size she needed was very close to the top end of the range.

After searching through the rails of another two shops, she was beginning to despair. One of the problems was that the dress shops were full of party wear – all glitter and tinsel – and she'd had to share changing-rooms with giggling office girls trying on impossibly short and tight-fitting confections in which they would grace their office parties the following week.

Finally, Nelly had overcome her pride and had gone into a shop in a little arcade that sold 'clothes for the more generous figure'. And here she found the perfect dress. It was in a colour that the assistant described as a 'loverly crushed raspberry', had three-quarter sleeves and a pretty scalloped neckline. It was high-waisted and the skirt fell in soft folds, hiding Nelly's portly figure. Before she went back to work, she popped into Boots to buy a new lipstick to match the dress. She smiled when she saw it was called Ripe Raspberry.

She was so pleased with her purchases that she didn't mind the smirks on the faces of Rosa and Poppy as she walked through the tea-room, not even when the word 'outsize!' floated in the air before the door into the kitchen swung behind her.

'So you sees,' said Albert Piggott to his drinking companions in The Two Pheasants the following day, 'I'll be at the wife's side when she gets her award come Thursday.'

Percy Hodge snorted. 'That's typical of you, Albert Piggott. You runs your wife down at every possible moment, but you're quick enough to go and bask in her glory.'

'It's a fair return,' responded Albert. 'After all, I took 'er back when she were down on 'er luck.'

Bob Jones stopped drying one of the pint glasses and eyed Albert on the other side of the bar. 'Well, if you're going to be there, what with all the photographers and reporters, you'll have to spruce yourself up. You're a right shambles at the moment. Your chin is a mess, your hands need a good scrub and goodness only knows when you last had a haircut.'

'My Nelly . . .' Albert paused when Percy Hodge gave another of his resounding snorts. 'My Nelly does me hair regular once a month. I were goin' to get 'er to do it for Chris'mas but I'll get 'er to do it tomorrer. An' these shavin' cuts,' he said, fingering his stubbly chin, 'will 'ave gone by Thursday.'

'What you goin' to wear, then?' asked Percy. 'Something a bit tidier than what you're wearin' now, I trust.'

'Course, I will. It'll be my funeral suit. Just the ticket. The ol' gel come back yesterday with a very posh frock. Must've cost 'er a fortune.'

'I just might turn up to watch this pantomime. Specially if there's to be cameras,' chortled Percy.

'Nelly said she'd be layin' on a bit of a celebration after closin' time,' said Albert, getting stiffly off the bar stool.

'Then I'll definitely come down,' Percy said.

'For staff only she said – an',' Albert added quickly, 'family, of course.'

The Fuchsia Bush was a hive of activity from before it even got light on Thursday morning. Nelly had arranged for Bert Nobbs, the Lulling taxi driver, to collect her from Thrush Green and take her to work. She wasn't going to risk creasing her lovely new dress by carrying it over her arm as she walked down the hill to Lulling. And there were her best high heels and handbag, too.

'See you this afternoon,' said Albert as Nelly was leaving to go out to the waiting taxi.

Nelly turned on the doorstep. 'What? You're not coming, and that's flat. You'd disgrace the ceremony.'

'Go on wi' you. Course I'm comin'. I'm not lettin' me wife receive her award and not be there for her big day.' Before Nelly could argue, he added, 'Anyways, I'm proud of you, gel.'

That stopped Nelly in her tracks. He'd never said that

before. 'Well, if you must,' she relented. 'But mind you tidy up, and have a good scrub first.'

On the way down to Lulling, Nelly thought about her lazybones of a husband. Now that he'd finally decided to hang up his churchyard boots, what on earth would he do with himself all day? Of course, she knew the answer to that – drink his pension away in The Two Pheasants – but she'd have to find something to occupy him. Then she pushed all thoughts of Albert to the back of her mind and ran through what there was still to be done.

With the award ceremony at four o'clock, it had been decided to close the tea-room at three, once the customers who had come in for a late lunch after an exhausting morning's Christmas shopping had gone. At first, Nelly had thought they would re-open for teas later but then she decided that she could afford to lose one afternoon's takings: after all, it wasn't every day that they got a Gold Award.

The hour after closing would give them time to clear away the lunch things, lay up some of the tables for tea for the visitors, and change out of their working clothes. The girls – Gloria, Rosa, Poppy and the kitchen staff – all seemed to be as excited as she was. Clare Border, who didn't usually work in The Fuchsia Bush in the afternoons, had arranged for her children to be collected from school by a neighbour and given their tea so she could be here. And quite right, too, thought Nelly. Clare had been such a help when they'd set up Nelly's next door. She was one of the team now. Gloria had decided to close the sandwich shop at two o'clock, once all the locals had been in for their lunchtime sandwiches and rolls, so she too could help with the preparations.

It was not just the award ceremony that was taking place that afternoon. Nelly had asked all the staff to stay on afterwards and she'd been busy preparing some tasty nibbles to go with the bottles of champagne that she had bought. Well, not real champagne, of course, since that cost the earth, but some sparkling white wine that the local off-licence had recommended. This was going to be her surprise. She had bought the bottles the day before, after everyone else had gone home, and had pushed them right to the back of the huge fridge in the kitchen, hiding them behind a stack of catering-size tubs of butter.

Word about the award had got round her most regular customers. A little paragraph in the local paper that came out each Friday had ensured that everyone in Lulling, it seemed, knew that the ceremony was going to take place that afternoon.

Nelly glanced at her watch. 'Oh lawks!' she exclaimed. It was just on three o'clock. Time to close, and she hurried through to the front.

Rosa had done her job well. She was holding the door open for the last customers who were now departing down the steps. She was about to close the door when three thin figures tottered down the pavement and the first had a foot on the steps.

The three Miss Lovelocks!

'Leave this to me,' Nelly said quickly to Rosa. 'Start clearing away then go into the back and change.'

As Miss Violet – the youngest of the three elderly ladies

– was about to put her hand out to open the door of The Fuchsia Bush, Nelly swung the door wide, filling the entrance with her considerable bulk.

'Miss Violet! Good afternoon to you, but I am afraid we are closing early this afternoon.'

'Ah yes, Mrs Piggott. We heard all about the award presentation when we came in for lunch today.' The Lovelock sisters came in to The Fuchsia Bush for a midday meal on Wednesdays and Thursdays, once the remains of their weekend joint had been used up. They would buy a piece of fish for Friday – very small, mind: the Lovelocks were notoriously parsimonious. 'And that's why we are here. We want to be present to congratulate you when you receive the award.'

'I'm afraid it's to be a private occasion,' Nelly responded, looking down on the demure hats that each of the sisters wore on their silvery hair.

'Oh dear, how disappointing!' cried Miss Ada, peering round her sister on the step above her.

'As some of your most regular customers,' continued Miss Violet, 'might we not be permitted to be here?'

'We would sit as quiet as mice in our usual corner,' wheedled Miss Bertha, who was still standing on the pavement.

Nelly's heart softened. They weren't all that bad, she thought, even though her own brief employment in the Lovelocks' house had been less than satisfactory. And it was true: they came in for lunch as regular as clockwork two days a week.

'Very well, why not? But could I ask you to come back

later, say at five to four. We need to close the shop now and get ready.' There was no way, Nelly thought, she was going to let them sit in the tea-room alone; Miss Bertha's light fingers had caused enough trouble in the past.

The three sisters retreated, chattering like excited children anticipating a special treat.

At a quarter to four, Nelly went into the front of the shop, to be ready to open the door as soon as the representatives of the Guild of Tea Shops arrived. It was only a few moments later that she saw a van draw up in the road outside. She watched as a young man opened the van's back door and began off-loading a pile of camera paraphernalia. The press! Nelly involuntarily patted her hair – not that there was a single strand out of place because she had asked the hairdresser, whom she had visited earlier that morning, to use plenty of lacquer. She ran her hands down the soft folds of her raspberry-coloured dress and adjusted the neckline so it sat squarely. The gold chain necklace that her erstwhile lover, Charlie the oilman, had bequeathed to her after his death hung in a double row round her throat.

'Afternoon!' cried the young man, coming into the shop and dumping camera equipment all over the floor. 'I'm Geoff from *Cotswold Highlights*. Got to take some shots of you receiving the award. But I'll take a few while the room is set up as I presume you usually have it.'

It wasn't long before he was snapping away. Nelly made sure she was out of range of his camera. She hated having her photograph taken.

'Now,' the young man said, looking round him, 'can we shift some of these tables? Anywhere they can go in the back?'

Nelly bridled. She wasn't going to be pushed around by a photographer chappie. 'No, there's no room anywhere else.'

The young man began pushing the tables back against the wall. 'Got to have room to move, haven't we?' he said.

Gloria came through from the back at that moment. She was wearing a navy blue skirt with a flowered blouse, and some pretty beads.

'I think it would be best if we could make a little more room in the middle,' she said. 'What if we push these tables back to the edge and the extra chairs can go through to Nelly's kitchen. They'll be out of the way there.'

'All right,' said Nelly. If truth be told, she was a tiny bit nervous about the forthcoming proceedings, and was happy to let Gloria take over.

'Rosa, Poppy!' called Gloria through the swing door. 'I need some help here when you're ready.'

Rosa joined her and together they moved most of the chairs out of the tea-room.

'Leave the chairs there,' said Nelly, pointing to a table in the corner by the window. 'I promised the Lovelocks they could have their usual place.'

Geoff the photographer continued to take photographs: the window with its Christmas decorations, the counter where Nelly had placed some of her best cakes, some scones and a plate of neat sandwiches. Just as he was pointing his camera at the back of the tea-room, the door from the kitchen swung open and Poppy came through.

'Oh, my!' crooned the young man. 'Hold it there, miss!' Click click.

Poppy, looking sparkling in a short tight dress, her slim legs seeming quite at ease in what Nelly thought were ridiculously high heels, preened and turned this way and that.

Nelly sighed. There had been a time, long long ago, when she'd had a figure like that.

The front door of The Fuchsia Bush opened, and a group of people unknown to Nelly swarmed in.

'Mrs Piggott,' said one of them, coming forward with his hand outstretched. 'I'm Mr Hunter from the Guild of Tea Shops. Many congratulations on your award!' He introduced the other people who were with him but Nelly's head was in such a whirl that she didn't remember any of the names. 'Now,' said Mr Hunter, looking around, 'can I suggest we present the award right away so Geoff can take his pictures and get off home. Perhaps then we might be able to have a cup of your excellent tea and,' he said, swivelling round to look at the counter behind him, 'taste one or two of your delicious cakes.'

Mr Hunter gently manoeuvred Nelly to stand in front of the counter, and then from a box he had stood on one of the tables, he pulled out a large teapot. It was one of the most beautiful teapots Nelly had ever seen: pale cream bone china, with gold leaf on the lid and handle. He then came to stand beside Nelly, while the photographer bent over his camera a little way away.

'Mrs Piggott,' boomed Mr Hunter in what was obviously his award-giving voice, 'on behalf of the Guild of Tea Shops, I am delighted to present this year's Gold Award for the Cotswolds area to you and The Fuchsia Bush of Lulling. I, and my committee and team of inspectors, would like to congratulate you on your excellent performance and to say what a credit you are to the tea business and, of course, tourism in the area!'

Mr Hunter then presented the fine teapot to Nelly who took it in trembling fingers. She read the gold inscription on the front: 'Awarded to The Fuchsia Bush by the Guild of Tea Shops' with the date in curly writing underneath.

'Look this way, Mrs Piggott,' called out the photographer, and his camera flashed.

From the corner of the room came a little smatter of clapping. Nelly looked across and saw the three Misses Lovelocks who must have crept in behind the contingent from the Guild and *Cotswold Highlights*. And beside them sat Albert, an unaccustomed smile on his pink, well-scrubbed face.

Then from near the kitchen door came more clapping – her faithful staff! Soon everyone was clapping. Clare Border lifted the recently received certificate from the wall and passed it to Nelly to hold, as well as the teapot.

'Can all the staff gather round, please?' called Mr Hunter. 'I'm sure everyone has contributed to this award.'

'Can you all move together, please?' cried the photographer. 'You,' he said, pointing to Poppy, 'will you move more to the front?'

Nelly swivelled round to ensure that everyone was in the photograph, and she caught sight of Gloria who had stayed by the kitchen door.

'Come along, Gloria,' she cried.

'No, I'm Nelly's,' the girl replied. 'This is the Fuchsia's award.'

'Nonsense, girl!' retorted Nelly. 'We're all part of the award, you too.' So Gloria shyly stood on the edge of the party.

Once all the photographs had been taken – apart from Geoff from *Cotswold Highlights*, there was a man they knew from the local Lulling paper as well as someone from the *Oxford Mail* – the girls slipped out to the kitchen to make the tea. Nelly and Clare re-positioned the tables that had been laid for tea in the middle of the room and chairs were collected from the back. Soon the guests from the Guild were seated, and while Rosa and Poppy put teapots and milk jugs on the tables, Nelly and Gloria handed round sandwiches and scones.

'Now then, Mrs Piggott,' called Mr Hunter, patting a chair beside him, 'you come and sit down and tell me all about yourself and your very fine tea-shop.'

Gratefully, Nelly sank down on the chair and accepted the cup of tea he poured for her. Across the table was a young woman who had a notebook open, with pencil poised.

'You don't mind if Jane takes a few notes, do you?' asked Mr Hunter.

'I'm from *Cotswold Highlights*,' the girl explained. 'We always like to write about the tea-shop that wins the regional award.'

Nelly was happy to talk about The Fuchsia Bush, making it clear that it was her first boss, Mrs Peters, who had set the standard. She skimmed over her own life but did point out that her husband, Albert, was over there with three of her most valued customers.

Mr Hunter accepted a second slice of coffee cake that Rosa offered him. 'This is really most delicious!' he said, brushing a few crumbs from his little moustache. 'There's coffee cake and coffee cake, but,' he said, patting a not inconsiderable stomach, 'this is truly the best I have ever eaten. I expect you have a special ingredient. Are you going to tell me what it is?' he asked mischievously.

'Of course not!' laughed Nelly, now much more relaxed. 'You wouldn't expect me to give away my trade secrets, would you?'

When the time came for the delegation from the Guild and *Cotswold Highlights* to leave, Nelly popped a fresh coffee cake into a box, tied it up with some pretty pink ribbon and presented it to Mr Hunter.

'Now it's my turn to give you something. I hope you have a very happy Christmas, Mr Hunter.'

To Nelly's surprise, Mr Hunter gave her soft cheek a little kiss. 'And a very happy Christmas to you, too! And to all your customers.'

When Nelly had waved them goodbye, she shut the door and leaned against it. 'Phew! Thank goodness that's over!'

'Well done, Mrs Piggott!' called Poppy. 'Well done, congratulations, Nelly,' echoed Gloria. Soon her staff were all round her, clapping her on the back.

'Now, then, steady,' puffed Nelly, quite overcome. 'Let's get this 'ere teapot into pride of place.' She cleared some space on the attractive Welsh pine dresser that stood to the right of the counter, and settled the teapot – gold lettering facing into the room – in the centre of the middle shelf. 'There, now, ain't that bonny!'

She asked the girls to clear away the tea things. 'Just put it all into the scullery. We can deal with it tomorrow. I hope none of you has any engagements this evening, cos I've got one or two nibbles for us to eat, and a bit of fizz for celebration.'

'Fizz!' squeaked Poppy, her pretty face aglow.

'Fizz!' repeated Miss Bertha from the corner where she and her sisters were still sitting.

Nelly had quite forgotten about them. Oh well, never mind. The more the merrier.

At that moment, she noticed a face peering in through the window from the street – Percy Hodge.

'Albert,' she said, turning to where her husband was still sitting, 'I think Perce has come to take you home.'

'Course 'e 'asn't,' retorted her husband who, Nelly had to admit, had turned himself out quite well. Though his best black funeral suit was a bit sombre for the occasion, he had found a brightly coloured tie which livened up the ensemble. ''E's come for the party!'

'Oh, go on then, let him in,' said Nelly. 'He can do some helping, though. You pass round those glasses, and Perce can get opening the bottles. I'll get 'em out of the fridge.'

An hour later saw the party at The Fuchsia Bush still in full swing. Miss Ada and Miss Bertha were quite pink in the face after a couple of glasses of fizzy white wine. Miss Violet, Nelly noticed, was being responsible and nursing her first glass. In fact, Violet had to admit she didn't really like champagne – the bubbles fizzed up her nose in a most uncomfortable way. She would have loved another cup of tea, but decided against asking for one.

Percy had had one glass in order to join in the toast but had then slipped out to the off-licence to get some cans of beer that he and Albert were putting away at an alarming rate. Nelly made sure they had a large plate of well-filled rolls on their table, to soak up the excesses.

She saw that Geoff the photographer had returned, and he and Poppy had their heads close together, and were laughing a lot. When Poppy returned to sit with the others, having waved Geoff off to another job he had that evening, her eyes were sparkling.

The Lovelocks departed at seven o'clock, and Clare Border offered to see them to their door. She helped them down the steps of The Fuchsia Bush, along the pavement, then up the steps of their own handsome house. Miss Ada fumbled for a while in her handbag for the key then found it in her pocket. 'Here we are,' she tinkled merrily. 'All safe and sound. Good night, Mrs Border, good night and thank you.'

The party went on for a little longer in The Fuchsia Bush then Nelly looked at her watch. 'If we don't go home now, we'll be in no fit state tomorrow.'

She rang Bert Nobbs and asked him to come and collect her. The girls cleared the glasses and plates away and promised they'd be in early in the morning to wash up. There was one bottle of fizz remaining, and Nelly pressed it on Clare Border. 'I couldn't have done it without you,' she said.

Clare left to return home to her family, and the girls went out into the cold night air, chattering about where they should go next. They were determined to make an evening of it, but Nelly was longing to go home and put her feet up.

When the taxi arrived, Nelly herded Albert and Percy

Hodge down the steps and then she turned to look back into the room. There, on the middle shelf of the dresser, gently illuminated by lights from the street outside, was her beautiful teapot, her award.

She pulled the door shut, locked it and went to join the others in the taxi. Bert Nobbs was holding the front door open for her.

'Madame,' he said, with a little bow.

Nelly got in the taxi, making sure that her dress was tucked in around her, and sank back against the soft leather upholstery. It had certainly been an exhausting day – but what an exciting one!

CHAPTER EIGHT

A Rescue Plan is Hatched

Preparations for Christmas continued at varying levels of urgency in most of the houses around Thrush Green. The big day itself was just a week away. Pretty wreaths made of holly and ivy, with flowing red ribbons, bedecked the front doors of most of the houses and cottages. The windows of The Two Pheasants were aglow with lights that winked and blinked in opposition to the lights Bob Jones had woven into the bay tree that stood in a tub outside the door into the saloon bar.

As was his custom, Albert Piggott had cut holly, sparkling with bright red berries, from trees and bushes in Lulling Woods. He placed the evergreen on an old tarpaulin and slowly dragged it back to the village. He made one stop on the way – to deliver a really nice bunch, together with a piece of mistletoe, to Dotty Harmer. The rest he left outside the church door where the flower ladies would find it when they came to decorate the church for the next day's Nativity play.

At Tullivers, Phil was gazing at a long shopping list.

'Lulling will be very busy, the supermarket especially, so the earlier you get there, the better it will be,' she advised.

Frank put aside the morning paper. There were two things he hated: one was shopping and the other was crowds. Put the two together, and it was purgatory. He knew Phil was right.

'If I were you,' Phil continued, 'do the supermarket stuff first and leave the High Street until afterwards. Nelly Piggott said the mince pies would be ready by ten.'

'I thought you always made your own mince pies,' said Frank, looking over Phil's shoulder at the shopping list.

'I do normally, but not this year, not with the Nativity and the party. And this isn't the main Christmas shopping list. I'll do that next week. This is just for the party.'

'Is Jeremy up yet?' Frank asked. 'I could do with some help lugging all the bottles and glasses to the car.'

Phil laughed. 'Jeremy up? It's school holidays and boys have to have plenty of sleep.'

'He shouldn't go to bed so late,' Frank grumbled, pulling on a jacket.

'I think he and Paul were running through their words for the play,' said the boy's mother, coming to his defence.

'What? To that ear-splitting pop music?' And with that, Frank opened the back door.

'Darling,' called Phil softly. 'The shopping list!'

Frank turned back and took the list from her hand, gave her a sheepish smile and this time made it out of the door.

Once he had left, Phil sat at the kitchen table and pulled a large pad of lined paper towards her. '<u>Nativity</u>' was written boldly across the top, and below was a list of the things that still had to be done before the performance. But would they get through the day without another member of the cast dropping out? They had lost another angel the day before, although not from chickenpox this time. Phil wasn't quite sure what was going on, but she had been told by Alan Lester that there were matrimonial problems in the home and the wife had decided to go and have Christmas with her parents, and was taking the child with her. Another little girl had been drafted in as a replacement.

Phil turned the pad over, and across the top of this page was written '<u>Party</u>'. She gazed at the number of things she had to do. Sitting here wasn't going to get things crossed off the list and she got to her feet, ready to put her shoulder to the wheel.

In the vicarage at Lulling, Charles and Dimity Henstock were also having breakfast. Charles was a great advocate of starting the day with a good breakfast. 'You never know if you're going to get lunch' was his maxim.

'What are your plans for the day?' Dimity asked.

Charles picked up an old envelope and peered through his thick spectacles at the list he had written there.

'I must spend a little time this morning finalizing the

plans for the Christmas morning services,' he said. 'I must ring Harold to make sure he's remembered that he will have to start the service at St Andrew's. Everyone seems to want to chatter so much after the ten o'clock service here that it's always a rush to get to Thrush Green for eleven-fifteen.'

'You'd have thought they'd all want to get home to their presents,' replied Dimity.

'And then I must go to Rectory Cottages. Jane rang yesterday to say that Mrs Miller isn't too well and asked me to go and see her.'

'In that case,' said Dimity, pouring herself a second cup of tea, 'could you double-check that Mrs Bates has remembered about the Nativity play on Saturday, and that the brights will need to be done early. She often does them on a Saturday afternoon.'

'She should remember because most of the Rectory Cottages crowd will be at the play. I just wish I could come, but there's so much to fit in at this time of year,' said Charles, rolling up his napkin and putting it neatly into its ring. 'What time are you meeting the others to do the crib?'

'I said I'd meet them at two o'clock. Lunch at one be all right for you?'

'Perfect,' replied Charles.

'Can we be sure to have lunch on time today?' Winnie asked Jenny as they were making the beds together.

'Yes, of course. It can be earlier if you like.'

'No, one's fine. I'm due to prepare the crib in St

Andrew's at two, but I'd like to get there a little before then if possible.'

'Then one on the dot it'll be. I thought we'd have that smoked haddock. Would you like a poached egg to go on top?'

Winnie laughed. 'Bless you, Jenny! You know all my weaknesses. It's a shame you never married. You would have made some man very happy.'

'And probably much too fat!' Jenny replied.

Neither woman said anything, but both thought back to the time when Jenny had been seriously pursued by Percy Hodge, who'd been looking for a wife after his Gertie had died. Marriage was fine, Jenny thought, but when one dies the other suddenly has to cope alone. Marriage was wonderful, Winnie thought, and once more counted her blessings that she had Jenny to keep her company.

'I must ring Edward in a moment, and see if he's remembered it's Crib Day,' said Winnie, giving the bed-spread a final tweak.

'I don't think that'll be necessary,' said Jenny, who was standing at the window. 'Mr Young's car is outside the church and he and Paul are offloading.'

'Ah, dear man! He's so reliable.'

The Youngs' large house had a very convenient attic floor where all manner of things were kept. Apart from the Nativity costumes, and the crib and its contents, there were boxes of bunting that were used for the summer fête, and various notices nailed to sticks: 'Car Park', 'Teas',

'Bowling for the Pig'. That last one hadn't been used for years, and Edward, as he pushed it to one side in order to get to the two boxes containing the figures for the crib, made a mental note to have a clear-out. I can make it my New Year's resolution, he thought, as he pulled forward one box. Then I won't have to think of any of those awful things that one should really do – like Take Off Weight, or Be Prepared to Talk at Breakfast.

He and young Paul now entered St Andrew's. The church was opened each morning and shut each evening by a member of a team of responsible people. When Charles Henstock had moved from being rector of St Andrew's to Lulling to look after four parishes, the PCC had discussed at length the question of whether to have the church open at all times, and be possible prey to those despicable people who were prepared to steal from churches – not only from the Donations box but candlesticks and other valuables as well – or to keep it locked and only open when services were to be held.

It hadn't been much of a discussion, really. No one wanted to see the church kept locked. For a time, Albert was given the responsibility but after the church had been left unlocked on three occasions when, due to drink taken, he had quite forgotten his duties, it had become necessary to set up a rota of willing people living round the green.

Harold Shoosmith was in charge of this rota and, accordingly, it worked like clockwork. If someone whose turn it was realised they couldn't do it that day, they rang Harold who either found someone else to do it or, more usually, did it himself. He always enjoyed the walk across the green to open or shut the church – even if it was raining. The years he had spent in Africa deprived of rain for much of the time meant that he took a strange pleasure now in getting wet.

Edward switched on the lights in the side aisle. 'We'll put the crib and boxes here. That's where Winnie and her team usually set it up.'

'Wouldn't it be helpful if we did it now, and save them coming over later?' Paul asked.

His father laughed. 'I don't think that would be a good idea at all. They are very proprietorial about setting up the crib. I think we should leave it to the women.'

As they were about to leave, the door swung open and Mrs Bates arrived to do the brasses. Everything, it seemed, was falling into place – in the church, at least.

Phil had spent the time while Frank was out shopping and, it has to be said, out from under her feet, getting down large platters not much used from the top cupboards in the kitchen. She was standing precariously on the little pair of steps when the telephone rang.

'Oh bother!' she muttered.

She leaned down and put a large blue-patterned plate on the top of the lower cupboards, and then carefully climbed down the steps and picked up the kitchen telephone.

'Ah, Phil, I thought you must be out.' It was Alan Lester.

'Sorry, Alan, I was up some steps. It's not more bad news, is it?'

'I'm afraid so. Mrs Todd has just got back to me and says Jimmy definitely cannot be a king after all.'

'But why?' cried the distraught Phil. 'You thought it would be possible.'

'Yes, I'm sorry. My fault. Because he took part in the little performance of *Robin Hood* we put on last summer, I thought it would be all right. But because it's the Nativity and in the church, it isn't allowed by the Plymouth Brethren.' As he heard Phil's groan down the line, he hastily continued, 'I've a couple of errands to do now, but then I suggest I come round and we'll go through the cast list together and see if we can juggle about some of the parts.'

'But no one will know their words if we do that – and the costumes, what about the costumes?' she wailed.

'Don't worry for the moment. We'll think of something. The show will go on!' And with that, the headmaster rang off.

Phil slumped onto a chair, and pulled her list headed 'Nativity' towards her. The original cast list was much rubbed out, crossed out and written over. She picked up a pencil and scored heavily through Toddy's name. Now what do we do? she thought.

At that moment, the back door banged open and Frank staggered in with a case of wine. 'Where shall I put this? In the hall? I'll probably have the drinks table there.'

'No, not there,' said Phil, quickly getting to her feet. 'I haven't cleaned yet. Can't they stay in the garage for the time being? I'll do the hoovering and dusting tomorrow and then you can set up.'

Frank executed a circle round the table and disappeared outside again. Phil picked up the big plates she had got out of the top cupboards and crossed to the sink to give them a good wash. Her head was still buzzing with how they could get over this latest defection from the cast. Perhaps Frank would have some ideas, she thought, as she ran warm water into the sink.

As arranged, Winnie and Jenny had their lunch promptly at one o'clock. Afterwards, Jenny waved away Winnie's offer to help wash up.

'You get off to the church. I know how you enjoy that,' she said. 'But wrap up warm, mind. That church can be very chilly and we don't want your bronichals to be affected again.'

Winnie smiled, and pulled on her tweed coat and wrapped a scarf round her neck.

'Here,' said Jenny, handing her a couple of dusters, 'you're sure to need these. And 'ave you got the piece of carpet?'

'Yes, it's ready by the front door,' and with that Winnie set forth on what was one of the highlights of her year.

She decided not to cross the green to the church, but sensibly walked round on the pavement. As she passed Ella's cottage, she saw the little front garden had a fine display of *Helleborus niger*, the Christmas rose. The plants' white, nodding, cup-shaped flowers shone out from their dark green leaves. How pretty they were!

A few minutes later, Winnie pushed open the door of St Andrew's and stood for a moment in the gloom. English country churches had a very special smell about them, and this one was no different. Just a bit musty. And then her nostrils picked up the smell of the flowers placed on the font nearby. That meant the flower ladies had been in. Muriel Fuller, one of the residents at Rectory Cottages, was a first-rate flower arranger and led the team.

After standing there quietly for a few moments, she turned on the church lights and made her way down the side aisle where she knew Edward Young would have placed the crib and boxes of figures. And she stopped short – and stared in complete amazement.

The crib had already been set up, but not with the much-loved figures that St Andrew's always had. Set around the crib were different figures, new figures, horrid figures.

Winnie's heart beat so hard that she could almost hear it herself. Staggering slightly, she sat down in a nearby pew. 'What on earth . . . ?' she cried. In her agitation, she realized she was twisting the two dusters round and round in her hands. She dropped them into her lap but then found her hands were shaking so much, she picked them up again and began twisting them once more.

After a minute or so, she felt a little calmer and got to her feet. Steadying herself on the end of the pew, she peered at the crib. Yes, that was the Thrush Green crib but the figures most definitely were impostors. The face of the Virgin was pert, with reddened curved lips. Joseph was not so bad although his robe was a hideous maroon colour. The figures of the two shepherds were much too boyish, and as for the Wise Men – they looked cheap and modern.

Winnie had a quick look round to see if there were any clues as to who might have placed these dreadful figures here. All she could find were the boxes of Thrush Green figures, and just as she was pulling the second one out from under the front pew where it had been pushed, the main door opened at the other end of the church.

'Hello, Winnie! We thought you'd get here first.'

That was Dimity's voice, and she and Ella now came down the side aisle to where Winnie was standing.

'Oh, you've already set things up,' cried Ella. 'You might have waited for us.'

But while Ella's failing eyesight didn't pick up the different figures, Dimity saw immediately, and clapped a horrified hand to her mouth. 'What in heaven's name has happened?' she cried.

Ella moved closer to the crib and peered at it. She now saw the horrible figures. 'Winnie! Did you put these beastly figures there?'

'Of course not!' responded Winnie sharply. 'Why on earth would I do that? Our figures are here,' and she pointed to the familiar boxes she had found.

Dimity tilted the figure of the new Virgin Mary towards her to examine it more closely. 'This is truly horrible. Who on earth has done this? And just look at the Baby Jesus – it's . . .' Her voice faded away. 'Charles will be horrified.'

Winnie seemed to pull herself together. 'It doesn't matter now. What matters most is that we should replace them with the proper figures. Did you bring the straw, Ella?'

Ella shoved her hand in a carrier bag she was holding. 'With Dotty's best compliments,' she said.

The three women silently went to work. Dimity found some old cardboard boxes in the vestry, and the offending figures were placed in a couple of them. Ella lifted the crib to one side so that Winnie could put down her piece of blue carpet that was always used for the occasion, then the crib was placed on the carpet and Ella sprinkled the fresh straw round the base of the crib. One by one, Dimity handed Winnie the figures that were placed in exactly the same position as they had been for the last twenty years.

All right, maybe they were a little shabby but, they all agreed, they were *the* Thrush Green figures and that was that.

Ella picked up one of the boxes that now held the unwelcome intruders and staggered to the vestry with it. From the noise, it sounded to Dimity and Winnie that she had dropped it onto the stone floor from some height. They guiltily smiled at each other. The second box followed suit.

'There!' said Ella, coming back from the vestry and wiping her hands down the sides of her trousers. 'Whoever had the audacity to put those dreadful figures in our crib can collect them from the vestry. Now, let's go. I am dying for a ciggy.'

'Jenny will have the kettle on for us,' said Winnie. It was a tradition that the crib party went back to Winnie's house for tea.

When the three of them were comfortably ensconced in Winnie's sitting-room, cups of tea at their elbows and plates of cherry cake on their knees, they returned to the events of the afternoon.

'The church is always open,' said Dimity, 'so it could have been anyone really.'

Winnie was the most methodical of the three, and liked to tackle such conundrums head-on. 'It must have been a regular church-goer. Why would they bother otherwise?'

This met with general agreement.

'Well, I can't believe it would be Isobel – she knows we three do the crib. And certainly not Harold. He reckons it's women's work. What about Phil?' Winnie asked.

Ella shook her head. 'I think she's much too busy with the Nativity play, and of course their party afterwards. No, it won't have been Phil.'

'Charles was going to Rectory Cottages this morning,' said Dimity. 'I'll ask him if he knows anything when I get home.'

'Surely no one from there would have put those *dreadful* figures there?' said Winnie. The offending impostors were now referred to as 'those *dreadful* figures' by all three.

'Charles said that Mrs Bates was going in to do the brasses today,' Dimity said, 'but she's so small she'd never have been able to carry across those boxes of figures. And she'd never have done such a thing anyway.'

'What about Muriel Fuller and her team of flower girls?' asked Ella, stretching forward to help herself to another slice of cake. 'Damn good cake, this, Winnie!'

'Thank you, Ella. I made it especially since I know it is one of your favourites and one gets so much fruit cake at this time of year.' Winnie then cocked her silvery head on one side, thinking, considering. 'Perhaps we could ask Muriel if the figures were there when they went in to do the flowers. If they weren't, we could find out what time they left the church so we shall know that the *dreadful* figures were put there between then and when I arrived just before two.'

'Quite the Sherlock Holmes, Winnie!' laughed Dimity.

'Almost as good as doing a difficult crossword,' she replied – and there the matter was left.

As arranged, Alan Lester arrived at Tullivers shortly before lunch and he and Phil sat at the kitchen table, with Phil's pad of paper in front of them. Names were arrowed and then crossed out, new names added, and then arrowed. It looked like a crazy game of snakes and ladders.

'And Frank didn't have any ideas?' Alan asked, leaning back in his chair and running his hands through his hair.

'No, we did much as we've done now,' replied Phil. 'Then he took himself off to The Two Pheasants – for inspiration, he said.'

'Well, I think we'll have to go with just the two shepherds, Patrick and little Tom, and move Harry up to being a king. I just hope his stammer doesn't get the better of him when he has to say his lines.'

'Perhaps we can have some sheep to make up for the lack of shepherds,' mused Phil, doodling a woolly ball on four legs on the notepad.

'Sheep? Real sheep?' asked Alan in some alarm.

'No, not real sheep. I've got an idea that might work. It should detract from there being only two shepherds.'

At that moment, there were noises outside the back door and Frank and Jeremy both came in.

'Is lunch ready?' asked young Jeremy. 'I'm starving!'

Phil laughed and ruffled her son's head. 'When have I heard that before? Yes, it will be about ten minutes.'

Alan got to his feet. 'I'll leave you making sheep then,' he said with a smile. 'And I'll phone Harry's parents and give them the news that he's been elevated to a king.'

Frank turned round from the sink where he was washing his hands. 'Is that a replacement for Jimmy Todd?'

'Yes,' Phil replied. 'It's the best we can do.'

'Hold that call, Alan,' Frank said. He had a great grin

on his face. 'I have The Solution – it's going to be good. No, it's going to be better than that. It's going to be brilliant!' And he proceeded to tell Phil and Alan his plan.

CHAPTER NINE

A Nativity Play with a Difference

'What a nerve!' Joan Young exclaimed. 'Poor Winnie, you must have been horrified to find someone else had set up the crib.' She continued to listen for some minutes, the telephone receiver tucked under her chin while she attempted to spread butter on her toast.

Across the table, Edward and their son Paul listened to Joan's side of the conversation with interest.

'Well, anyway,' Joan said, 'the right figures are in place. Thank heavens for that. And if that awful woman comes to the Nativity tonight, I shall cut her dead!'

There were words from the other end, and Joan laughed and said, 'All right, but I won't go out of my way to speak to her. I'm glad it's ended up all right. I'll see you there – five-thirty! Bye.'

Having replaced the receiver, she exhaled noisily. 'We–ell! What about that then!'

'So?' asked Edward. 'Go on, tell us!'

Joan relayed what Winnie had told her, how she'd gone into St Andrew's to set up the crib the previous afternoon and had found 'those *dreadful* figures' already there.

'And have they discovered who did it?' asked Paul.

'Indeed they have. Mrs Burwell!' replied Joan.

Edward's reaction was like a mini-explosion. 'That bl— that wretched woman, that ghastly burbling Burwell woman! It *would* be her, wouldn't it?' He got to his feet and paced round the kitchen table like a tiger in a cage. 'Why can't she keep her blithering nose out of every damn thing in the village?'

'Calm down, dear,' said Joan, worried about her husband's blood pressure. She knew that anything to do with the Burwells was apt to send him into orbit.

'I've only met her once or twice,' said Paul. 'I didn't think she was that bad.'

Edward swung round to face his son, and gave him two minutes' worth of his opinion of Mr and Mrs Burwell and their house. Joan just sighed and finished off her breakfast.

When Edward had run out of steam, Paul asked his mother, 'How did Mrs Bailey discover it was her who did it?'

'Dimity talked to Muriel Fuller who had done the flowers in the church earlier that morning. A group of them do the flowers for Christmas, and Mrs Burwell was one of them. Apparently she suggested a large arrangement should be set just where the crib goes, and was told why space had to be left there. Muriel saw her peer into the boxes holding the Nativity figures, and apparently she remarked to one of the other flower women that she thought they were very tatty and she had better ones at home. So Winnie and Dimity put two and two together.'

'Have they had it out with the wretched woman?' asked Edward.

'Dimity thought it would be better if Charles rang her.'

'Poor Charles! He's always draws the short straw. Do we know what the ghastly woman said?'

'You really don't like her, do you, Pa?' Paul said, laughing.

'No, I don't. She and her dreadful husband are total menaces.'

'Well,' Joan said, 'she didn't apologize, if that's what you were hoping for. She went all high and mighty apparently, and said she thought her figures were much better, more modern.'

'We don't *want* modern figures,' scowled Edward. 'We want our traditional figures.'

'We've got the right figures now, that's the main thing.' Joan looked at the kitchen clock. 'What time are you due at St Andrew's for the dress rehearsal, Paul?'

'Mrs Hurst said we should be there at eleven, that we would be about an hour, then everyone connected with the Nativity are wanted back again at four-thirty.'

'Before you disappear now,' Joan said, 'let's go upstairs and just check that you've got clean trousers and shirt for this evening.'

'And make sure your shoes are clean,' added Edward.

'But my feet won't be seen,' the boy protested.

'That makes no difference at all,' responded his

father, 'as you well know,' and he ruffled Paul's hair affectionately.

At Tullivers, preparations were under way for the party after the performance. On either side of the morning's dress rehearsal, Phil hoovered, dusted and polished the sitting-room and hall, and Frank set up the table for the bar just inside his study that led off the hall. They had decided this would be the best place since it would give more room for people to circulate. It did mean, however, that whenever Frank wanted to get something from his study, he had to crawl under the table.

By mid-afternoon, the glasses had been taken out of their boxes and set out on the table. Orange juice had been decanted into jugs and was waiting in the fridge. Frank had been down to Lulling to collect some ice, and the white wine was now residing among it in a plastic dustbin that was resting on a sheet of plastic in the study.

In the kitchen, there were trays of sausage rolls, vol-au-vents and mince pies ready to go into the oven to warm. Jeremy had been set to spreading garlicky cream cheese down the middle of sticks of celery and then cutting them into bite-sized pieces. 'Now sprinkle a little – just a little – paprika over the cheese to make it look more interesting,' directed Phil.

She had kept the smoked salmon squares to do herself. She knew if she asked Frank to help, he would eat half of the smoked salmon pieces that she had bought. Anyway, having set up the drinks table, he had gone out, saying he would meet them at St Andrew's later.

As Phil buttered the brown bread, cut off the crusts, then laid on the smoked salmon, she ran through the Nativity for the enth time. The morning's final rehearsal had gone as well as could be expected considering the changes to the cast. But would the Plan work that evening? Oh goodness, she hoped so.

'I'm off now,' Harold Shoosmith called up the stairs to Isobel who was still changing. 'I'll see you there.'

Since he was standing in for Charles Henstock, Harold felt he should be at St Andrew's in good time to welcome those who came to see the Nativity play. As he walked down the garden path, he sniffed the air appreciatively. There was a delicious smell of wood smoke in the air. As he exhaled, his breath plumed out in front of him. There was going to be a frost tonight for sure.

Just as he reached the church, Bert Nobbs pulled up in his taxi and Harold, knowing who the passengers would be, gallantly opened the passenger door and helped out Miss Ada Lovelock. He made sure she was steady on the pavement before turning to give his hand to Miss Bertha. Miss Violet was checking with Bert Nobbs that he knew when he was to return to take them home.

'Dear Charles would have brought us,' twittered Miss Ada, 'but of course he is committed to the Christingle service in St John's this evening.'

Harold gently ushered the three old ladies into the church and saw they were settled in a pew. It seemed that Albert Piggott had done as requested and turned on the heating soon after lunch to ensure the church was really warm. It was not only the thin old bones of the Lovelock sisters that felt the cold so terribly but also most of the residents of Rectory Cottages who were the next to arrive, ushered in by the ever vigilant Jane and Bill Cartwright, the wardens at the retirement homes. Mrs Jenner arrived and sat with the Cartwrights; Jane was her daughter.

The level of chatter increased as more people turned up, and leaned backwards and forwards in their seats to talk to friends around them. The Thrush Green Nativity was always a highlight of the year.

'It's the beginning of Christmas proper,' said Mrs Jenner to her daughter, and waved to Nelly Piggott who was seated close by.

As Winnie walked to her usual pew near the front, she was pleased to see that Gladys Hodge, a chapel-goer, had come with Percy; they were sitting with Nelly and Albert. When Connie arrived with Ella, they joined Winnie. Ella, it seemed, had been regaling Connie with the story of the crib and, before sitting down, Connie went to look at the Christmas scene.

'It's as lovely as ever, Winnie,' she said a moment later as she settled herself in the pew.

And so the church filled up, although of the Burwells there was no sign. Latecomers found they weren't able to sit together as a family, and had to squeeze in where they could. Mrs Biddle found herself in with the Misses Lovelock and the parents of one of the angels, while her two elder children were in the pew in front with the Hodges and the Piggotts.

Molly Curdle arrived, carrying fourteen-month-old Billy under her arm, and went to a seat at the far end of the choir stalls. These were already almost full with congregation, but Molly squeezed in and placed the young child on the floor beside her.

Shortly after five-thirty, Harold Shoosmith made his way to the chancel steps and then turned to face the congregation. The chatter faded away. The last to be quiet were the performers who were out of sight in the vestry at the back of the church but after some loud hushes, they too fell silent.

'Good evening, everyone, and welcome to St Andrew's church for this year's Nativity. I am standing in for Charles Henstock since, as most of you know, he has the Christingle service at St John's. He has asked me to say that he hopes to see as many of you as possible at the Christmas morning service here at eleven-fifteen. Now, before I hand over to Phil Hurst, I would like to open the proceedings with a short prayer.'

There was a rustle as people leaned forward in their seats, and lowered their heads.

'Lord, may we be like the Wise Men who were guided to You by a star. Give us the wisdom to seek You, light to guide us to You, courage to search until we find You, graciousness to worship You and generosity to lay our gifts before You, who are our King and our God for ever and ever.'

'Amen' resounded round the church, and the congregation sat back in their pews.

'Harold has such a lovely voice,' whispered Joan Young

who was sitting next to Isobel, who nodded her agreement.

'Now, Phil, if everyone is ready, let the Nativity begin,' and Harold walked back down the aisle to take his place next to his wife.

The church lights dimmed, and finally the congregation fell silent. A small figure who had been sitting quietly on the pulpit steps now made his way up into the pulpit and switched on the reading light there. It was Paul Young, his usually unruly hair wetted and smoothed down.

' "And in the sixth month, the angel Gabriel was sent from God unto a city of Galilee, named Naz'reth. To a virgin espoused to a man whose name was Joseph of the house of David, and the virgin's name was Mary." ' Paul paused, and then continued. 'Well, you all know the official version, so Mrs Hurst decided to write some of the words a little differently. She's asked me to say that she hopes it won't give offence to anyone. I don't think it will, cos I think it's much more fun.' He then switched off the reading light and receded into darkness.

As he did so, a light towards the back of the church came on, and the congregation all turned round in their seats to look down the main aisle. There stood little Annie Curdle, in a long blue dress with a gold cord round her waist. She wore a simple white headdress. In front of her stood a taller girl, dressed in white, a pair of cardboard wings attached to her back, and a wobbling halo on a stick above her head.

'Who's playing Gabriel?' whispered Joan to Isobel.

'I think it's the Hooper girl.'

In the gallery that stretched across the back of the church, another light came on, illuminating Jeremy Prior.

'The Archangel Gabriel visited Mary, and told her . . .'

' 'Ello, Mary. I'm Gabri'l. I've come to tell you that you're goin' to 'ave a baby.'

'What?' cried little Annie Curdle in a rather squeaky voice. 'You're 'avin' me on!'

Isobel nudged Joan. 'Adorable!' she whispered.

'Do you know anything about this, Joseph?' cried Annie, turning to her brother, George.

'Nope, news to me.'

'You've got to get to Beth'lem – quick-fast,' said the Archangel, one wing tipping dangerously sideways.

'Who says?' demanded Joseph.

'Er . . . er . . .' The Archangel turned desperately to where Phil was standing nearby.

'Cæsar Augustus,' she prompted in a stage whisper.

'Ah, yes. Cæsar Gustus,' gabbled the Archangel.

The reading light in the pulpit came on. ' "And it came to pass in those days, that there went out a decree from Cæsar Augustus, that all the world should be taxed," ' read Paul. ' "And Joseph went from Galilee, out of the city of Naz'reth, into Judæa, unto the city of David, which is called Bethlehem." '

As he switched off the reading light, so Mrs Hope – who was seated at the old upright piano in the side aisle – played the opening line of 'Once in Royal David's City', and from the gallery alongside Jeremy, the infant choir began to sing, not very evenly, the first two verses of the carol.

As they began, so the main lights were turned on, illuminating the slow procession down the aisle of Mary and Joseph hand in hand. They were preceded by a small child holding his arms stiffly out in front, and from the arms hung a notice proclaiming: 'Bethlehem this way'.

Baby Billy Curdle, who had shuffled on his bottom away from the choir stalls and had been sitting quietly in the middle of the chancel floor, now saw his brother and sister approaching. With a gurgle of pleasure, he bumped his way surprisingly fast towards the chancel steps.

Winnie caught sight of him, and nudged Connie. 'Just look at the darling!'

Connie turned to look. 'He's supposed to be a lamb. See, he's wearing a sort of fleece tunic.'

Molly crept forward and rescued Billy and just got back to her place as Joseph and Mary arrived at the chancel steps.

' "And so it was," ' read Paul, ' "that whilst they were there, the days were accomplished that she should be delivered. But there was no room for them in the inn." '

Once more the nave lights dimmed and those in the chancel went on.

'Who's on the lights?' Isobel whispered. 'Must have a very good crib sheet.'

Joan craned round and peered to the back of the church. 'It's Alan Lester. He's doing a good job. I know Ben spent ages this week setting them up.'

Andrew, a large lad who was playing the innkeeper, had been sitting in the choir stalls and he now came forward, and an altercation ensued between him and Joseph, with much arguing about available accommodation in Bethlehem that evening. Finally, the innkeeper relented and admitted Joseph and Mary to the area just above the chancel steps that was designated the stable. Little Annie gave a great sigh as she dropped down on the stool set in the middle.

'Oooh that's better. Me feet were killin' me,' she said, and the congregation tittered in response.

' "And she brought forth her firstborn," ' read Paul, ' "and wrapped him in swaddling clothes, and laid him in a manger." '

Someone from the choir stalls now pushed an old

wooden orange box, filled with straw, towards Joseph who rather inelegantly hooked it with his crook and dragged it across the floor to rest beside his wife. Mary leaned down and picked up the Baby Jesus – one of Annie Curdle's favourite dolls well wrapped up in a shawl – and rocked it. But the congregation's attention was diverted once more by Billy Curdle who had bumped his way on his backside down the chancel and ended up at his sister's feet, stretching up a hand towards her.

Annie, with great presence of mind, dropped the doll back in the orange box and bent down and heaved Billy onto her lap and rocked him instead.

'Aaahh,' crooned the congregation.

The lights changed again. The chancel went into darkness while the light in the gallery went on, illuminating Jeremy once more.

' "And there were in the same country shepherds abiding in the fields, keeping watch over their flock by night. And, lo, the angel of the Lord came upon them, and the glory of the Lord shone round about them, and they were sore afraid." '

Lights came on at the back of the church where a little group was gathered, and the Angel of the Lord – the Archangel Gabriel doubling up – bid the shepherds go to seek the Baby Jesus.

'Where do we go?' demanded one.

'We don't know the way,' said another.

The Angel of the Lord then put her fingers into her mouth and produced a most unfeminine and ear-splitting whistle and the 'Bethlehem This Way' signpost, who had been sitting quietly at the top of the nave, scurried back and took his place at the head of the procession which now walked slowly towards the Holy Family. The main lights were turned on, and in the gallery the infants began to sing 'While shepherds watched their flocks by night', although Alan Lester was sure he heard at least one voice singing the forbidden version of 'While shepherds washed their socks by night'.

'Oh look,' gasped Nelly Piggott as the little group passed the end of her pew. 'Just look at the sheep!'

All round, people were craning their necks to see the sheep. Dotty Harmer's Bruce, the West Highland terrier, was straining at his lead held by young Patrick. 'Heel!' the lad demanded, to no avail. The other shepherd was dragging a rather reluctant Scottie terrier that was owned by one of the families who lived on the Nidden Road. The dog's black back was covered with a white coat made out of a piece of sheep's fleece. The intended third sheep was sitting quite content on Mary's lap.

As the shepherds with their charges got into their positions behind Joseph and Mary in the chancel, a group of very little angels came down from where they had been sitting by the altar, as quiet as church mice, to gather round the Holy Family. They took up the singing of the carol's last verse, piping: 'All glory be to God on high, And to the earth be peace. Goodwill henceforth from heaven to men, Begin and never cease.'

Winnie Bailey fleetingly remembered Mrs Burwell but equally quickly dismissed the thought.

The church lights dimmed once more and Paul switched on his reading light in the pulpit.

'He's doing awfully well,' Isobel whispered to Joan.

Joan nodded. She was hugely proud of her son, and just prayed she would be able to say the same about the rest of the family.

' "Now when Jesus was born in Bethlehem, in the days of Herod the king, behold, there came wise men from the east to Jerusalem, saying . . ." ' Paul switched off his light, and the church was in darkness apart from a small light on the Holy Family in the chancel.

There was total silence. Winnie wondered if someone had forgotten their words.

Then the church's main south door crashed open, and what sounded like an army of people fell into the back of the nave.

'Watch out!' cried a male voice.

'I can't see anything,' said someone else. 'Where's that dratted star we're supposed to be following?'

A beam of torchlight obligingly appeared and shone down the nave.

'Come on, we've got to follow the star,' said a voice that Joan recognized as belonging to Edward. She knew he was involved in some way but didn't know how. 'This way, lads, follow the star!'

'Wait for me!' cried a third voice. 'This wretched camel is as slow as an old donkey.' This was followed by another crash, and Alan Lester decided that it would be safer if the lights were turned on.

Everyone in the pews craned round to see what the

noise was all about, and the sight that met their curious eyes was – well, it was difficult to tell what was going on. However, once the heap on the floor, which had collided with a table at the back of the church on which the visitors' book rested, had got to its four feet, a sort of procession was beginning to form.

And the congregation burst out first into laughter and then into applause.

The three figures struck a theatrical pose and, despite their costumes, they were easily identifiable as Frank Hurst, Edward Young and John Lovell. They were dressed up as hippy pop stars of the seventies – wigs of long hair, dark glasses, leather jackets, tight jeans and winkle-picker shoes.

'Hi!' called Frank, who was in the front. He strummed a chord on the guitar that hung round his neck. 'We are the Three Kings or, if you prefer, the Three Wise Men.'

'Not very wise, I'm afraid, but we do try,' called out Edward. 'He's Gaspar,' he said, poking Frank in the back, 'I'm Balthasar, and him at the back' – and he dropped his voice a little – 'not very bright, I'm afraid, but he's all right with the animals, he's called Melchior. Come forward, Melchior, and introduce Charlie the Camel.'

John Lovell/Melchior jerked the piece of rope in his hand, and the pantomime camel ambled forward. 'Say hello to the people, Charlie.'

'Ba-aa-aa,' replied the camel rather worryingly.

Frank struck another chord on his guitar. 'Now, all the children here, say hello to Charlie.'

'Hello, hello, Charlie,' rang out round the church. One

or two children climbed onto the pews in order to see, while some of the infant choir were leaning dangerously over the edge of the gallery in order to get a better view, totally ignoring Mrs Hope's gesticulations from where she was sitting at the piano. The church was echoing with the sound of laughter.

Mrs Hope struck up the opening bars of 'We Three Kings of Orient Are' on the piano, and the procession set off down the nave. Everyone was laughing so much that very little of the carol was heard, which was probably just as well since half the choir was still shuffling back into position.

'Howdee,' said Edward Young, grasping the hand of Violet Lovelock and pumping it so vigorously that Miss Violet's hat shook on her ancient head.

'Hi, man!' cried Frank Hurst, slapping Nelly Piggott so hard on her broad back that her ample front wobbled dangerously, but her face was wreathed in smiles.

John Lovell, much more reserved than the other two, restricted himself to leading the camel but had to stop suddenly as Gaspar made another dive into one of the pews to shake someone's hand.

'Ouch, you've trod on me heel!' came a muffled cry from inside.

'Sorry,' came the reply from the back end. 'You shouldn't stop so sudden.'

Finally, the crazy group made their way to the chancel steps and made their presentation of gold and frankincense and myrrh to the Holy Family. Little Billy had been upset by all the laughter, and when he had started to grizzle, Molly darted forward to retrieve him, and now clasped him firmly on her lap. The Virgin Mary leaned down and retrieved the doll from the orange box.

Once the Three Kings had presented their gifts, they joined the shepherds behind Joseph and Mary. Bruce the Westie-cum-sheep had started barking when everyone laughed at the Three Kings, and Patrick had quickly picked up the dog and was holding him tightly in his arms.

Mrs Hope struck up on the piano once more and everyone sang 'Silent Night, Holy Night'. George Curdle took his sister's hand and stroked the doll's hair.

As the carol ended, Paul Young called from the pulpit: 'And they all lived happily ever after. And that's the end.' He paused, then added, 'I hope everyone enjoyed the play. I must say it was jolly good from up here. Dad, you were brilliant!' and he waved to his father below him.

There was a burst of applause from the congregation, and the buzz of voices seemed to confirm they had indeed enjoyed it.

Harold stepped out into the nave from the pew where he'd been sitting, and held up a hand to ask for quiet. 'Thank you, thank you, everyone! That was truly marvellous. And a special very big thank you to Phil and Alan for pulling it all together. Just one thing before you go home. I would like to quote from a familiar nursery rhyme.

> *Christmas is coming, the geese are getting fat,*
> *Please to put a penny in the old man's hat.*

If you haven't got a penny, a ha'penny will do,
If you haven't got a ha'penny, then God bless you!

Which is one way of saying,' he continued, 'that there'll be a retiring collection on your way out. Thank you, good night and a safe journey home.'

To round off the extravaganza, Frank strummed a series of running chords on his guitar, and as he finished, the Three Kings all cried, 'Olé!'

Edward pulled off his long black wig and then smoothed down his own hair into place. 'Phew!' he exclaimed. 'Thank heavens that's over. I could do with a very stiff drink!'

'If you will excuse me from the clearing up here,' responded Frank, taking the guitar from round his neck, 'I'll get back home and get things going for the party. Come across as soon as you can.'

'We'll be over in a jiff,' replied Edward. 'Take Phil with you. She's done more than her fair share here. What a wonderful evening.'

'And so say all of us,' said Winnie, coming up. 'Charles and Dimity will be furious to have missed it. Perhaps you could put on a second performance for those who weren't here tonight.'

'Winnie!' cried Edward in horror, and then he saw the twinkle in her eye, and bent down to give her a hug.

CHAPTER TEN

The Hursts Entertain

After the Nativity at St Andrew's, no one seemed very keen to disperse to their various homes. They stood around in the church, chattering about the performance. The infant choir had come tumbling down the stairs from the gallery and were slapping their thespian playmates on the back.

Several families had gathered round the crib, which was gently lit by a light Ben had attached to one of the columns in the side aisle. One parent was pointing out the various figures to her young daughter who listened quietly, but then declared, 'I think the people we've just seen were much better. And there's no camel here.' Her smiling mother led the child away.

Harold Shoosmith stood at the end of the pew where the Misses Lovelock had been sitting. They were now gathering together their gloves.

'Did you enjoy it, ladies?' he asked.

'Oh yes,' squeaked Miss Ada.

'We were very sorry to miss the service at St John's,' said Miss Violet. 'We apologized to Charles, of course, but the Nativity play here is always much more fun. Now we must go and see if Bert Nobbs has arrived to take us home. We said to be here at six-thirty.'

She turned to check that the third Miss Lovelock was ready to go but Bertha was still sitting in the pew, hunched over and scrabbling round her feet.

'What are you doing, Bertha?' she cried. 'We're going now.'

'I'm looking for my muff,' came the reply from some-where near the floor.

'Oh dear,' said Violet, shaking her head. 'Come along, Bertha dear, you didn't have your muff with you this evening,' and then added for Harold's benefit, 'She hasn't used that muff for years!'

Bertha straightened up, her normally pale face a little flushed. 'Oh, didn't I?' she said rather vaguely.

'I'll just go and check that Bert has arrived,' said Harold. 'We don't want you standing around in the cold.'

On his way out, Harold passed two separated ends of the camel. The very red-faced occupants were standing up, glad of the fresh air that was coming in through the church door. Frank Biddle had been at the front and Ben Curdle at the rear.

'Well done, you two,' said Harold, pausing by them. 'You were so funny, and the children loved you. Did you feel hands stretching out to pat you as you passed up the aisle?'

'I was doing my best not to pass out inside the wretched costume,' said Ben, and wiped his perspiring face with a huge red-spotted handkerchief, 'but I'm glad we were the butt of so much amusement.'

'Young Davey will be so sorry to have missed this evening,' said Frank Biddle. 'I've promised to take the costume home and put it on for him – with the wife at the other end. She doesn't know about that yet,' he added.

Harold could see from the church porch that Bert Nobbs was ready to take the Lovelocks home, so returned to the group who were still chatting in the aisle.

'Yes, Bert's there. Now, let me escort you to your carriage,' and he took the arm of Miss Bertha, the oldest and frailest of the three sisters.

There was an ulterior motive in his gallantry, of course. The way out led past the table on which the platter for the retiring collection was placed. He naturally didn't expect the parsimonious sisters to contribute but he knew Miss Bertha had a roving hand. He was then made to feel very guilty when he heard the tinkle of coins in the platter behind him as one of the other sisters proved him wrong.

Jane Cartwright clapped her hands and called for the residents of Rectory Cottages. 'Come along, now, time we were home for supper.'

Jane's mother, Mrs Jenner, turned to Gladys Hodge. 'Jane always gives them supper after the Nativity play each year,' she explained. 'It's become a bit of a tradition, see. They gather in the communal sitting-room and have it on trays on their knees. It's macaroni cheese tonight, Jane said.'

'Very warming, too,' commented Gladys. 'Now come along, Perce, we must be off.' When she caught her husband glancing at Albert Piggott, she sighed. 'Oh, all right, then. You go to the pub with Albert if you must, but you can walk home because I'm taking the jeep.'

'I'll take you,' said Mrs Jenner, 'and Percy can come home later.'

Percy Hodge's face lit up.

'Mind, not more than one pint or PC Darwin will catch you with his breathalyzer-thingy.'

'You go on, Perce,' said Albert. 'I've got to lock up and it seems folks will be nattering here for ages.'

In another group, Winnie, Ella and Isobel were chatting.

'Do you think we've given Frank and Phil enough time? It would be wrong to arrive before they were ready.'

'Phil said to go over as soon as we liked, and to take pot luck. We don't want to get chilled now that the church door is letting in all the cold air,' said Isobel.

'I'm going to pop home on the way,' said Winnie, 'and change into some proper shoes. I wore these fleece-lined boots for the service. I know the draughts of old in this church.'

'Talking of fleeces, weren't the "sheep" wonderful,' said Isobel. 'And Billy Curdle! I've never seen a baby manoeuvre so fast on his bottom.'

'I'm off now to relieve Kit,' said Connie, joining the group. 'He'll be coming up to Tullivers for the party and I'll give Aunt Dot her supper. And I must get this young man back to his mistress.' She looked down at Bruce whose lead she held firmly. 'He's got very over-excited,' she continued. 'The children have been all round him and the Scottie, petting them.'

Bruce's pink tongue was lolling out, and he was looking around for some more attention.

'I think we're all going now,' said Isobel. 'Let's walk over together, and then you and I, Ella, can go on to Tullivers while Winnie pops in to change her shoes.'

They moved together out of the church into the sharp night air. Harold had been right about there being a frost that night. Alan Lester and his family were walking home to the school house down the middle of the green, and

their passage had left four sets of tracks across the white grass.

'While shepherds washed their socks by night,' the two youngsters sang in high-pitched voices, and then skipped out of the way of their father's reach.

'I'm dying for a ciggy,' Ella said, 'and I know I won't be popular if I smoke at Tullivers so I'll go home for a quick one and join you at the party in a tick.'

'You know you should give them up,' Winnie said disapprovingly, but with a smile.

'It's one of the few pleasures left to me in life,' replied Ella, and the other two women made 'Aaah!' noises, and they all laughed.

Thank heavens for good friends, thought Winnie as she did up the top button of her sensible tweed coat.

At Tullivers, Phil and Frank Hurst had about a ten-minute start on the first of their guests. As soon as they were back, Frank ran upstairs to change out of his seventies' pop-star clothes. Phil could hear him above her, the floor-boards creaking as he moved around their bedroom, drawers opening and shutting.

As she slid trays of sausage rolls and vol-au-vents into the oven, which had been left on low, she hummed 'We Three Kings of Orient Are'. She was delighted, and not a little relieved, that the Nativity play seemed to have gone so well, better really than if they'd had their original pre-pox cast. And she was inordinately proud of Frank. She was stoking the fire which had been left well-banked before going out when he clattered down the stairs again.

'Now, what can I do?' he said coming into the sitting-room, running his hand over his thinning hair. 'I think I'll give myself a drink. I've deserved it!'

'Darling, you were wonderful,' said Phil, giving her husband a hug. Still holding him but standing back from him, she continued, 'I think you must do things like that more often. Keeps you young!'

'Thanks, but no thanks,' replied Frank. 'I think you can reckon this evening will be both my debut and my finale at that sort of thing. I'm much too old.'

'Well, it was the performance of a lifetime. Now,' she said briskly, disengaging herself, 'I must go and change. When the boys arrive back, put them to work!'

Jeremy had asked if he and Paul could help at the party and Frank had been more than happy to agree.

'I'll get some bottles open,' said Frank to Phil's retreating back. He went down on his knees and very carefully crawled into his study under the drinks table, being careful not to take the tablecloth with him. 'I'm too old for this sort of caper, too,' he muttered, as he clambered to his feet the other side. 'Now, where's my corkscrew?'

He looked on the table: not there. On his desk: not there. He then remembered it was in the kitchen so, with an ungentlemanly oath and a good deal of grunting, he warily wriggled back under the table. He found his cork-screw and was just making his way back under the tunnel of tablecloth when the first guests arrived.

'Hello!' called Isobel Shoosmith, coming through the

front door. 'Are we too early for you?' She looked around at the empty hall. 'Anyone at home?'

'Yes, yes, I'm here,' replied Frank, scrambling to his feet on the business side of the table, bright red in the face. 'Phil will be down in a moment, she's just changing. Pop your coat on that chair.'

At that moment, Phil came running down the stairs and gave Isobel a big hug. 'Lovely to see you. Harold's coming, isn't he?'

'Yes, of course. He's sent Albert on to the pub and will stay to lock up. Well, what an evening! Everyone was marvellous,' said Isobel, laying her coat on the chair at the bottom of the stairs. 'And well done, you, for persevering when all those children went down with chickenpox.'

'It was Frank, really,' she said, giving her husband a loving smile.

'To be fair,' Frank said, pausing a moment to extract a cork, 'the three of us cooked it up at the pub that lunchtime. I think the second pint gave us Dutch courage. It was good fun, but I'm not sure I would do it again. Now, what can I give you, red or white?'

Phil welcomed some more people who came through the front door at that moment, and as soon as they had drinks and had moved through to the sitting-room, she bustled into the kitchen to take the clingfilm off the plates of squares of brown bread and smoked salmon. She squeezed some lemon over the top and was grinding on black pepper when Jeremy and Paul arrived.

'Hello, you two. Well done, you did the readings really well. Now, Jeremy, you're just in time to help. Can you take that pile of coats upstairs and put them on our bed – tidily! – and keep your eye on that chair for a bit. You don't need to go upstairs with every coat, but don't let the pile get too big. Then you could see if Frank needs any help.'

Jeremy disappeared and Paul asked, 'What can I do to help, Mrs Hurst?'

'Would you like to hand these round?' she said, handing him a platter of smoked salmon squares. 'I expect people will be peckish.'

Paul took the big plate carefully and disappeared, but not before Phil saw the first of the squares disappear into the boy's mouth.

She had bought some French bread, and when Jeremy arrived back into the kitchen, she pointed it out and said, 'You are probably both starving. There's bread and butter there, and some cold chicken in the fridge. Make yourself some sandwiches when you've a moment.'

'Thanks, Mum,' said Jeremy and cut himself a big chunk of bread.

Harold had seen the last of the congregation out of St Andrew's and he stood for a moment in the now-silent church. 'What a very good evening,' he said out loud. The retiring collection had received a generous amount, and was safely in a cloth bag he was holding. After he had locked up the church, Harold set off across the green to his cottage. He followed the Lesters' tracks over the frosty grass but diverted, as usual, to pass close to the statue of Nathaniel Patten.

'I'm not sure what you would have made of that Nativity, old chap,' he said, pausing to look up at the statue. 'But it's all in a good cause,' and he lifted up the bag holding the retiring collection. 'I'll see that half of this gets out to the mission hospital.'

He continued on his way to the house where he hung up the church key and put the money in a safe place. Then he set off to join Isobel at Tullivers.

The party was in full swing when he arrived. Young Jeremy was just about to take an armful of coats upstairs, and Harold added his to the top. He wove his way through the people standing in the hall, glasses in hand, chattering nineteen to the dozen, and found his way unerringly to Frank's table of bottles.

'Ah, Harold, well done! You've made it. All locked up? Red or white?'

'Thank you, red, please, and yes, all safely locked up,' said Harold. He took the glass of wine and took a generous sip. 'Ah, I needed that. I hope you're finding time to have a drink, too, because you've certainly deserved it. I had no idea you could play the guitar.'

Frank laughed. 'I can't really, not any more. I used to play a bit at university. It's Jeremy's and he showed me a few chords. It's rather like bicycling – once learned you never really forget. And with a guitar, there's no danger of falling off!'

Harold laughed. 'I am totally hopeless at music, and tone deaf as well. Isobel begs me not to sing in church, but I love carols and don't care what I sound like.'

'Quite right, too!' said Frank. 'Now go on through to

the sitting-room. Isobel's in there and you should find some food. Ah, Charles and Dimity! Well done, you've arrived! How was the Christingle service?'

'Good, good, thank you,' replied Charles, his eyes twinkling behind his little round spectacles. 'And how did the Nativity go?'

Frank handed him a glass of red wine, and a glass of white to Dimity. 'Very very well. I think we can safely say it was a huge success. Go on through, and I'm sure you will hear all about it.'

'Is Ella here?' asked Dimity. 'I've got some magazines to pass on.'

Frank looked around. 'Actually, I don't think Ella has arrived yet. Perhaps she went home first, some did. Do you want me to put them in here, out of the way?'

Dimity handed a carrier bag over the drinks table, and Frank put it on his desk. Returning to the table, he hailed Jeremy who had just bounded back down the stairs.

'Do you reckon everyone is here?' he asked. 'I'm longing to come out from behind this table.'

'It's difficult to tell, but there's certainly quite a scrum in there,' the boy said, turning towards the sitting-room. 'It's hard to get round with the food. I should say everyone is here. If you want to come out, I'll hold the tablecloth up for you.' He hooked up the cloth to give Frank an easier hands-and-knees passage.

'Thanks, Jeremy,' his stepfather said, dusting down his knees. 'You're being a great help.'

'Mum has said to stop taking food round for a bit, to

give it a rest. Is there anything I can do to help you?' he asked.

'I tell you what would be useful. Get rid of some of the empty bottles and orange juice cartons from in there,' he said, pointing back into the study, 'and put them out by the dustbin. Get Paul to help you. Thanks.'

Frank picked up a glass of wine for himself and shouldered his way into the sitting-room to join the chattering throng.

Frank had been right. Ella hadn't arrived for the simple reason that she had tripped in her kitchen and had had a crashing fall. She had put a hand out to save herself but she had landed heavily and awkwardly.

'Oh, no! No, no, please not!' she cried out loud. But she knew her wrist was broken when she tried to put some weight on it in order to lever herself upright. She moaned in pain. 'Oh, drat and double drat! Now what am I going to do?'

She managed to roll cumbersomely onto her side, and then with the help of her good hand she heaved herself cautiously into a sitting position and leaned back against a cupboard. And here she sat, her heart pounding in protest at the fall. What she wanted more than anything was a cigarette but she knew she could never make one of her noxious roll-ups with just one hand.

And that was where Kit found her quarter of an hour later.

When Isobel had expressed concern about Ella not appearing, Dimity smiled and said of her old friend, 'But you know how Ella is. Hates a crush. She's probably having a second cigarette and will come over when it's thinned out a bit.'

'But when we were walking over,' said Isobel, 'she was definitely going to come straight over after just one cigarette. She said she wanted to talk to Kit about what to give Dotty for Christmas, and she knows Kit won't be staying long.'

Dimity looked round her. 'Well, there's Kit. Perhaps he'd pop back to Ella's to see what's going on.'

'And he could look at some of Ella's handiwork while he's there, to see what Dotty might like.'

'Or not like,' said Winnie, and everyone laughed. Ella's Christmas presents of peg bags or lumpy hand-made ties were a source of annual amusement.

And so it was that Kit walked the short distance to Ella's cottage. He found the front door ajar and walked in. 'Ella? Are you here, Ella? Everyone's asking for you at the party.' He pushed open the kitchen door and saw the great bulk propped against the cupboard. 'Oh, my dear Ella, whatever has happened to you?'

He knelt down on the floor, and peered at his friend who looked decidedly ashen-faced.

'My wrist, gone and broke it,' said Ella, holding up her left arm, then squeaked with the obvious pain and put it hastily back in her lap. 'Fell, didn't I? Over that wretched piece of lino that's come away from the floor.'

'Let's get you up,' said Kit, 'and then I'll go and get John Lovell.'

He hooked his arm through Ella's good arm and heaved

and pulled and, with a great deal of huffing and puffing, he managed to haul the big woman to her feet, and then guide her to the safety of an upright chair that stood at the kitchen table.

'Now you sit there,' he commanded, 'and I'll fetch John.' And, with just a backward glance to make sure Ella was all right, he hurriedly left the house to get help.

The news of Ella's accident was greeted with dismay by everyone at the party.

'Thank goodness you went over,' cried Dimity. 'She might have lain there for ages, poor lamb. What a disaster – and just before Christmas, too!'

John Lovell put down his glass with regret. 'I'm actually off duty tonight, but because it's Ella I'll go over at once. Thank goodness I've only had this one glass of wine. I'll have to call in at the surgery to get my bag.' He turned to Dimity. 'Do you think you could go and sit with her until I get there?'

'Of course,' replied Dimity. She'd do anything for her old friend.

Frank looked round for Jeremy so he could fetch Dimity's coat, but there was no sign of the boy and Dimity said it would be much quicker to pop upstairs to find it herself. A couple of minutes later, she walked into the familiar kitchen in Ella's house that she had shared with her friend for many years, and was horrified to find Ella in floods of tears.

'Dearest Ella, there, there,' she cried, and put out an arm to encircle Ella, but Ella jerked away.

'Careful, it hurts, it all hurts,' and she burst into a fresh wave of tears.

'I'll put the kettle on and we'll have a nice cup of tea,' said Dimity, who was herself very shaken by the sight of her old friend in such distress.

'I'd rather have a ciggy, but I can't roll them one-handed,' sobbed Ella.

'There's absolutely no point you having a cigarette,' replied Dimity, 'since your tears would put it out at once.'

That made Ella laugh, and then she gave a great big sniff. Dimity found a box of tissues and handed it to her. Ella grabbed a handful, wiped her wet face and then blew her nose noisily.

'At least it's my left wrist. Won't make me quite so helpless. Now,' she said to Dimity, sniffing again, 'can I have that ciggy?'

It was her turn to laugh, a laugh that was more relief than anything else. Relief that Ella's sense of humour hadn't totally disappeared.

'What happened?' she asked.

'Fell over that dratted piece of lino,' said Ella, tilting her head and peering at the offending tile on the floor.

'But it's been like that for years,' said Dimity.

'I know, that's what makes it so much worse,' said Ella. Then, dropping her voice to a hoarse whisper, added, 'It's my eyes, Dim. They're getting worse every day. Things I used to be able to see clearly are not much more than a blur now. I don't know what I'm going to do.'

At that moment, John Lovell walked in and took over, his calm, professional manner quickly soothing the distraught woman. He only needed a quick but gentle examination of Ella's left wrist to confirm that it was indeed broken.

'We'll get you to hospital straight away and get it X-rayed. I am pretty certain it's a Colles' fracture, but the X-ray will tell us. Now, will you be all right to walk to the car, and I'll take you straight up? It'll have to be Dickie's, of course, because there're no X-ray facilities at Lulling's Cottage Hospital, but with me there I'll ensure that you're seen quickly.'

Dimity hung Ella's sheepskin jacket carefully over her friend's shoulders and John propelled Ella forward out of the kitchen.

The rector's wife touched the doctor on the arm, and he turned back to her. 'Bring her to the vicarage when she's been plastered, and she can stay with us for a few days.'

'I heard that,' said Ella as she pulled open her front door. 'I'll only come if I'm allowed to smoke. No ciggies, no me!'

Dimity laughed. 'Of course you can smoke. I'll clear a space in the shed, and you can puff away in there.'

And with a harrumph – that Dimity recognized as Ella's way of saying thank you – the doctor led his patient off to hospital.

CHAPTER ELEVEN

A Haven for Ella

In St Richard's Hospital, in the nearby large town, John Lovell was as good as he'd promised, and Ella was sent for X-ray quickly, and a Colles' fracture was confirmed. Back in the Emergency Department, the duty doctor looked at both the swollen wrist and the X-rays and pronounced that the fracture 'could have been worse'.

'Thanks for nothing,' muttered Ella.

'It means,' the doctor said tartly, 'that we won't need to manipulate it before it is plastered.' He left the cubicle to attend to another patient.

While they were waiting for the plaster to be applied, John sensed that Ella was obviously very upset.

'It's rotten luck, Ella,' he said. 'I broke my arm when I was at school, and I got very frustrated at not being able to do the things I wanted to, and felt so useless. People are usually very kind, however, and you're sure to get all sorts of offers of help.'

'I don't want to have to ask for help,' Ella growled. 'I'm used to living on my own, and I don't want people barging in all the time offering help.'

John Lovell was used to gruff Ella and her independent ways. 'I'm afraid you'll definitely need a bit of help to start with, but later you'll find ways of using your fingers. In fact, it will be good to get them moving so you don't stiffen up too much.'

Ella turned her head away. She just didn't want to hear the bad news.

'Come on, Ella, cheer up. It could have been so much worse,' John said. 'Your friends will be only too pleased to help you. I'm afraid Ruth will be run off her feet because my brother and his family are coming for Christmas, but I'm sure Joan would, or Phil or Isobel.'

'You don't understand,' Ella mumbled and then fell silent.

'What don't I understand? Come on, Ella,' John said gently. 'Tell me and I'll see if I can help.'

Ella looked at John Lovell, then looked away again. John waited.

'It's my Christmas presents. I was all behind with them because of my eyes, and now with this wretched hand, I won't be able to finish making them. I'll have to give horrid *bought* ones,' and Ella curled her lip at the word 'bought'. 'And someone will have to take me. It's bad enough Christmas shopping in all those crowds for one's own Christmas presents, but to hang around while someone else is shopping – well, no one will want to do that. And it would end up,' she said, with a toss of her head, 'with me shopping too quickly and buying a load of rubbish.'

'Well, don't give presents this year. Everyone would understand,' John proposed.

'Not give presents? What an awful suggestion!' Ella was obviously scandalized at the thought, and it seemed to give her more resolve. 'Well, if someone would take me down on Monday . . . then that would be very kind.' She laid her good hand on John's arm. 'Thank you.'

'I'll find someone to take you shopping on Monday, I promise,' said the doctor. 'Now bring me up to date about your eyes.'

While Ella's wrist and lower arm were being plastered, John went to telephone Dimity. The telephone rang in an empty vicarage, so he rang Tullivers.

Frank answered. 'They left about fifteen minutes ago,' he said. 'But they were going via Ella's cottage to pick up some nightclothes and other necessities. I think they're going to offer to have her to stay over Christmas.'

'How kind of them. She'll kick and scream, of course, but it's the right thing.'

'Dimity is the one person who can make Ella see sense. How is she?'

'Kicking and screaming!' Both men laughed. 'But, seriously, she's very down but that's to be expected. I'm sure she'll be fine with Dimity's TLC. Is the party still going strong? I was very sorry to have to leave it, especially since I had carefully arranged to be off-duty tonight.'

'Most people have gone – including Ruth who said she

has a busy day tomorrow. Relations or something coming to stay.'

'Yes, I'm afraid my brother and his family have invited themselves for Christmas and Ruth's going to try to do some cooking in advance,' responded John.

'The Shoosmiths and a couple of others are staying for some lasagne. Come and join us when you've delivered Ella to the Henstocks.'

'How kind, but I won't. I'd better get back home and help Ruth. Thanks for everything, Frank, it's been a great evening.'

'Just before you go, John,' said Frank hurriedly, 'do you have any suggestions for hangovers, junior hangovers?'

'What do you mean, *junior* hangovers? Do you mean just a little bit of a hangover?'

'No, I'm afraid I mean hangovers in juniors.'

John twigged and laughed. 'Oh dear, did young Jeremy drink too much wine?'

'Sort of, but it's not quite how it sounds. He and Paul were initially very helpful and then I asked them to take the empty bottles out to the dustbin, get them out of the way. And from what I can gather from Paul when we woke him up to go home, they drained each bottle. And you know what it's like, when one's rushed and pouring out lots of glasses, sometimes the bottle isn't finished. We've counted fifteen bottles out by the dustbins, so they could've had quite a lot. Certainly more than they're used to.'

'Oh dear,' laughed John. 'Well, they've got to learn some time.'

'We found them in Jeremy's room, sound asleep and, would you believe it, half a bottle with them. Phil's put Jeremy to bed, and Edward managed to get Paul to walk home. I think he was rather cross!'

'Yes, he would be,' said John. 'My brother-in-law doesn't like anyone to be out of control. Anyway, my advice is to let Jeremy sleep on in the morning.'

'That's what we're planning, and then he can get stuck into the washing-up. We are leaving it all for him to do. That'll learn him!'

When Ella woke the next morning, it took a moment to get her bearings, and then she remembered the beastly accident and her broken wrist. She didn't know what time it was, but a little light was showing through a crack in the curtains. The radiators were popping so she guessed the central heating had just come on. She lay there, pondering how she would cope while she was so incommoded.

She shortly heard movements in the rest of the house and it wasn't long before the door opened a bit, and Dimity's head peered round.

'It's all right,' said Ella, 'I'm awake.'

Dimity came in, and went to draw back the curtains. 'How are you feeling, and did you get any sleep?'

Ella cocked an eye at her old friend. 'I hardly slept a wink, thanks.'

'Oh dear, I'm sorry. Well, stay in bed for as long as you want. You might doze.'

'No, I'd rather get up. I hate lying in bed doing nothing.'

Dimity sat on the side of Ella's bed. 'I'll get you a cup of tea, and when you've had that, we'll get you dressed.'

She was about to get up off the bed when Ella stretched out her good hand to stay her. 'Dim?'

'Ella, yes?'

'Dim, I'm frightened. I've lain awake all night, worrying. Not about this bally wrist. That'll mend. No, about my eyes. I've been lying here, going through the events of yesterday evening. I tripped over that damn tile simply because I didn't see it. I've never tripped over it before because I've always seen it and automatically stepped over it. But this time I didn't see it.' She paused and when she saw Dimity was about to say something, she continued quickly. 'But at the Nativity, I realized I couldn't see the faces properly. I heard people whispering all round me things like, "Oh, look at Annie," or "Look at our Patrick," but I didn't know which child they were talking about. I couldn't make out the detail on their faces. It was like looking at people in those magic mirrors – you know, the ones that distort images.'

Ella now fell silent, the anxious fingers of her good hand plucking at the eiderdown.

'Oh, Ella, I'm so sorry. What a worry it must be for you,' Dimity said.

'What frightens me most is how long I'll be able to go on living in the cottage. Alone. I'm afraid John Lovell will pack me off to an old folk's home, and I'd commit suicide rather than let that happen.'

'Ella!' Dimity said sharply. 'You *mustn't* speak like that. It is very unChristian for one thing and . . . and . . . and . . .'

'And what? That old people's homes can be quite nice?' Ella said, her mouth puckering. 'I couldn't go into one, Dim, I really couldn't.' A tear escaped down her pale cheek.

Dimity now got up from the bed. 'We'll think of something, Ella. And I promise you, it won't be an old people's home. Although I believe they can be quite nice.'

This brought a smile to Ella's lips, and she flapped at Dimity who moved nimbly out of reach.

'That's better. Now I'll go and get that cup of tea. Charles is busy all morning with services, of course, so we can have the place to ourselves and have a really good talk.'

'Thank you, Dim. I don't know what I would do without you.'

Later that morning, Isobel Shoosmith was preparing Sunday lunch. Both she and Harold had been to the 8 a.m. service in St Andrew's and Harold was now helping Edward and Frank pack away the costumes used for the Nativity play. Isobel was, as they say, miles away when the telephone rang, startling her. She put down the sprouts she was preparing, dried her hands and hurried to answer the insistent ringing – there was nothing more annoying than reaching the telephone just as it stopped.

'Isobel?' came a familiar voice down the line. 'It's Agnes.'

'How lovely to hear you!' Isobel cried. 'How are you, and Dorothy?'

'We're well, very well, thank you.'

Isobel missed her friend after the two schoolmistresses had retired and moved to Barton-on-Sea. They kept in regular touch by telephone, of course, but it wasn't the same as their living next door to each other. It was unusual for Agnes to ring Isobel, however, rather than the other way round, because Agnes was very conscious that her fairly meagre pension covered far less than a half share of the expense of running the house and she never wanted Dorothy to think she was being profligate.

Isobel now said, 'Is everything all right, Agnes?'

'Yes, of course. Things are getting busy in the lead-up to Christmas, needless to say. We're going to our church's carol service this afternoon, which will be nice. Have you had the Nativity play yet?'

Isobel regaled her with some of the previous evening's happenings, and was pleased to hear Agnes laugh at the other end of the line. There didn't seem to be anything amiss.

'Are you spending Christmas quietly at home, or is Dorothy splashing out and taking you both to the Ritz?'

Agnes laughed. 'Heavens, no – although that would be very nice! No, we're spending it here, of course, but there's quite a lot going on. Each year there seems to be more. I suppose it's as we get to know more people and, you know, one thing leads to another. Snowballs.'

'I do know. Sometimes I feel that Christmas just goes on too long. By the time we get to New Year, I'm exhausted. The Youngs are having a New Year's Eve party, and I'll probably fall asleep long before the witching hour,' said Isobel. She glanced at the clock. It was lovely talking to Agnes but she had lunch to cook. 'Frank and Phil Hurst had a lovely party yesterday evening, after the Nativity. Oh, and Ella had a fall and has broken her wrist.'

'Yes, I heard about that,' said Agnes, much to Isobel's surprise.

'Goodness, news travels fast! Who did you hear that from?' she asked.

'From Joan Young. I've just been speaking to her.'

'Oh, I see,' said Isobel.

'And she's asked if Dorothy and I would like to come up for their party. And we would if, if . . .'

'If you can stay,' finished Isobel. 'Of course you can. It will be lovely to see you both. Will you come on the day, or can you come earlier?'

'No, we would like to come that afternoon, if we may, and we shall only stay a couple of nights because Dorothy wants to get back for the Lifeboat charity lunch on the second of January.'

'It will be wonderful to see you both,' said Isobel and, tucking the receiver under her chin, wrote it in the diary.

At that moment, the front door bell rang.

'Agnes, dear, I must go – that's the front door. We'll talk again before you come up. Have a lovely Christmas! Bye.'

Somewhat thankfully, Isobel replaced the receiver and went to see who was calling on a Sunday morning.

It was Charles Henstock.

'Charles, come in, come in!' she cried.

'I'm not disturbing you, am I?' said the good rector. 'Is Harold around?'

'I'm afraid not. You'll find him next door at the school, I think. They're packing up the costumes from last night's Nativity. But come in, I don't think he will be that long. His nose starts twitching at about 12.30 on a Sunday. But would you mind coming through the kitchen. I *must* put in the beef or Harold won't get his lunch until mid-afternoon, I'm so behind.'

Charles sat himself at the kitchen table while Isobel told him of the forthcoming visit of Dorothy and Agnes.

'What fun! Dimity will be so pleased. We've been

invited to the Youngs, too – what a party it's going to be.'

At the mention of 'party', Isobel swung round from the sink. 'Goodness, I'd quite forgotten. How's Ella, poor Ella?'

'She wasn't up when I had to leave for the early service here in Thrush Green,' said Charles. 'She was understandably very shaken yesterday – more fearful about the future, I think, than actual pain. I believe it's what is known as a Colles' fracture, and she'll be in plaster for about six weeks.'

'Brittle bones,' said Isobel, carefully placing the piece of beef among the potatoes and parsnips that were already browning in the pan of sizzling fat, and then spooning the spitting liquid over the meat and vegetables.

'I beg your pardon?'

'A Colles' fracture is usually indicative of brittle bones, osteoporosis – that disease that every woman dreads,' replied Isobel.

'Ah, yes,' said the rector. 'I believe that that is what one of my parishioners is suffering from. She's fairly incapacitated.'

Having put in the joint, Isobel wiped her hands on her apron, looked at the clock and said, 'I'm sure Harold won't be long. Let me get you a glass of sherry. Everything's done in here for the moment. Come into the sitting-room where the fire's lit.'

A few minutes later, Harold returned, and came into the sitting-room rubbing his hands together. 'Hello, Charles. Jolly cold out there, isn't it?'

'Yes, but very beautiful. I love these winter mornings, when the sky's so blue, like today. The road to Lulling Woods was pretty icy, but all the frost on the trees looked lovely in the sun. It's beginning to melt now – that'll certainly make it easier to get around, anyway!'

Harold, having checked that Charles had got a glass of sherry, poured himself one and joined his old friend with his back to the fire.

'You have a good life here, Harold,' Charles said, a cheerful smile on his round face. 'A welcoming fire, surrounded by all your books, music on the player and—'

'And a beautiful wife to look after me!' cut in Harold, smiling at his wife sitting in one of the fireside armchairs. 'I know, I'm very lucky but you don't do so badly yourself.'

'And I know it, too,' Charles replied.

'What *would* men do without women!' added Isobel mischievously.

'Now, now,' said her husband, 'don't let's start on that subject. What's most important is Ella. How is she this morning?'

Charles once more said that he wasn't sure since he'd had to leave the house before she was up. 'I had a word with John Lovell when he brought Ella back last night. She was predictably very depressed about the fracture. Dim and I had a talk early this morning, and we are determined that Ella should stay with us now, and right over Christmas. She can't go back alone to her cottage, and we've got so much room.'

'What a sensible idea,' said Isobel.

'I don't for a moment think she will agree,' said Charles, and both Isobel and Harold nodded. They knew Ella of old. 'But we'll insist and that's the end of the matter.'

'And then what?' asked Harold.

'I don't know, I really don't know. I think we will have to take it day by day.'

At that moment, the pretty little clock on the mantelpiece struck one o'clock.

'I must go!' cried Charles. 'Lunch is usually at one-fifteen on Sunday, which gives me time to digest it before the next service. It's the carol service at St John's this afternoon.' He put his empty glass down on a little table. 'Thank you for the sherry.'

Harold saw him to the door. 'You will keep us in touch about Ella, won't you? And let us know if there is anything we can do to help.'

'Thank you, and yes, of course, both Dim and I will keep you posted.' And with a cheery wave, the rector made his way down the garden path to his car.

At Tullivers on the other side of the green, there was a clattering noise on the stairs, and Jeremy burst into the kitchen.

'What's for lunch?' he said. 'I'm starving.'

His stepfather looked at him over the top of the newspaper he was reading. 'Good afternoon, Jeremy. And how are we feeling?'

'Fine! Great! Good party!'

'Ah yes, good party,' Frank repeated. 'And after every

good party, there's the clearing up. So where've you been?'

'Growing boys need plenty of sleep,' Jeremy replied cheekily. 'And I'm here now to help. But first I must have some food. What time's lunch?'

Phil came into the kitchen at that moment. 'Morning, darling. We've decided not to have lunch today, but have a decent supper instead.'

Jeremy's face fell and he looked so disappointed that his mother immediately softened her resolve to be strict with him on 'the morning after'.

'Some people got up and had a proper breakfast. Have some cereal now, to keep the wolf from the door, then you can fill up with bread and pâté when we eat in about half an hour, and there's plenty of cheese.'

Jeremy grunted, at which Frank shook his head and returned to his newspaper.

However, Phil wasn't going to let Jeremy off so easily. 'In between your breakfast and lunch, there's some washing-up for you to do,' and she indicated a pile of large platters standing on the draining-board.

Jeremy had reached for the box of cereal and was pouring a huge heap into a bowl he had taken from the cupboard. 'They can go into the dishwasher,' he said, pleased that his chore had been so easy.

'Not those plates, they can't,' replied his mother. 'First, they're too big for the dishwasher, and second they're too good. They're old plates and I don't want them anywhere near the machine. All the stuff now on the draining-board has to be hand-washed, and you have been designated Chief Washer.'

Jeremy wasn't really listening. Having spooned three large teaspoonfuls of sugar onto his cereal, he now went to the fridge to get the milk. His eyes lit on a covered bowl of food.

'What's this? Can I have this?'

'That's the remains of last night's lasagne. Yes, I suppose you can have that for lunch.'

'Lasagne? I never had any lasagne,' Jeremy said, slopping milk into his cereal bowl so fast that cereal bits went out over the back edge. The boy nonchalantly scooped them up with his fingers.

'Well, no, you didn't,' Frank said, giving up on his newspaper and folding it up. 'You and I need to have a chat, young man, but it can wait until later. Are you coming with us to the carol service at St John's this afternoon?'

Jeremy's spoon paused halfway between bowl and mouth. 'Paul and I had planned to go for a bike ride and,' he said, looking out of the window, 'it looks a super day for one. To be honest, I think I've had enough of church for a bit.'

'Fair enough,' Frank replied. 'You can go round to the Youngs when we go down to Lulling, so long as you've done your duties here.'

His voice was firm and Jeremy knew his stepfather well enough to know when he meant what he was saying. 'OK,' he said, and then concentrated on devouring his bowl of cereal.

Frank watched him for a minute. He was fairly used to teenagers. Robert, his son from his first marriage, had four children, and the youngest of those was about Jeremy's age. Frank usually spent a week or so down in Wales each year with Robert and his family, and knew all about growing pains. He wasn't worried about Jeremy. The boy had natural exuberance and the bike ride would do both him and Paul good – but only once the chores had been carried out.

Having finished the bowl of cereal, Jeremy got up from the table and gently pushed his mother away from where she was leaning with her back against the sink.

'Move. How can I wash up with you standing there?' And a moment later, with a sinkful of frothing suds, Jeremy set to work.

As Charles Henstock drove back to Lulling, he mused about the coming week which was the busiest in the year for him. The morning's hard frost had mostly gone although he noticed there was still a little patch of white beneath one wall where the weak winter sun hadn't reached. As he crossed from the garage to the back door, he heard the squabble of starlings as they battled for position on the bird-feeder that was hanging from an old apple tree.

Opening the back door, he was greeted by warmth and the delicious smell of Sunday roast. Rubbing his hands together gleefully, he went into the kitchen and tilted his little snub nose to sniff appreciatively. 'That smell must be the best smell in the world. Sunday lunch!'

Dimity turned round from the stove where she was making gravy. 'Just in time, I was beginning to think we'd start without you.'

'Where's Ella? How is she?' Charles asked quietly.

'She's in the drawing-room with the Sunday papers. She's very down, but that's understandable. Would you go through and tell her we're about ready to eat.'

And a few minutes later, Sunday lunch at the vicarage was under way.

'Pass Ella's plate to me,' Dimity said, 'and I'll cut it up.'

Charles put down his carving knife and passed the plate of nice pink lamb to his wife.

'I feel so helpless,' said Ella, 'and I'm afraid you're going to get very tired of me saying that all the time.'

'Then don't say it!' responded Dimity gently. 'We'll just take it for granted. I'll cut those potatoes up a bit, but you'll be able to manage the carrots and beans yourself.'

Over lunch, the three of them discussed Ella's immediate future. Charles was slightly surprised that their doughty friend didn't put up more of a fight about staying on at the vicarage until after Christmas but, later, Dimity quietly explained to him that getting Ella washed and dressed that morning had been such a performance that Ella obviously realized that she couldn't return to her cottage and fend for herself.

Over the apple crumble and cream, they made plans for the afternoon. Dimity was going with Charles to the carol service, and Ella was deputed to keep the fire going in the drawing-room. Before leaving, Charles carried in a big armful of logs and dropped them into the wicker basket by the fireplace.

'That should keep you going while we're out,' he said, and Ella smiled gratefully.

'You are very dear friends. I don't know what I would do without you.'

CHAPTER TWELVE

Albert Plans a Party

Lulling High Street on the Monday before Christmas was crowded with shoppers frantically trying to buy the last of their presents. At the beginning of December, the men from the local Fire Brigade had arrived with their ladders and strung lines of white lights across the fronts of the first floor of all the buildings. It was a time-honoured tradition that these brave men would undertake this job and, as usual, little knots of children had gathered to watch them and offer unhelpful advice. The following day the firemen returned to attach small Christmas trees to brackets above many of the shops' front doors, and the trees now twinkled with little white lights.

However, few of the shoppers now had time to appreciate the decorations; they were all intent on ticking names off their Christmas lists.

'That's Auntie done,' puffed one stout woman as she came out of the chemist's shop. 'Now, what would Dad like?' she asked no one in particular. And no one answered.

Sounds of Christmas music floated in the air sporadically as the doors of W.H. Smith opened and shut behind shoppers. A huge poster in its window proclaimed '3 shopping days left'.

As she was coming out of the shop, Isobel Shoosmith bumped straight into Joan Young who was with Paul.

'It's a scrum in there,' laughed Isobel. 'Are you sure you need to go in?'

'I think it's the best place,' replied Joan, standing to one side to let other shoppers go in. 'We've only popped into Lulling since Paul needs to buy a present for his father, and we thought a book token would be just the thing.'

'Have you time for some coffee?' Isobel asked. 'I'm almost done but I've half an hour before meeting Harold. He's gone down the other end of the High Street to buy some wine.'

Joan looked at her watch. 'Yes, why not. The Fuchsia Bush?' She turned to Paul who was looking at the display of books in the window. 'Paul, what do you want to do? Come and have some coffee with us – and perhaps some of Mrs Piggott's chocolate cake – or meet us somewhere at twelve?'

Paul looked undecided. The lure of chocolate cake was certainly compelling, but he wasn't sure he wanted to be seen sitting with his mother and Mrs Shoosmith.

'I think I'll go in here,' he said, indicating the shop Isobel had just come out of. 'There's some music I might get.'

Joan arranged to meet him at the till nearest the door at noon, and she and Isobel crossed the road and walked up the steps of The Fuchsia Bush. The tea-shop wasn't very full – the lunchtime trade hadn't started and most people were intent on their Christmas shopping.

'Harold might well run into Edward,' Joan said, settling herself into a chair. 'He thought he'd better buy the wine for the New Year's Eve party now, in case they run out.'

'That's hardly likely, is it?' asked Isobel.

'No, of course not, but you know Edward. Always wants to get everything just right, and if he found they were out of his favourite quaffing wine, he'd say the party wouldn't be the same. Now, what are you having? Coffee and some cake?'

Rosa, the waitress, was hovering nearby, her pen and pad at the ready.

'I'll just have coffee, thanks. Harold and I are going to have a snack lunch with Dimity, and then I'm bringing Ella shopping afterwards.'

'Of course,' said Isobel. 'Dimity told me when I rang this morning to find out how poor Ella is. Apparently she's very worried about her Christmas presents. I offered to take her round the shops but heard you'd got in first.'

'I don't think she's got much to buy,' Joan said. 'Most of the presents have been made – or knitted – for some time,' and both women laughed. Ella's hand-made presents were awaited with trepidation each Christmas, and often found their way to distant cousins the following year. 'Dimity said she's very down, which isn't really surprising. I wonder what the future holds for her.'

'Well, she's definitely staying with Charles and Dimity over Christmas, and then Dimity told me they'd have another think. See how she gets on with her plastered arm and wrist.'

The waitress, Rosa, standing beside the table, shifted from one leg to another, and Joan was sure she heard a sigh.

'We must get our order in. Two cups of coffee, please, and a slice of chocolate cake.'

The girl scribbled on her pad, and then left to fill the order.

'Always so chatty, that one,' Isobel remarked. She swivelled in her chair, and pointed to the pine dresser near the till. 'See that teapot? That's the big award that Nelly Piggott got the other day.'

Joan nodded. 'Yes, I read about it in the local paper. Now, how's your shopping coming along? I expect you've done it all!'

'Well, we don't have that many people between us,' Isobel replied, 'and Harold is very good at helping. What about you?'

'Oh, I finished mine weeks ago but I've still got Paul and Edward's lists to finish off. Men are so hopeless about shopping. I've done most of it but I've still got to get Edward's present to me.'

Isobel looked shocked. 'Don't tell me that he leaves you to buy your own present?'

'It's better than getting something I don't want,' replied

Joan. 'So difficult pretending that it's just what one wanted. I know someone's husband who said to his wife that his present to her was hanging on the tree. She found a Christmas tag tied to the end of one of the branches which read "IOU £20".'

'How awful!' exclaimed Isobel. 'What a cheek!'

'It was the beginning of the end, really. The marriage finished soon afterwards.'

In St Andrew's church on Thrush Green, Albert Piggott was showing Bobby Cooke how the heating worked.

'When I'm finished 'ere at the end of the month,' he said, 'don't you think you can come runnin' to me, askin' me this, askin' me that. When I retires, I retires – final. So listen, look sharp, boy!'

The sulky lad sniffed noisily and then unprettily wiped his nose on the sleeve of his less than clean jacket.

'An' you can't do that when you've got yer best suit on, neither,' Albert reprimanded.

'Yeah, well, I ain't got the suit yet, 'ave I? 'Ow long are we goin' to be, Granddad?' the boy asked. 'I'm meetin' our Cyril at twelve.'

'What's the time now, then?' asked Albert, suddenly alert. 'An' don't you go callin' me granddad, neither,' and he made to cuff the boy's ears.

'Nearly twelve o'clock, pub's open,' the boy said, neatly dodging out of the way of Albert's flailing hand.

'You finish off in 'ere,' ordered Albert, indicating the small pile of dust that had been swept together and was waiting to be collected and taken out, 'an' we'll go through the 'eatin' again this af'ernoon. I've got some business to attend to,' he said, somewhat pompously, 'an' I'll see you back 'ere at two.'

Just at that moment the church door flew open, crashing back against the table that stood just inside and Cyril Cooke came sauntering up the aisle. He was younger than his brother, but stockier and just as ugly.

'Come on then, Bobby,' the boy said, totally ignoring Albert. 'I've got somethin' to show yer up the Woodstock Road.'

Bobby turned on his heel and walked away with his brother.

'Hey, come back 'ere and finish off,' called Albert, but they didn't even bother looking back.

Albert sighed. Why should he care? He only had another week to go, and then the dust, and the leaves in the churchyard, the heating and the graves would all be someone else's problem. His mouth felt dry. There was only one way to alleviate that, and he left the church not far behind the Cooke boys.

As he walked the few yards up the road to cross over to The Two Pheasants, he heard a clattering noise behind him on the green. Looking over his shoulder, he saw Bobby Cooke had upended the litter bin and the pair of them were kicking it across the grass, paper flying out in all directions.

'Proper tearaways,' he grumbled, but then didn't give them a further thought as he entered the hallowed interior of his favourite hostelry.

Young Cooke might have bet even money that he knew

Albert's business had meant 'the business of drinking' but he would have been wrong. All right, Albert did mutter 'Same as usual,' as he dragged out a bar stool and arthritically pulled himself up onto it, but he did in fact need to talk to the landlord about a matter he had been turning over in his mind for some days.

It wasn't every day that a chap retired and he thought he would have a little celebration. Nothing big, of course, just a get-together with a few of his cronies. He hoped that if he put money behind the bar for the first round – or possibly the first two rounds – then the others would pick up the tab for the rest.

' 'Nother 'alf, Albert?' asked Percy Hodge, pushing his own glass forward across the bar a short time later.

'No thanks, Perce, not for me today. I needs to 'ave a word with you, Bob,' he said to the publican who was drawing half of bitter for the farmer.

'Yes, go ahead,' replied Mr Jones, easing the pump forward gently to add a little bit more to the glass.

'No, private, like.'

Mr Jones looked at Albert with some surprise. 'What do you want that can't be said in front of Percy here?'

'Never you mind. I just wants a *private* word with you,' replied Albert rather crossly. He tapped his fingers on the bar while another customer was served then, when Mr Jones jerked his head towards the saloon bar where no one was sitting, he stiffly got down from the stool and shuffled through to the adjoining room.

Mr Jones merely moved down to the far end of the counter which served both the public and saloon bars, and addressed Albert when he appeared. 'So what can I do for you? Must be something pretty big that you can't talk about it in front of your mates.'

'Well, you knows I'm retiring?' Albert began.

Mr Jones gave a bark of a laugh. 'Know you're retiring? You've talked of nothin' else for weeks.'

Albert wasn't going to be put off. 'Well, I wants to have a party – in here.'

'What do you mean, in here? In this room?'

'Yes, I don't see why not,' responded Albert. 'This room don't get much used in the evenin's winter-time. Always crowded other times, though.'

Bob Jones knew this was true enough. 'When were you thinkin' of, then? And what time?' he asked.

Albert turned slightly, and looked at a calendar hanging beside the bar. 'I finishes at the end of December, so why not that evening, the thirty-first?'

Mr Jones gave another of his short laughs. 'Come on, Albert, be sensible! That's New Year's Eve and the place'll be packed.'

Albert Piggott was never one to care about the change from one year to the next and was invariably tucked up in bed long before champagne corks started popping.

'Ah, forgot that. Well,' he said, looking at the calendar again, 'what about the night before? I don't want dinner-time, cos not all folks can make it then.'

'Sorry, can't do that neither,' said Mr Jones.

'What? Why not?' demanded Albert peevishly.

'Because there's another party that night, that's why.'

Albert looked again at the calendar. 'Well, I suppose

it'll 'ave to be the Monday night then. Seems wrong, some'ow, havin' it so long before I finishes.'

Mr Jones reached a hand to the back of his bar, and found a dog-eared diary. He flicked through the pages.

'Sorry, no can do. I've got another private party that night.'

'*What?*' exclaimed Albert, aghast that his Grand Plan was fast disappearing. 'What do yer mean, *another* party? No one never 'as parties in 'ere. Why's it so popular all of a sudden?'

Bob Jones smoothed his sandy hair back over his head. 'Ah, popular, that's my middle name. People wants the good service, good food that I can provide, see. You should 'ave got in earlier.'

Albert was stumped. 'I'll 'ave me other 'alf in here, while I thinks.'

He hauled himself up onto a bar stool, took the calendar off the wall and laid it on the bar in front of him. Mr Jones pushed the beer across the bar, which Albert swapped for some of his hard-earned cash.

'S'pose it'll 'ave to be the evenin' of New Year's Day then,' he grumbled. 'Or are you goin' to tell me that's booked an' all?'

Mr Jones looked at his diary again. 'That's clear, Albert. I'll put you down now. What time? And do you want food doin'?'

All this decision-making was too much for Albert. He pushed his greasy cap back on his head and scratched at his thinning hair.

'Make it seven o'clock, when folks 'ave 'ad their bite of supper. Then I won't have to feed 'em.'

Crafty parsimonious old fellow, thought Mr Jones, writing in the diary.

'I'll call it me Freedom Night,' Albert declared. 'I'll pay for the first round. Then they can pay for themselves – and me, I hopes.' And with that, he drained the last dregs of beer from his tankard, got down off the bar stool and ambled out of the pub without so much as a 'See you then' to the landlord.

Later that afternoon, Edward Young drove northwards out of Thrush Green to Woodstock. He knew that Joan would have bought her own Christmas present from him – they had discussed it – but he wanted to get a little something extra, to surprise her. There was a gift shop in the main street where he hoped he might find an attractive knick-knack for her.

As he drove past Blenheim Lodge, he slowed down. He suspected the Burwells would have some dreadful over-the-top Christmas decoration on their front door but his eye was drawn immediately to the lion and unicorn statues on the gate pillars. Round their necks hung large, evergreen Christmas wreaths. Edward swore out loud, and pressed his foot on the accelerator. Where would their vulgarity end?

He spent longer in Woodstock than he had intended. For a start, he couldn't find anything he thought Joan might like in the gift shop, and he'd had to go into one or two others and they were all busy. He was about to give up when he saw just the thing in the window of one of the little town's antique shops. Set on a small velvet cushion among a number of items of jewellery was a pretty brooch – a gold pin with a petal-shape of little turquoises. Joan loved turquoise and he was sure she would like this.

Coming out of the shop a few minutes later, feeling pretty pleased with himself, he ran into a friend, a fellow architect who worked in Woodstock.

'Edward! Just the man I wanted to see. I was going to ring you. Have you a moment to come into the office as there's something I want to discuss with you? With any luck, Julie will make us a cup of tea.'

Shopping, especially Christmas shopping, was thirsty work and Edward agreed at once.

It was nearly five o'clock and dark when he left Woodstock and set off for home. His mind was full of what his friend had talked to him about: going together to the Euro-Architects Conference which was being held in Brussels in the spring. Edward didn't usually attend conferences of that sort since his work was mostly local and involved designing new buildings to fit in with the local softly coloured Cotswold stone, but a couple of days at this conference would be valuable. It was important to keep abreast of new ideas.

He dropped his speed automatically as he came down the Woodstock Road towards Thrush Green. He could see Christmas trees twinkling in many of the windows of the houses set back on either side. One or two people had looped Christmas lights round their front doors and into the branches of small trees. Everyone to their own, thought Edward charitably.

As he drew alongside Blenheim Lodge, he turned his head – and immediately slammed on his brakes. Luckily there was no one immediately behind him but a car further back blew his horn as he drew out to overtake Edward's now stationary car.

It was one thing to put Christmas wreaths round the necks of the lion and unicorn, but not winking lights! He hadn't noticed the lights woven in among the yew and holly when he had passed earlier, but now you couldn't avoid seeing them.

'Holy Moses! What will those dreadful people think of next!' he exclaimed.

Five minutes later, after putting the car away in the garage, and ensuring that the little box containing the brooch for Joan was safely out of sight in his jacket pocket, he barged into the kitchen, sending the door banging against a cupboard and setting all the china shaking.

'Edward! Whatever's the matter?' Joan asked in some alarm.

Paul, who was sitting at the table, also looked up – a large piece of bread spread with peanut butter and jam halfway to his ever hungry mouth.

'Those ghastly Burwells! You'll never guess what they've done now! As if those *ghastly* uplighters weren't bad enough, they've gone and draped the poor innocent lion and unicorn with the most *excruciating* Christmas wreaths – that *twinkle*, for heaven's sake,' and he proceeded, rather breathlessly, to describe what he called 'an abomination of bad taste'.

Joan stood in front of her husband and ran her hands over his shoulders and down his arms. 'Poor Edward, what an affront to your dignity! But you must calm down or your blood pressure will go through the roof.'

'I agree with Dad,' said Paul through a mouthful. He swallowed, then continued: 'I think Christmas decorations should be discreet but beautiful. That's why I like your Christmas tree with just the white bows and white lights, Mum.'

Edward ruffled his son's head. 'There's my boy!' He

peered at the half-eaten piece of bread in Paul's hand. 'Horrible! How *can* you mix peanut butter and jam together?'

'It's brilliant. Here, have a bite,' and Paul held the bread towards his father.

But Edward waved it away and went out of the kitchen, banging that door behind him, too.

'Oh dear,' said Joan. 'Your father gets so upset when someone does something that he considers bad taste.'

'Yeah, but a twinkling lion and unicorn does sound fairly ghastly,' said Paul, cramming the last of the bread into his mouth.

'Well, it's all a matter of what people like. After all, you like peanut butter and jam together on your bread. Let the Burwells have their twinkling statues.'

After supper that evening in the kitchen at Lulling Vicarage, Ella was doing her best to do her share of clearing up. She obviously couldn't help Charles dry the cutlery and plates that Dimity was washing, but she had learned where they lived, and she had put them away in the right drawers and cupboards. It was the bowls and large plates that she couldn't find homes for, and there was no point guessing.

Dimity, glancing over her shoulder, saw her friend just standing there, four-square, the other side of the table. 'That blue bowl goes in the middle cupboard, just behind you,' she said, and Ella gratefully picked up the bowl and turned to put it away.

'And where does this go?' she said, lifting up a little cream jug.

'Ah, I know that!' said Charles. 'In that top cupboard there.' And Ella walked a few paces to where he had pointed.

'I shall learn in time,' Ella said. 'Probably just as I go back home.'

Neither Dimity nor Charles made any comment to that. It was a subject that had been avoided.

Once they were settled in the drawing-room, with cups of coffee, Dimity decided to tackle the problem but not head-on. She thought it would be better to approach it from round the corner.

'Did you get everything you wanted in the shops this afternoon, Ella? Will you need to go back tomorrow?'

Ella stirred her coffee. 'I always think that coffee isn't the same without a ciggy,' she said, ignoring Dimity's question. 'It's like strawberries without cream.'

Dimity didn't respond to this, but Charles looked up. 'Of course you can smoke in here, Ella,' he said. 'It's not banned in this house.'

'It's just that smoking's not good for your health,' said Dimity.

'Oh, pah! to my health,' retorted Ella, scrabbling in her pocket for her cigarette-making equipment.

'And how are you going to put one together, with only one hand?' asked Dimity, smiling at her friend.

'You're going to do it for me,' Ella replied. 'You know how.'

And Dimity did. There had been a number of occasions

when, during the time they were sharing Ella's cottage, Ella had been incapacitated in one way or another, and Dimity had learned how to roll the cigarettes.

'If you are going to continue to smoke,' she said, moving across to sit beside Ella on the sofa and taking the tin from her, 'I think you'd better move on to proper cigarettes, the sort that you buy in a packet.'

'I hate those. They don't taste of anything.'

'Well,' said Dimity firmly, 'I think it's either that or not smoking.'

Ella remained silent. She wasn't really in a position to argue, not with her wrist in plaster and in a sling.

'Now, what about your shopping? Have you got everything you need?' Dimity asked again.

'Yes, I think so,' said Ella somewhat meekly. 'Thank you.' She knew how much she owed to Charles and Dimity for taking her in. Then she added, 'Tomorrow, do you think we could go back to the cottage so I can get the presents that are there? Most of them are already wrapped, but I shall need help with a few others and those I bought today. And then they'll need delivering round the village – please.'

'Of course,' replied Dimity, handing Ella the cigarette. 'Sorry it's a bit raggedy. Out of practice.'

'It's fine, thank you,' said Ella, and lit it with a lighter she produced from another pocket. 'Aah!' she breathed out in great contentment, blowing a cloud of smoke into the air.

Dimity waved the smoke away, and returned to her chair beside the fire. 'I suggest we call in at the cottage on the way to Rectory Cottages tomorrow – it's the Trustees' Christmas party at teatime,' she added by way of explanation.

'That would suit me well,' said Ella. 'While you're entertaining the old folk, I can busy myself around the cottage. There're things I will need if I'm going to stay here for a few more days.' She paused, then added, 'I can stay here over Christmas, can't I, Dim? I don't think I want to face the cottage on my own yet, not until that lino has been mended at any rate.'

'Of course you can stay,' Dimity cried. 'We love having you, don't we, Charles?'

And the good vicar looked up from his book. 'Yes, Ella, we love having you,' he echoed. 'You must stay as long as you want.'

CHAPTER THIRTEEN

Vandals About

The next morning at Tullivers, Phil took a cup of tea upstairs to Frank who was still in bed.

'What have I done to deserve this?' he said, struggling up into a sitting position. 'It's only just after seven o'clock and you're already dressed.'

'Shopping,' said Phil shortly.

'More shopping? It's not possible!' said Frank, accepting the cup from his wife.

'The butcher will be open at seven-thirty,' Phil said. 'And if I leave it till nine, there'll be a queue all down the street as everyone with any sense will be collecting their turkeys today rather than tomorrow. And the supermarket will be hell, too. I may as well get it over with. Tempers get so dreadfully frayed later on.'

Frank grunted. Thank heavens the womenfolk do the shopping, he thought.

Phil sat down at the dressing-table and brushed her

thick blonde hair. 'Have you anything specific planned for today?'

'I'd really like to finish the article for the *Listener*,' he said. 'I know it's not due in until the first week of January, but I'd rather finish it now. I find articles are never as good if there's a gap during the writing. What's Jeremy doing when his lordship deigns to get up?'

'I expect he and Paul will find something. If you see him before I do, encourage them to go out – for a bike ride, or something. And now,' she said, bending over the bed and giving her husband's forehead a kiss, 'I must be off. Is there anything I can get for you while I'm there?'

'No thanks. Have fun.'

'I doubt it,' said Phil. 'Thank goodness Christmas only comes once a year.'

Edward Young pulled his front door shut and walked a few steps down the garden path. Then he stopped and sniffed the air. The sky was steel grey above him, and the weather forecasters – if they could be trusted – had murmured something about the possibility of some snow. Since there had been a frost the previous night, the ground was still hard and any snow might settle. He crossed the little road outside his house, and walked onto the green, intending to cut across it to Winnie Bailey's house. He had promised to help her set up her Christmas tree.

His progress was delayed when he saw that Harold Shoosmith, also on the green, was in the throes of picking up a trail of rubbish that had been jettisoned from the litter bin which was inexplicably in the middle of the green, on its side. Edward went across to help.

'Ah, morning, Edward,' Harold said, straightening up. 'Beastly mess, this. Can't stand litter at the best of times, but certainly not on our green.'

'I can't think what the bin is doing here,' said Edward, stooping to pick up a drinks can. 'There wasn't any wind yesterday.'

'Urchins, probably.'

Edward laughed at Harold's use of such an old-fashioned word. 'Well, if I catch said urchins, I'll shove 'em in the bin along with the litter.'

'I'm just going across to see Albert,' said Harold. 'I'll ask him if he knows anything. I expect he'll lay it at the door of the Cooke boys, even if it wasn't them.'

'Thing is, he'd probably be right,' said Edward. 'Right little scoundrels. I'll see you later, won't I, at Rectory Cottages?'

'I'll be there,' replied Harold. 'Wouldn't miss the sweet sherry for the world!' And with a cheery wave, he grabbed the rim of the litter bin and, dragging it behind him, set off across the green towards the church.

Edward continued his progress to Winnie's house, and she was standing at her open front door as he approached. The Christmas tree, which had been delivered the day before, was lying on the drive.

'Well done, you two, for clearing up that mess. I saw it lying about yesterday. And you're so kind to help with the tree. Everything's ready.'

Edward peered through the open door into the hall

where the tree would stand. Winnie had already positioned the tub for the tree into an angle of the staircase, and she had neatly draped the front of the tub with red crêpe paper.

'I asked for a slightly smaller tree this year. I shouldn't really bother to have one at all, but Donald always said that Christmas wouldn't be Christmas without a tree so I'll keep going as long as possible.'

'Quite right, too!' said Edward. 'Now, if you're ready, I'll bring it in.'

Edward stood the tree upright on the drive, put his arms round and through the prickly branches and lifted. He carried it towards the front door – it was more awkward than heavy. Having manoeuvred it through the door, he paused momentarily on the front door mat and carefully wiped his feet.

'Don't worry about any mud!' cried Winnie. 'We can sweep up afterwards. Now walk forward and I'll guide you to the right place.'

Jenny had appeared from the kitchen and now went a little way up the stairs, and took hold of the top of the tree. 'Back a bit more. Over to the right – no, the other way, your left. There, that's it. Now down.'

And Edward gently lowered the tree into the tub. He extricated his arms from the branches and the tree immediately tilted to one side but Jenny was ready for it, and pulled it back upright. They had done this many times before.

'Now where's the stuffing?' asked Edward, and Winnie handed him a bucket of kindling. Edward got down on his knees and shovelled handfuls of kindling wood round the base of the tree in the tub, and then packed in balls of newspaper Jenny had prepared until the tree was steady. He felt the trunk once more, declared it 'as good as it will ever be', and then got to his feet.

As he dusted down his trousers, Winnie thanked him. 'You're a dear man, Edward. What would I do without you!'

'It's a pleasure, Winnie, you know that. Now, can you and Jenny manage the rest?'

'Yes, we're fine now. We can reach the back by leaning over the banisters. And Jenny is quite happy to stand on the step-ladder to do the top at the front. We shall have a lovely time decorating it. And I expect Donald will be hovering somewhere, telling me that I've tied something on crookedly.'

Winnie laughed, a little embarrassed at what she'd said, but Edward was used to it. Everyone knew that Winnie frequently chatted to her late, much-loved husband.

Edward kissed her soft, wrinkled cheek and to Jenny said, 'You'll come over on New Year's Eve, won't you, Jenny?'

'Thanks, Mr Young, but I won't. I'm going to have supper with some friends in Lulling and will be back here in time to see Mrs Bailey is tucked up safe and sound. I'll pop in for a moment when I come to collect her.'

'I won't stay until midnight, Edward,' Winnie explained. 'That's much too late for me.'

'You stay just as long as you want, and not a moment more. I'll see you both at church on Christmas Day?'

'Of course,' said Winnie. 'And here's a present for you and Joan.'

'Oh, Winnie, you shouldn't have,' protested Edward, taking what felt remarkably like a bottle wrapped up in pretty festive paper.

'It's more a thank you for helping with the tree. Open it whenever you want.'

'Oh, I wouldn't dream of opening it until Christmas Day,' replied Edward and, with a wave, he went out of the front door, closing it quietly behind him.

Winnie and Jenny stood looking at the bare tree.

'Let's have our elevenses first,' said Winnie, 'then we'll get to work. What fun we'll have!'

Shortly before a quarter to four, Charles Henstock's car drew up outside Ella's house. The forecasters had been right. Light snow was falling. There wasn't yet enough to settle on the grass, but the bushes and shrubs in the gardens surrounding Thrush Green looked as though someone had sprinkled icing sugar over them.

'You go on across to Rectory Cottages, Charles,' Dimity said. 'As chairman, you should be there before it starts. I'll see Ella into the cottage.'

As Charles made his way to Rectory Cottages, he recalled the happy years that he had lived in Thrush Green rectory. He knew many people, especially Edward, cheered when it had burned down but he had been fond of it. Also, living inside it meant that he didn't have to look at its somewhat unlovely Victorian embellishments on the outside.

Meanwhile, Dimity helped Ella from the car, taking care to protect the broken wrist. She took Ella's good arm as they went through the gate but Ella shrugged it off.

'I'm perfectly capable, thank you!' she said gruffly, and Dimity left her to it.

However, a moment later, Ella had to ask for help since the key to the front door was in the bottom of her huge untidy handbag and, after rummaging in it for a moment, she shoved it at her old friend and said, 'Go on then, you find it.'

Dimity never took offence at Ella's abruptness. After all, they had shared this cottage for long enough, before Charles had swept her off to the rectory, and she knew all Ella's foibles and forgave her for them.

'At least it's warm in here,' Dimity said, having opened the front door and gone in. 'It would have been so silly to have turned off the heating and ended up with frozen pipes.'

Ella had tried to persuade Dimity to drive up to the cottage on Sunday to turn off the heating since there was no one in the house, but Dimity had rightly told her it was a false economy.

'Now, are you going to be all right on your own?' she asked Ella. 'I don't have to go to the drinks party. I can stay here and help, if you like.'

'I don't like,' said Ella, shuffling through a pile of post that she had picked up from the front door mat.

'Fine!' replied Dimity, not in the least put out. 'We'll be about an hour. But promise you'll ring me if you need any help. You've got the Cartwrights' number.'

Ella didn't answer but Dimity persevered. 'Ella, do you promise?' she said firmly.

'Yes, yes, yes,' said Ella. 'Now off you go. I'll be fine.'

Dimity looked back as she left the kitchen. Ella was gingerly holding an envelope in her bad hand, slitting it open with a kitchen knife held in her good hand. Dimity shuddered and hoped she wouldn't return to a bloodbath.

The Christmas party was held in the communal sitting-room at Rectory Cottages and its adjoining conservatory. When the retirement cottages had been built, the room had been included in the plans for occasions such as this. However, Edward Young, who was the architect engaged, had not envisaged that the residents would use it so much and it soon became obvious that it was too small. The problem was rectified by the addition of a conservatory which, for a time, had proved satisfactory.

However, Mrs Thurgood – one of the Trustees – had later pressed for even the conservatory to be enlarged. She had nagged poor Charles Henstock, and any other Trustee within range, like a dripping tap. For a time, Charles had parried her demands by saying there was no money for a further extension but then an angel – in the guise of an American with connections back to Mrs Curdle and the May Day Fair – had appeared and donated the funds.

Edward had been able to extend the conservatory without spoiling its overall appearance and it seemed that everyone was happy, including Mrs Thurgood. Looking round the room and the conservatory now, filled with all

the residents and most of the Trustees, Charles had to admit the extra space had been needed.

Jane and Bill Cartwright, the wardens, had decorated the rooms festively. Albert Piggott had paid a second visit to Lulling Woods, and had again dragged back a tarpaulin heaped with fine sprigs of holly and mistletoe which he delivered to Rectory Cottages. The brightly berried holly was now tucked behind the pictures on the walls, and coloured streamers criss-crossed both the main room and the conservatory. In one corner, a small Christmas tree stood on a table, its pretty lights winking.

The elderly residents were in their favourite chairs, while the Trustees perched on other chairs brought in for the party or sat on the conservatory window seat. Cups of tea had already been poured and handed round and now Bill Cartwright circulated with the sweet sherry much favoured by the residents. It was perhaps a bit early for sherry but it had become a tradition. Jane Cartwright handed round plates of sandwiches and squares of Christmas cake, and later there would be mince pies.

Like small children, the residents had clamoured to be allowed to pull the crackers the Trustees always provided, and now most present were wearing paper hats. Mrs Thurgood, however, declined to take off her large blue felt hat with its jay's feather tucked into the ribbon round its crown. She felt that paper hats were rather undignified for people of their age – not that she was as old as the residents of Rectory Cottages, she thought hastily.

Charles Henstock sat near his old friend Tom Hardy. Both men were wearing their paper hats, Charles's somewhat askew on his round bald head. Tom had aged and slowed up a lot in the past year, he thought, and the old man's once very blue eyes were rheumy, but he seemed content enough.

'Will you come to St Andrew's on Christmas morning, Tom?' he asked.

'Course, I will, sir,' Tom replied. 'Those that can will walk to the church but John there' – and he waved a hand towards his friend John Enderby – 'I'm not sure he'll make it. His bronchitis is bad again, and Dr Lovell told him to stay indoors and keep warm.'

Across the room, Harold Shoosmith was talking to Mrs Bates and Miss Fuller, congratulating them respectively on the brasses and flowers in St Andrew's. 'Wonderful, quite wonderful,' he said, in his best churchwarden's voice. 'I don't know what we would do without you good ladies.'

And the good ladies simpered appreciatively.

As promised, mince pies were brought round and Harold pretended not to notice when he saw old Mr Cross carefully lift the lid and pour a slurp of his sweet sherry inside.

Jane Cartwright suddenly clapped her hands, calling for hush. 'The carol singers are here!' she said. 'They will sing the two carols we requested, so if you all like to go into the conservatory you will be able both to see and hear them in the garden.'

This, too, was a tradition. Alan Lester with a merry band of carol singers of both children and parents made Rectory Cottages their first port of call, while the annual party was in progress. This year, the residents had chosen 'Hark the Herald Angels Sing' and 'The Holly and the Ivy'. During the singing of the second carol, little Annie Curdle came round with a collecting box marked 'For St Richard's Hospice', and the residents and Trustees generously dropped their coins into it.

As the carol singing party left the garden, Jane Cartwright stood at the gate with a plate of mince pies.

Bill Cartwright brought the sherry bottle round once more and filled up the glasses. Dimity caught Charles's eye from the other side of the room, and when she slightly raised her glass, Charles remembered it was his duty, as chairman of the Trustees, to give the annual Christmas toast. He patted Tom Hardy's arm, and then rose to his feet, clearing his voice as he did so. The room hushed.

'Ladies and gentlemen, dear friends in Rectory Cottages, it only feels a short while ago that we were here toasting last Christmas. But I know how time flies as one gets older.' There was a murmur of agreement. 'I would like to thank Bill and Jane for another lovely party.' He paused while the residents variously raised their glasses to the two wardens, or called out, 'Thank you, happy Christmas!'

Then Charles continued: 'We lost our dear friends Eric and Carlotta Jermyn during the year, but are so pleased that Martha and Stephen Hill have settled in so quickly.' The newest residents, sitting side by side on the window seat, beamed. 'We, the Trustees, wish you all a very happy Christmas and a healthy and happy New Year.' And, raising his glass, he called out, 'To the residents of Rectory Cottages, a very merry Christmas!'

'Everyone seems very happy there,' said Dimity a short while later, as she and Charles were walking back to Ella's cottage. They made their way with great care since the snow was now falling more seriously and the pavement had been quickly covered. Their feet crunched on the virgin snow in a most satisfying way.

'Yes, it gives one such comfort to see them so settled,' replied the good rector, 'but Tom Hardy indicated that John Enderby isn't very well, rather frail now.'

'I expect it comes from all those years he spent out of

doors, working in people's gardens,' Dimity replied. 'Jane will keep a close eye on him.'

'Just as we must keep a close eye on Ella,' said Charles.

'She's far more stubborn than John Enderby,' Dimity said. 'And proud.'

Charles was about to push open the garden gate of Ella's cottage when the party of carol singers came down the road.

'Hello, Vicar,' called Alan Lester. 'Would Miss Bembridge like us to sing her a carol?'

'I think that would be a lovely idea,' cried Dimity. 'Just hang on a tick and we'll go and fetch her to the door.'

Dimity found Ella sitting in the kitchen, an extremely frayed roll-up sticking out of her mouth. It was a very familiar scene, apart from her plastered arm.

'Ella, the carol singers are here. They'd like to sing you a carol. Here, put your coat round your shoulders and come to the front door.'

As Ella lumbered to her feet, she had the presence of mind to leave her cigarette in the ashtray on the table, and pick up her purse.

'Now, what carol would you like?' Dimity asked, as the two old friends made their way to the front door.

'Oh, golly, I don't mind. Hello, Alan,' Ella said, greeting the schoolmaster. Then, as a snowflake landed gently on her nose, she looked up. 'Goodness, I didn't realize it had snowed so much. Is there a carol with snow in it?'

'I think it had better be "Good King Wenceslas", hadn't it?' Alan replied. 'The children like that one.'

The three friends stood on Ella's doorstep and listened,

smiling, as the words of the carol floated out in the snowy evening air, and when the carol had finished, they clapped appreciatively and more coins tinkled down into the proffered collecting box.

'Good night, merry Christmas,' the singers called and they walked down the path, stamping their feet to keep out the cold, and set off to find another audience.

Back in the kitchen, Ella sat down on her chair again, picked up her cigarette and re-lit it. Only when she had sent the first cloud of pungent smoke into the air, did she speak.

'Had a good time at the old folk's home?' she asked gruffly.

'Yes, indeed,' Charles replied. 'Mrs Bates and the Angells sent their best wishes for a speedy recovery. Now,' he said, 'are you ready for us to take you home?' And as he said it, he knew he'd made an error.

'*This* is my home,' snapped Ella. She paused a moment, then continued quietly, 'I love this cottage, I really do. I couldn't bear to have to leave it.'

She looked round at the familiar room: the scrubbed pine table in the middle of the kitchen, and the little Welsh dresser against the wall between the two windows. Dimity noticed Ella had lit the candle on her favourite Christmas decoration: the heat from the candle made a whirligig of angels slowly move round in circles, tinkling gently.

She then took a deep breath, stubbed out the cigarette, and said, 'And, yes, I'm ready. That needs to come with me.' She pointed to a bulging carrier bag containing wrapped parcels, and a roll of Christmas paper. 'I've put a few clothes out on my bed,' she continued and then stopped. Neither Charles nor Dimity said anything and, after a moment, Ella went on in a quiet voice. 'I can't get my little suitcase down off the top of the cupboard without standing on a chair, and I didn't think it would be very safe for me to climb up one-handed.'

Dimity shuddered at the thought. 'I'll go up and pop them in the case. Why don't you and Charles take the rest of the things out to the car? I won't be a moment.'

'Thanks, Dim,' said her old friend. 'Thank you both very much.' She heaved herself to her feet, crossed to the Welsh dresser and blew out the candle on her Christmas decoration. She watched the circling angels slowly come to a halt and then turned to Charles who was waiting quietly by the door. 'I'm ready now. Shall we go?'

At about the same time as the Thrush Green carol singers were entertaining the residents of Rectory Cottages, another group of carol singers arrived outside The Fuchsia Bush, which was serving tea to the last exhausted shoppers. It was nearly five o'clock, and the shops' brightly lit windows shone out onto the pavement. The white Christmas lights, strung high across the fronts of the High Street shops, twinkled cheerfully.

Poppy, who was idling at the back of the tea-room and wondering how quickly these last customers might leave because she was going out that evening with Geoff, the photographer who had attended the award ceremony, pushed open the door into the kitchen and called through, 'Mrs Piggott, the carol singers is come.'

Nelly came bustling through into the tea-room. 'Well, open the door, girl, so as we can hear them!'

Poppy dutifully opened the door, letting in the cold evening air. Ha! she thought. That'll shift the dawdlers.

The carol singers' voices followed the cold air in. 'God rest ye merry gentlemen,' they sang. It was the choir from St John's and Nelly waved to a few people she knew. The remaining customers smiled and sat back to enjoy the music.

Nelly pulled the last remains of the cakes resting on the counter towards her, and sliced great chunks of rich fruit cake, chocolate cake and coffee cake. When the carol singers had finished their second carol, 'In the Bleak Midwinter', she handed two plates piled with cake to Poppy and Rosa.

'Look sharp now!' she said. 'Take the cake down to them and make sure you come back with empty plates. It's nippy out there, and this'll keep 'em warm.'

The singers gratefully stretched out for slices of cake, and one or two popped an extra slice into their pockets. Then, calling out their thanks, they moved off down the road towards their next stop. As Nelly held the door open for the last of the customers to leave, she thought that the singing was sounding a little muffled – no doubt the slices of cake had something to do with it.

At six-thirty that evening, Derek and Jean Burwell arrived home having spent the afternoon in Oxford. As Mr

Burwell turned the car across the Woodstock Road to enter his driveway, he let out a surprised cry, and stopped the car between the two stone pillars.

'What's happened to the lights?' he spluttered.

'Oh dear, there must be a power cut,' Jean Burwell said.

'Rubbish, woman!' snapped her husband. 'There are lights on in the house next door.'

He backed the car a little, so the headlights lit up the stone gateposts, and then got out of the car, crossing to peer more closely at them. When his wife saw him bending down and fumbling around the base of the pillars, she realized that the uplighters were not shining either.

'Come on, dear,' she called. 'It's perishing cold with your door open.'

Derek got back into the car. 'I think they've been vandalized, but I'll be able to see better with a torch.'

Having parked the car, he grabbed a large torch from a shelf in the garage and marched back up the tarmac drive to the gateway, leaving his wife to take all their shopping into the house. She was pouring boiling water into a teapot when her husband marched into the kitchen, slamming the back door behind him.

'I was right – vandalized!' he exclaimed. 'What a nerve! The wreaths round the lion and unicorn seem to be all right but I've found at least two of the little lights smashed which has shorted the rest. And the bottom lights have been kicked to one side.'

'Who'd have done such a thing?' his wife asked indignantly.

'Lord knows,' he replied. 'Some of the kids, I expect.

That Cooke family that lives down the Nidden Road, they're always making trouble. It came up at the PCC meeting the other day.'

'Ring Harold Shoosmith, then,' Jean Burwell said. 'It's not right to damage people's property like that. The lights were so pretty, too.'

'I'll go down to Lulling in the morning and get some replacements.' He waved away his wife's proffered cup of tea. 'I'll have it in a moment. I'm going to ring Shoosmith now. Got to get to the bottom of this,' and he stormed out of the kitchen.

'Tell him it's scandalous behaviour,' called his wife to his retreating back. 'And at Christmas time, too!'

CHAPTER FOURTEEN

A Very Happy Christmas!

Christmas Day was the busiest day of the year for Charles Henstock, with services in all four of his churches, and he was up long before dawn started to glimmer on the eastern horizon. Dimity was still asleep in bed; she had been to the midnight service with him the evening before in St John's, and they hadn't got home until after one o'clock.

She had left out the box of cereal on the kitchen table for him, and he poured a generous helping into a bowl as he waited for the kettle to boil.

'You must have breakfast before you leave for Nidden, dear,' Dimity had said. 'And make sure you wear your thermal vest – that church is never warm enough for the eight o'clock service.'

As Charles opened the back door a quarter of an hour later, he could smell the frost outside rather than see it for it was still very dark. He stood for a moment and sniffed the air as a curious rabbit might. Much to the disappointment of the local children, the snow that had fallen two days previously had not lingered. Rain on the morning of Christmas Eve had melted it swiftly and all that remained were a number of sagging snowmen. The previous night's frost would mean an awkward drive to Nidden. The vicar tilted his round face up to gaze into the dark sky; he could see stars high above – and shining brightest of all was the Morning Star. How apt, he thought, as he crossed the gravel to the garage.

Charles set off for Nidden, passing through Thrush Green as he went. The village was beginning to stir. He was glad to see the figure of Albert Piggott pushing open the church gate; he would be going in to turn on the heating, ready for the eleven-fifteen service. There were lights on in the Curdles' home next to the Youngs'. No doubt George, Annie and Billy were opening their stockings.

As he turned up the Nidden Road, he dropped his speed. Although the steep hill from Lulling to Thrush Green had been dry and frost-free, the gritting lorry would not have come up here the evening before. He passed the ramshackle cottage where the Cooke clan lived. It was still in total darkness. He wondered if the youngest children would have any sort of Christmas. Cooke senior was still serving time at Her Majesty's pleasure and he didn't know if Mrs Cooke had any work. It was certain that none would appear in church, and he made a resolution to call on them in the New Year.

He hoped there would be more than the usual four

worshippers at the eight o'clock communion service but doubted it. He sometimes wondered how long the little church could continue to remain open. There were only ever two services a month here, the regular worshippers having to go to one of his other parishes if they wanted to attend every Sunday. After Nidden, he would have the nine o'clock service at Lulling Woods, a dash back for the ten o'clock service at St John's in Lulling and then, finally, he'd have to hurry to get to St Andrew's in Thrush Green.

Christmas Day was always a rush – but it was worth it. Churches fuller than usual, children, happy faces. Yes, a very good time of the year, he declared, as he pulled into his regular parking place outside the little church.

The rector had been right about the Curdle household: it had had a very early start. Much too early, Ben had chided, sending Annie back to her room when she'd appeared beside his bed and his clock told him it was not yet five o'clock.

'But Father Christmas has come, an' I want to open my stocking,' she'd whispered so as not to wake her mother.

'If you don't go back to bed, Father Christmas might come and take it back,' her father had said sternly. 'You can come in at seven. And no opening of the stocking beforehand,' he added to his daughter's retreating figure.

It had been closer to six-thirty when Ben and Molly's bedroom door had burst open, and two over-excited children had come in, dragging their stockings behind them.

'Happy Christmas, Mum, Dad!' they cried.

Ben opened one eye and saw the time. Well, they'd

managed an extra hour and a half's sleep. 'Happy Christmas, George. And happy Christmas, Annie,' he said, sitting up, running a hand through his tousled hair.

The two children scrambled up onto the end of the bed, and Annie wriggled her way towards her mother. 'Are you awake, Mum?' and she shook a shoulder under the bedclothes.

'Yes, I'm awake. Now get off me so I can go and fetch our Billy.'

Their youngest had pulled himself up on the bars of his cot in the little single room next door, and was shaking the side vigorously.

'Just as well you're the last,' said Molly, lifting the child out. 'That cot won't last much longer.' She took him off to the bathroom to change his nappy.

Five minutes later, everyone was squeezed onto and into the double bed, and Ben called, 'Ready, everyone? Right, one, two, three, go!' And the two elder Curdle children delved into their stockings – long green woollen stockings that had been in the Curdle family for years – and the room was soon filled with cries of delight and the bed covered with pieces of discarded wrapping paper.

Molly stretched out a hand to her husband. 'Happy Christmas, Ben.'

'Happy Christmas, darlin',' he replied, and gave her a hug.

Winnie Bailey stood at her bedroom window in her dressing-gown. The sky was beginning to lighten, and was softly streaked. A well-wrapped-up figure was bicycling slowly past and Winnie wondered where on earth anyone would be cycling to at this hour on Christmas morning. A blackbird's alarm call brought her gaze into her own garden. The grass was white with frost and the bushes round the bird table were already a-twitter with expectant sparrows and finches. She resolved to put out an extra large helping of bread as soon as she'd had her breakfast. She could already hear Jenny downstairs in the kitchen, and remembered that scrambled eggs were on the menu. Winnie had to admit that Jenny's scrambled eggs were the best in the world.

When her nephew Richard had telephoned one day a few weeks earlier to say that he, Fenella and the children were going to stay in London for Christmas, Winnie had felt immense relief. She was too old, she decided, to have a house full of over-excited youngsters. They had all come to stay a few years before and she had been exhausted even before lunchtime. On top of which she found it very difficult not to show her disapproval of the way the children opened their presents with abandon, hardly glancing at one before tearing the paper off the next. Richard had done his best to keep a list of who had given what, but she doubted many bread-and-butter letters were written.

Isobel Shoosmith had been with her when Richard had rung. She had popped over to get a recipe for a sherry trifle that had been handed down to Winnie by her mother, and which Harold had declared 'the most delicious ever' when they'd been having lunch there one day.

'That was Richard,' Winnie had said, putting down the

telephone. 'Not coming for Christmas, thank goodness. It will be nice to be on our own.'

'You must come and have Christmas lunch with us,' Isobel had said immediately. 'There's no point the four of us sitting down to huge lunches on separate sides of the green.'

When Winnie had demurred that it would be too much trouble, Isobel had insisted. 'We tend to eat at about two o'clock,' she'd said, 'so have a good breakfast to last you through.'

And so, the evening before, Winnie and Jenny had planned their breakfast of scrambled eggs on toast, with grilled bacon. Afterwards, they would open their presents before getting ready for church at eleven-fifteen.

She turned away from the window and crossed the room towards the bathroom. She paused by the chest of drawers on top of which stood her favourite photograph of Donald. He'd been asleep in a deck-chair under a shady tree in the garden, and the book he had been reading had fallen sideways in his lap. She loved the peaceful look on his face, and she had never regretted creeping up on him and taking the photograph.

'Happy Christmas, dearest Donald,' she said now, and gently touched his face in the photograph. 'It's scrambled eggs for breakfast!'

'Are you awake?' called Connie, pushing open her aunt's door. She was still in her dressing-gown and was carrying a tray carefully in front of her.

'Yes, been awake for ages,' replied Dotty.

Connie set the tray down on the bedside table, and went to close the window. 'There's been a hard frost. Perfect for Christmas Day. Happy Christmas, Aunt Dot.'

'If there's a frost, I must get out quickly to see that the goats have got plenty of hay, and we must give extra to the ducks,' cried Dotty, ignoring the niceties of seasonal greetings in her concern for her beloved animals and birds and, pushing the bedclothes aside, started to get out of bed.

'No, you don't!' Connie said, gently pushing her back. 'Kit will see to the feeding as soon as he's dressed. We don't want you slipping on the icy ground.'

Once Dotty was back under the bedclothes, Connie plumped up the pillows behind her aunt and then laid the tray across her knees. 'Boiled egg and toast this morning.' She perched herself at the end of the bed. 'Do you feel like coming to church with us today?'

Dotty looked towards the window. The rising sun had flushed the sky a gentle peach colour.

'Yes, I think I'd like that. So long as the animals have been fed, of course,' she said firmly.

'Excellent!' said Connie. 'I know Charles will be delighted to see you. The service is at nine and we must leave ten minutes before that. I'll go and get dressed now, and then come back and help you.'

'I must wear a hat,' Dottie declared. 'That nice straw one with ribbons will do nicely.'

'Of course,' Connie said. Come summer or winter, rain or shine, Dotty invariably wore no other hat. She smiled lovingly at her ancient aunt, and left to get dressed.

*

When Harold Shoosmith pushed open the door of St Andrew's at ten forty-five, he rubbed his cold hands together in pleasure. Albert had done his job; the church was nice and warm. He switched on the lights, and looked around. The flowers on the altar, on the font and by the rector's chair were lovely. It was not the most beautiful church in the county, he admitted, but it had such a good atmosphere.

He picked up the three collection bags from the vestry, and laid them on the table with the hymn books. He and Frank Hurst would take the collection in the main body of the church, and he hoped Ben Curdle would climb up into the gallery to collect from the congregation that invariably overflowed up there at the Christmas morning service.

He was standing at the lectern, checking the ribbons were in the right places for the two lessons, when the first people arrived, those who had walked the short distance from Rectory Cottages. He went forward to greet them, and show them to their seats. Frank and Phyllida with Jeremy were the next to arrive: Phil and her son went to sit down while Frank took a pile of hymn books to hand out at the door.

Harold was greeting Winnie Bailey and Jenny when he felt a tap on his shoulder. He turned to find Derek and Jean Burwell behind him.

'Well, have you talked to that Cooke family, then?' demanded Derek.

Harold bridled. 'And a happy Christmas to you, too,'

he said. He wasn't going to be pushed around by this unpleasant man. He had had Derek Burwell on the telephone for half an hour two days earlier, demanding that – as chairman of the Parochial Church Council – he had to bring to justice whoever it was had damaged his Christmas decorations at Blenheim Lodge.

'Well?' said Derek, thrusting his face closer to Harold's.

Harold took a step back. 'I don't think this is the time or the place for having this conversation. I suggest we leave it until after the Christmas holiday.'

'We've had to spend a great deal of money replacing the lights,' cut in Jean Burwell, her face pink with indignation.

'Yes, well, I'm sorry about that. Now, if you will excuse me, I must get ready to begin the service. Perhaps you would like to find yourselves somewhere to sit.'

Derek gave him a look that said he didn't think much of the chairman of the PCC, and moved off down the aisle.

'Sit somewhere,' said his wife in a stage whisper, 'where we don't have to look at that tatty crib.'

Very soon, the nave and side aisle were full, and families clumped upstairs to the gallery. There was a general hubbub of chatter as friends wished each other 'Happy Christmas' and children excitedly described what presents they had had. No one seemed to be paying attention to what the organist was playing but when he saw that Harold was ready to leave the vestry, he pulled out the stops, the music swelled to fill the church and the talking soon died away.

Harold walked down towards the reader's chair and

turned at the chancel steps to face the congregation, which was now standing.

'Good morning to everyone, to all the families from Thrush Green and around, and especially to all the visitors here in St Andrew's today. As you know, our good rector Charles Henstock will be with us as soon as he can get away from the service in St John's and, in the meantime, I will start this morning's service. And the first hymn on this beautiful Christmas morning is "Christians Awake, Salute the Happy Morn".'

After the four church services he had taken that morning, Charles Henstock was still not really able to relax, but after the service in Thrush Green he'd gone, with Dimity and Ella, across the green for a glass of sherry with Harold and Isobel.

Later, having dropped Dimity and Ella off at the vicarage, Charles drove to the local hospital to see his parishioners there who had not been able to go home for Christmas. He returned to the vicarage for a late lunch of cold ham and salad and after the Queen's speech, which they watched on television, they opened their Christmas presents.

Instead of the usual hand-made present, Ella had bought Dimity a beautiful screen-printed silk scarf.

'Oh, Ella, it's lovely. And just the right colour – it will go with my coat perfectly. How clever of you!'

'You've got a pair of gloves that colour, and when I saw you wear them with the coat, it gave me the idea. So I popped a glove into my pocket when we went shopping the other day, and the nice assistant helped me choose the right colour. I couldn't risk my dratted eyes getting the colour wrong.'

'So that's where my glove went to! I lost it – and then it appeared again.'

Ella laughed. 'And for you, Charles, a bottle of your favourite port!'

Dimity then handed quite a bulky present to Ella. 'From both of us.'

'I don't need a present from you,' said Ella rather ungraciously, and then added, 'Being here with you both is present enough. But thank you.'

She unwrapped a box containing a cassette recorder and, separately, two plastic boxes containing audio tapes. She looked at them then put them on the sofa beside her. 'Thank you. Very useful.' After a moment's silence, she said, 'Shouldn't you be going over to the Lovelocks'? It's nearly four.'

On their way to the traditional Christmas tea with the elderly sisters, Dimity was worried that they had upset Ella with their present.

'The cassette player is sort of ramming home that she's going blind,' she said. 'I wasn't sure if she was more upset or cross.'

'She can't bury her head in the sand,' said Charles. 'According to the optician, her eyesight is deteriorating fast. And for someone who has been as active as she has, that's a bitter blow. She's got to face up to things, and it'll be so much better if she can do that in the company of true friends.'

'You're so right, dear,' said Dimity. 'How wise you are.'

Together, they climbed up the steps of the Lovelock residence and Charles banged the knocker on the front door, not failing to notice the cracked and flaking paint.

'Come in, come in,' cried Miss Ada as she opened the door.

'Happy Christmas, dear Charles,' called Miss Violet from the drawing-room door.

The third sister, Miss Bertha, was already seated at the tea-table. She was wearing a paper hat from a cracker, and it was sitting rather lop-sidedly on her silver-grey head.

Dimity was concerned at the trouble the three sisters

had obviously gone to. There was thinly cut bread, spread with the faintest amount of butter possible. There were scones that bore Nelly Piggott's hallmark, and – considering their usual parsimoniousness – a quite sizeable Christmas cake. That too, Dimity was sure, came from next door at The Fuchsia Bush. And why not? she thought. She doubted any of the Lovelock sisters had ever baked a cake in their life.

To have tea with the Lovelocks was a tradition that Charles had inherited from his predecessor, Anthony Bull. In normal circumstances, Charles wouldn't have minded having tea with them one little bit – but he was very tired. It had been a long day. Thankfully, Dimity knew just how tired he was and chattered away, leaving Charles to smile benignly and enjoy a slice of Nelly Piggott's absolutely sublime fruit cake.

'We must be going!' Dimity said quite soon, springing to her feet. Charles looked at her in some surprise; he thought they'd have to be there for at least another half-hour. 'We must get back to Ella,' Dimity explained.

The Lovelocks knew all about Ella's accident and that she was staying at the vicarage with them. They twittered their best wishes, and begged Dimity to bring Ella to morning coffee quite soon.

'And you, my darling,' said Dimity, tucking her arm through Charles's as they walked down the High Street towards the vicarage, 'are going to bed when we get home.'

'Bed? But I haven't had my Christmas dinner yet!' Charles said rather plaintively.

Dimity laughed. 'And you shan't go without it. We'll eat at eight, which will give you at least two hours' shut-eye. Either that, or you'll fall asleep over your turkey.'

And Charles did just as he was told, and was asleep a moment after he had laid his head on the pillow.

At half-past seven that evening, the three friends gathered in the vicarage's elegant drawing-room. Charles, much refreshed from his nap, had put on a dark blue smoking jacket and a blue and white spotted bow tie. Dimity was in a very pretty dove-grey chiffon dress, and even Ella had made an effort. She was wearing a long woollen tartan skirt, with a bright red jacket with black trimmings. It had wide sleeves – which is why she had brought it with her from the cottage – through which she had gently threaded her left arm. The white sling stood out startlingly across its front.

When she made her way into the drawing-room from upstairs, Charles jumped to his feet. 'Ella, my dear, you look ravishing!'

Ella dutifully turned a little pink at the compliment.

As Dimity handed her a glass of sherry, she peered at her old friend. 'Good heavens, Ella! You're wearing lipstick! Well, I never!' And that made Ella turn even pinker.

Dimity and Ella had laid the dining-room table together and it looked magnificent. The best silver was shining brightly, and the flickering of the candles reflected in the polished surface of the table. The turkey was cooked to perfection, and the roast potatoes that had been cooked in goose fat were wonderfully crispy.

The three of them had discussed whether or not to have

a Christmas pudding since each admitted to not liking it very much. In the end, Dimity bought a small one from The Fuchsia Bush.

'It's not that I dislike it,' Ella had declared, 'but if I have too much, there's no room left for the cheese and the nuts and bolts.'

'Nuts and bolts?' Charles had queried.

'You know, walnuts, figs and dates, stem ginger – to my mind, the best part of Christmas dinner,' said Ella, her troublesome eyes shining as brightly as a child's.

'Er, not sure about some of those, not very keen on figs and dates,' Charles had said.

'Typical of a man,' Ella had grunted in response.

'Just as well I didn't buy the smallest pudding,' remarked Dimity now as Charles gave himself a second helping. 'Oh, I see – a little bit of Christmas pudding and a great big spoonful of brandy butter.'

Charles beamed with pleasure. 'And when I've finished this, I shall have some of that fine Stilton with a glass of the port you gave me, Ella, and will leave all the figs and dates for you two.'

Dimity looked at her husband sitting so contentedly at the head of the table. Then she looked across at her old friend sitting on Charles's right. How well she and Ella had got on when they had shared Ella's cottage before she had married Charles. On this Christmas night, it seemed as though fate had brought the three of them together.

CHAPTER FIFTEEN

Ella Does a Runner

Most households had a fairly quiet start to Boxing Day morning. The weather had changed again. Gone were the blue sky and crisp frosts, and back came leaden skies and a sharpish wind.

Percy Hodge, of course, had had to get up at his usual time because cows had to be milked whatever the day, whatever the weather. However, he whistled as he went about his work, knowing that when he went in for breakfast, there would be a slice of fried Christmas pudding with his usual fry-up.

'Aren't you havin' any?' he asked, as his wife carefully lifted the sizzling slice of pudding from the frying pan onto his plate.

Gladys Hodge gave a shudder. 'Certainly not!' she said. 'What a dreadful mixture.'

'Luverly,' pronounced Percy, spearing open the fried egg that he had directed should be placed on top of the

Christmas pudding. 'What makes it so special is that I only gets this once a year.'

'You can have it tomorrow, too,' Gladys said. 'There was that much left over from yesterday.'

There was silence in the farmhouse kitchen, broken only by Percy's old sheepdog having a scratch in a corner, setting a tall rack of saucepans rattling as his backside bumped against it.

Gladys knew better than to disturb her husband at his breakfast, but once he had cleaned his plate with a piece of white bread, she poured more tea into his huge cup and asked what his plans were for the day.

'I thought I'd go down into Lulling mid-morning an' see the hunt. It's always such a fine turn-out, the Boxing Day meet. You comin'?'

'No, too much to do here. You haven't forgotten Doreen, Bobby and Suky are arriving round dinnertime, have you?'

Doreen was Gladys's daughter by her first marriage and Bobby and Suky were Doreen's children. The boy's father was a ne'er-do-well who had led Doreen a merry dance. She had finally seen sense and returned home to live with her mother and, for a time, the tongue-wags of Thrush Green had thought that Percy Hodge was paying court to the girl. 'Much too young for him,' said one; 'cradle-snatcher!' said another. In the event, it was Gladys Lilly on whom Percy Hodge had set his sights.

Mother and daughter were both married within a few months of each other – Gladys Lilly to the Thrush Green farmer, and her daughter to a nice young man she had met while living in London, where he had a window-cleaning business.

'Plenty of work up there,' Percy had said to his cronies in The Two Pheasants. 'What with all that smog.'

Bob Jones, polishing a glass, had paused and said, 'Smog? That's out of date, that is. Ain't no smog any more.'

'Well, I wouldn't know, would I?' Percy said defensively. 'Never set a foot there. Did plan to go once, to visit Smithfield Market, but then that wretched Foot an' Mouth come in, and I never moved far from 'ere. That would 'ave been 1968. Anyways, the boy seems to get plenty of winders to clean. Got other chaps workin' for him now.'

The window-cleaner appeared to be a dutiful son, and he was going to see his elderly mother who lived not far away in Cirencester, dropping off Doreen, Bobby and the new baby, Suky, on the way. He would collect them the following afternoon.

'I'll be back for me dinner,' said Percy now, pushing back his chair and reaching for his old jacket and cap. 'Got a few chores to do in the parlour first, then I'll be off.'

'Don't be late,' cautioned his wife. 'No poppin' in to the pub, and then gettin' stuck in for one of your sessions. We're sittin' down proper today, what with the children here.'

Percy grunted and clicked his fingers at the old dog which followed his master out of the back door into the yard.

Well, I didn't say I wouldn't, Percy thought smugly; always a good crowd in the Pheasants on Boxing Day. A swift half wouldn't hurt.

Before they had gone to bed the previous evening, Dimity had encouraged Ella not to rush to get up in the morning. 'Boxing Day is a day of rest in this household,' she'd said. 'Charles is always exhausted after the busy Christmas Day, and we take it very quietly.'

'I'm not one to lie in bed, as you know,' Ella had responded. 'However, I'll keep quiet for Charles's sake and hold off making the fire, doing the washing-up and hoovering right through until he's up and dressed.'

Dimity had laughed. She'd known Ella was joking. Her friend still found it very difficult to use her plastered arm and wrist. 'You can help me with the washing-up later in the morning,' she'd said.

The house was quiet when Dimity went downstairs that Boxing Day morning in her dressing-gown, a few minutes before nine o'clock. Although she didn't have the same arduous Christmas Day programme as Charles, she had welcomed the unaccustomed lie-in. She was determined that he should have a really quiet day. They were due to have lunch with the Shoosmiths the following day, Saturday – and then it was Sunday again, with services in three of Charles's four parishes.

The kitchen was as they'd left it the night before, and she was pleased that Ella had not crept down early and tried to tackle the washing-up single-handed. After their Christmas dinner, they had put the plates and dishes in to

soak, and she had put away the brandy butter and covered the remains of the turkey and cheese. These had been
stored in the vicarage's cool north-facing larder.

On the kitchen table was a bowl of crusts, left from the
bread sauce that they'd had with the turkey. Dimity
looked out of the window. It seemed to be a miserable
grey sort of day and she decided that the birds at least
should have their breakfast on time. She sat at the table
and dreamily broke up the bread into small pieces. She
found an end piece of loaf in the bread bin and crumbled
that up, too.

The bird table was set in the grass at the edge of the
gravel drive, and Dimity knew she would be able to take
the food out without getting her slippers wet. She went to
unlock the back door and, to her surprise, found it was
not locked.

Surely it was locked last night? she thought. It was one
of those things that was done automatically by Charles
each night: lock the back door, check the front door was
locked, raise the blinds in the kitchen windows – Dimity
hated to come downstairs in the morning to dark rooms.
Yes, she distinctly remembered his locking it because he
had asked if there were any milk bottles to put out, and
Dimity had had to remind him that there would be no
milk delivered on Boxing Day.

Dimity stood in the middle of the kitchen and looked
round. Everything seemed in place. She went through into
the dining-room and nothing appeared disturbed there.
The candlesticks were still on the table, as were the silver
coasters in which the bottle of wine and Charles's port

had stood. Well, it didn't appear they'd been burgled. But why was the door unlocked?

Then she remembered her unpredictable house guest. Lifting up the edge of her dressing-gown in one hand to ensure she didn't trip over it as she went upstairs, she set forth to find if Ella was still in her room.

She wasn't – and, somehow, Dimity wasn't that surprised. Ella had muttered the evening before that she thought it was time she went home, but Dimity had hoped she'd persuaded her to stay on for a few more days.

She looked round the room: the little case they had brought from Ella's cottage only a few days before had gone. She opened the drawers in the mahogany chest of drawers – they were empty, as was the wardrobe apart from the tartan skirt and red jacket. The bedclothes had been roughly pulled up, and on the eiderdown was the box containing the cassette player she and Charles had given her for Christmas. The bird had flown!

Dimity returned to her bedroom and quietly began to dress. Charles, who had been asleep, now woke up and sleepily asked her what the time was.

'It's a quarter past nine. You stay there as long as you want. Ella's done a runner, and I'm going to find her. She's obviously walked home – lugging her case with her. Goodness only knows how she managed to dress herself.'

'Oh dear,' said Charles, now sitting up in the bed. 'If you wait a moment, I'll come with you.'

'No, dear, there's no need. I don't know what time she went. I found the back door unlocked which alerted me. If she only went a short time ago, I'll be able to pick her up in the car. I'll try to get her to come back with me but if she insists on going home, I'll ring you from there.'

By the time Dimity had got the car out of the garage and set off through Lulling, it was drizzling. It had obviously rained during the night since there were puddles in the road. There weren't many people about: just a few brave dog-walkers and a couple of lads showing off on what were obviously new bicycles.

Dimity saw Ella from quite a long way off. She had reached the steepest part of the hill leading to Thrush Green and had stopped to have a rest, the little case beside her. The sheepskin jacket draped round her shoulders – her plastered arm prevented her wearing it properly – was some protection against the rain, but she had nothing on her head, and her short straight hair was plastered to her skull.

Dimity felt a surge of both concern and affection for her old friend. She stopped the car beside Ella who, as soon as she saw who it was, picked up the case and trudged on up the road.

'Ella, stop!' Dimity cried. 'Don't be so silly. You're soaking wet.' Then she drove on a little way, this time stopping some yards ahead of Ella. She quickly got out of the car and went round to confront the sorry figure that was her dearest friend.

Ella tried to push past, but Dimity stood firm. 'Ella, you're mad! Stop—'

Again, Ella tried to pass Dimity but she was obviously exhausted by the walk up the hill. 'Just let me go home, Dim,' she said. 'I just want to go home.'

'Then let me drive you,' Dimity replied, opening the passenger door. She was relieved when, after a moment's hesitation, Ella plonked herself down in the seat. Dimity picked up the abandoned case and put it on the back seat.

Nothing was said during the few moments it took to drive up the rest of the hill and to park outside Ella's cottage.

'Have you got the key?'

Ella took the front door key out of the pocket of her jacket, and handed it to Dimity, who said briskly, 'Come on, then, let's get you inside, and get those wet clothes off.'

It was as though a bubble had burst. Ella allowed Dimity to hold her good arm and guide her down the short garden path, and waited patiently while Dimity unlocked and opened the front door. Ella stumbled over the lip of the doorstep and might have fallen had Dimity not got a firm hold of her.

They went upstairs together to Ella's bedroom, Dimity carrying the case.

'Now, let me take your jacket. It's soaking.' Dimity dropped the sodden garment on the floor.

Ella just stood there, a picture of misery.

'Oh, my! You must have been freezing as well as drowned,' exclaimed Dimity. All Ella had been wearing under the jacket was her nightdress, more a night-shirt than anything. It had wide sleeves through which Ella had been able to put her plastered arm. It had been roughly tucked into the elasticated top of her skirt.

Gently, Dimity helped Ella off with the wet clothes. She

wrapped her in a bath-sheet she'd fetched from the airing-cupboard, the big woman snuggling into the towel's warmth. When she was dry, they found a clean pair of trousers and a sort of fisherman's smock that they eased gently over the arm.

'Now you get on some clean socks, find some shoes you can manage, and I'll go and put the kettle on. I think we both need a good cup of tea.'

'And a ciggy,' muttered Ella.

Dimity was almost relieved by that remark; it showed that her old friend had not lost all her spark.

Dimity put on the kettle and then telephoned Charles to tell him that Ella was safe, and that she would ring again when they'd had a talk.

By the time Ella clomped heavily down the cottage's narrow stairs, the tea was made and there was a plate of biscuits from a packet Dimity had found in the cupboard, along with some powdered milk, the fridge naturally being empty of the fresh variety. Not having had breakfast, Ella was ravenous and ate three biscuits before touching the tea.

'Thanks, Dim,' she said finally, brushing some crumbs off her ample front.

While she had been making the tea, Dimity had pondered how to tackle this latest drama and had decided that this time a head-on confrontation was perhaps the only way.

'What possessed you to do such a damn silly thing?' she asked. 'If you wanted to come home, you only had to ask, you know that.'

'I know, but I didn't want to be a nuisance. I thought that if I asked you to bring me home, you'd say I couldn't cope. So I thought I'd see if I could manage, muddling along as best I could. And I didn't want to disturb your day by asking you to drive me back. You have no idea how beastly it is to have to continually ask for things to be done. "Can you tie up my shoelace?", "Can you cut up my meat?", "Can you drive me home?"' The flood-gates were open and words now came tumbling out. 'And it's so awful not being able to help, do my share. You've been very kind but I don't want to be beholden to you and Charles any more.'

Dimity snorted. 'Beholden? For heaven's sake, Ella, beholden doesn't come into it. We're your *friends*. I like to think I'm your best friend. You would've been the first person to come to my aid if it'd been me who had fallen down and broken my wrist. You'd have been down to the vicarage in a flash, organizing me and ensuring that Charles and I still had a good Christmas.'

Dimity paused momentarily to gather breath, and into that pause Ella said, very very quietly, 'But it's not just my wrist, Dim. That'll mend in time. It's my eyes – I can't see very much. They've deteriorated even over the past few days. When I saw the specialist eighteen months ago, he warned me that my eyesight might go downhill suddenly.' The large woman gave a wheezy cough, as though it gave her time to gather her thoughts. 'I didn't let myself think about it but now I'm frightened that that's what's happened. I'm beginning to see things, too. Odd patterns on the wall or floor, patterns that I know aren't actually there.'

'Poor Ella!' cried Dimity, and leaned over to give her friend a big hug. 'But if you can't see, then why on earth come back to the cottage instead of letting us look after you at the vicarage?'

'Because I need time to think,' Ella replied, now very calm. 'I need to sit here, in *my* kitchen, with *my* familiar things around me, and think about *my* future. Don't you understand that?'

'Yes, I think I do understand,' said Dimity slowly.

'What I would like to do is to spend the rest of the day here. See how I manage. I'm not totally blind. I can see shapes, just not details. Could you come and fetch me this evening?'

'Yes, of course. What about food? You must eat.'

'I think I ate enough yesterday to last me through today. But if I get peckish, I've got some spaghetti. Easy enough to cook that up, and throw on some ketchup and herbs. I won't starve – and yes,' she said, anticipating her friend's next remark, 'I will be careful with the pan of boiling water.' She helped herself to another biscuit. 'Now go, Dim, I'll be all right. And I know where you are if I need you.'

Dimity understood her friend well enough not to argue, so she finished her cup of tea, kissed Ella's cheek and left the cottage to return home, mindful of the fact that Charles would not only be anxious for news but would also be wanting his breakfast.

*

Paul Young came into the kitchen still wearing his pyjamas, and rubbing the sleepy-dust out of his eyes.

'Good afternoon!' said his mother, turning round from the sink where she was washing glasses.

'It's not *that* late,' mumbled Paul. 'And you said I could sleep in.'

'I know. Only joking.'

They had had a very happy Christmas evening. Paul had been given a chess set by his father. The boy had learned to play at school the previous term, which had pleased Edward since he would now have someone to play with. He and Joan both played bridge occasionally, but Joan professed chess was beyond her.

After their Christmas dinner, Joan – who was wearing the pretty turquoise brooch that Edward had bought for her in Woodstock – was content to sit by the fire with a new book. Edward and Paul had settled down, the chess-board between them and a glass of port each at their elbows.

'You're old enough to appreciate a nice glass of port,' Paul's father had said. 'Much better than draining off the dregs of wine bottles.'

Paul had reddened slightly at the memory of the Hursts' drinks party before Christmas.

One game had led to another, and it was late when Edward finally put the fireguard in front of the dying embers, and they'd gone to bed.

Paul now reached into the cupboard for a packet of cereal.

'Go and get dressed first,' reprimanded his mother. 'I'm

not having you eating your breakfast in your pyjamas, not at this hour. If your father saw you, he'd have a fit.'

When Paul returned, duly dressed, Joan said, 'Jeremy rang about half an hour ago. He asked if you could go round – wants to show you his Christmas present.'

'Did he say what it was?' Paul asked. 'When I asked him yesterday in church what he'd got, he said he hadn't had his main present yet. They were keeping it back until after church.'

'Ah,' said his mother enigmatically. 'Well, have your breakfast and then go round. We're only having a light lunch because we'll eat properly this evening.'

A quarter of an hour later, Paul banged on the front door of Tullivers. It was opened by Jeremy and in his arms was a squirming, wriggling bundle of black and white silky hair.

'What? What on earth's that?' burst out Paul.

'Meet Alfie. I got him for Christmas,' beamed Jeremy proudly.

'Come in, Paul,' called Phil from the hall. 'Come in and shut out the cold. Jeremy, go into the kitchen. You know how he wees when he's excited.'

In the kitchen, Jeremy gently placed his Christmas present on the floor. The animal shook himself and once his hair had fallen into place, Paul recognized the head and long ears of a spaniel.

'He's a blue roan cocker spaniel. Real pedigree and everything. Isn't he super?' said Jeremy.

Paul crouched on the floor by the little animal, and

stroked his domed head and silky ears. The puppy re-warded him by rolling onto his back and immediately had his tummy tickled.

'Gosh, you're lucky, Jeremy,' he said. 'Dad doesn't like dogs so I'll never be able to have one.' He stood up. 'But what about term time? Won't he get fat if he doesn't get walked?'

'That's the whole point. Mum will walk him when I'm not here. To stop her getting fat, she says.'

'I heard that, young man!' said Phil, walking into the kitchen. But she was smiling. 'Isn't he lovely? Have you told Paul about how we kept the secret?'

Jeremy was dancing around in front of the puppy which was bouncing forward and mock-attacking his young owner's feet. 'He spent the night before Christmas next to you! The Curdles had him, and brought him over when we got back from church.'

'We knew that Molly wouldn't be going to church,' explained Phil, 'since she had the lunch to cook and they thought Billy had had enough church experience for one year. So Frank collected him on Christmas Eve and delivered him to Stable Cottage.'

'They were afraid he'd bark, and you'd hear, and then you'd spill the beans,' said Jeremy, his face aglow with happiness.

'But your mother said she hadn't heard a thing,' added Phil.

'You mean Mum knew all about it?' asked Paul.

'Yes, she was in on the secret.'

Paul tried not to show how envious he was, but made a bad job of it. 'I wish I could've had a dog. Much nicer than a silly old chess set.'

Phil put her hand on Paul's shoulder. 'When he's older, you and Jeremy can walk him together. Can't he, Jeremy?'

'Of course! We'll share Alfie,' Paul's young friend said generously. 'We can have loads of fun with him. Walks, bike rides, everything.'

'Gosh, thanks,' said Paul.

Phil looked out of the window. 'It's not raining at the moment so why don't you two take your bikes out now? Something tells me it's time for this young fellow's mid-morning nap,' and she picked up the puppy which had collapsed into a heap by Jeremy's feet. 'And I'll ring your mother, Paul, to say you're staying here for lunch. OK?'

'Very OK. Thanks, Mrs Hurst.'

The two boys rushed out of the kitchen. Jeremy's Christmas present appeared to have been a success.

CHAPTER SIXTEEN

A Friend in Need

When Dimity returned to Lulling Vicarage, Charles was up and already having breakfast.

'I'm sorry to have abandoned you, dear,' she said, taking off her coat. 'And I'd got a nice piece of smoked haddock for your breakfast, too.'

'Never mind that,' said Charles. 'How's Ella?'

And Dimity recounted the sorry, sodden tale and then Ella's fears about going blind.

'What happens now?' Charles asked.

Dimity fetched herself a cup and poured some coffee out of Charles's pot, then settled herself opposite him.

'She wants to spend the day thinking, she said. I don't think there's any point in our trying to sort things out. You know Ella, she's as stubborn as anything and will only do what she wants, when she wants.'

'Maybe the time has come,' said Charles, 'when she's going to have to learn that her own frailties and incapacities are going to mean she'll *have* to rely on other people, even if she doesn't like it.'

'Which she won't,' said Dimity. 'But I think she'll listen to us if no one else.'

Neither spoke for a while. The kitchen clock ticked quietly to itself on the wall.

Then Charles said, 'Could we have the smoked haddock for lunch – with a poached egg on top?'

Dimity laughed. 'My darling husband! Always thinking of your stomach. I think it would be an excellent idea. Now, if you would re-set and light the fire in the drawing-room, I suggest you settle yourself down with one of your Christmas books, and I'll clear up in here.'

When Charles protested, saying that he would help her with the washing-up that was still stacked neatly on the side, Dimity shooed him away.

'No, this is your day of rest. Go and enjoy it.'

A short while later, with her hands deep in the frothy washing-up water, Dimity turned her thoughts once more to Ella. It was obvious that she wasn't going to be able to continue living on her own, not even when the wrist was mended. It just wouldn't be safe, not with all those steps up and down in the cottage, and other hazards just waiting to cause accidents. She decided she would talk to John Lovell over the weekend and ask his advice.

Charles, having cleaned out the grate and re-laid the fire, didn't actually light it but went instead to his study. It was warm and snug in there, and he wanted to make some notes for the sermons he was due to give on the coming Sunday. He settled down at his desk, switched on the anglepoise lamp, and pulled a sheaf of papers towards him. Sunday would be 28 December, known as Holy Innocents' Day, held in commemoration of the slaughter of the male infants in Bethlehem during Herod's attempt to kill the infant Jesus. Since it was so soon after the Christmas festivities, the congregations would be small, and Charles didn't see why he should inflict a sermon about that dreadful massacre some two thousand years ago on his faithful parishioners. He decided merely to add some prayers for those who were currently involved in working for peace in the many areas of world conflict.

He stretched out his hand, and took down *The Oxford Dictionary of Quotations* from the bookshelf, a favourite source of inspiration for his sermons.

He ran his finger down the index of entries for 'Innocent'. 'I am i. of the blood' – no, that was too close to the Holy Innocents; 'i. is the heart's devotion': Charles turned to the page referred to and found the quotation had come from Shelley's poem 'To— I Fear thy Kisses'. No, that didn't seem a very good idea.

Charles checked a few more 'Innocent' entries but there was nothing suitable. He went higher up the index to the word 'Innocence': 'companions, i., and health': ah, that sounded promising. It turned out to be from Oliver Goldsmith's poem 'The Deserted Village':

> *His best companions, innocence and health;*
> *And his best riches, ignorance and wealth.*

Charles hummed to himself – he found humming always helped him think. Was there some way he could use those words? They seemed apt for the post-festive period. But maybe a bit censorious. He returned to the index. 'I. is closing up his eyes'.

Immediately, all thoughts of his sermon went from his head, and the vision of Ella sitting alone in her kitchen, struggling to come to terms with her future, flooded into his mind. What was going to happen to her? He agreed with Dimity that she wasn't going to be able to continue to live alone in the cottage, well, not for long anyway. She might be able to cope there for a little while but the time would come when she would need to have fairly constant help. She could either stay there, with someone living in – and he knew how dreadfully expensive that was – or she could move into a residential home and be looked after.

Apart from Rectory Cottages in Thrush Green, Charles regularly visited two old people's homes on the outskirts of Lulling and he knew the specific difficulties faced by two residents – one in each home – who were blind. While most of the residents were, he had to admit, rather senile and appeared content to sit in their chairs all day, either just nodding at nothing or gazing at whatever programme the television was tuned to, the two blind people were in total control of their wits, but just happened to be blind.

It was a terrible conundrum, but one to which he had given much thought. He was going to suggest to the administrators of the two homes that, when possible and with the relevant families' approval, one should move to join the other; then at least they would have each other's companionship.

But he just couldn't visualize Ella going to live in such a home. She would absolutely loathe the necessary regimentation.

Charles continued to sit at his desk for some time, turning the problem over in his mind, his sermons quite forgotten.

Isobel was carving some slices off the Christmas turkey, ready for lunch, when Robert Wilberforce telephoned that Boxing Day morning.

'Robert!' she exclaimed. 'How lovely to hear you. A very happy Christmas to you. Thank you for your card . . . Oh, good, you got ours, too! . . . And how's Dulcie?'

Just at that moment, Harold came noisily through the front door, banging it behind him. Isobel clapped her hand to her ear. 'What? Oh, that's marvellous news. I must tell Harold, who's just come in.' She called through the door to where Harold was taking off his coat. 'Dulcie's going to have a baby. Isn't that wonderful?' Then she spoke again into the receiver, 'When? Oh, you must tell me everything! Is she there? I'd love to speak to her.'

Much as Harold would have liked to have a word with Robert Wilberforce, he knew better than to interrupt women's talk, especially about babies. Having given the sitting-room fire a poke, and added another log, he settled down in his armchair, ready to do battle again with the crossword in the newspaper.

When Isobel came in a minute or so later, she was glowing with excitement. The baby was due in April, she said, and Dulcie seemed to have got through the morning-sickness stage, and wasn't it exciting – oh, and they were coming to stay.

'What? When?' asked Harold. This was much more interesting than the problems of impending motherhood.

'On New Year's Eve. What fun it'll be.'

'But I thought Dorothy and Agnes were coming then?' Harold queried.

'Well, yes, but we can fit everyone in. It will just mean Dorothy and Agnes sharing.'

'You know they'd much rather not,' Harold said. 'Also, had you forgotten that we're going out to the Youngs?'

'No, of course I hadn't. I'll ring Joan in a moment. I'm sure they'd love to have Robert and Dulcie.'

'Well, I think it's much too much. This house will be groaning at the seams. Could Dorothy and Agnes go and stay somewhere else? What about with Winnie?'

Harold's suggestion brought Isobel to her senses. 'No, of course not! I couldn't possibly push out one of my oldest friends and, besides, they asked ages ago if they could stay. But why not Robert and Dulcie somewhere else? What about with Charles? After all, Charles knows them as well if not better than we do.'

'But Ella's staying at the vicarage,' reasoned Harold.

'Of course, I'd temporarily forgotten that.' Isobel frowned in concentration. 'Still, they've got masses of room there. I'll give Dimity a ring now.'

'Hang on, hang on,' said Harold quickly. 'Don't rush

into anything yet. Let's just think this one through.' And he persuaded Isobel to sit down on the other side of the fire from him.

It was at a dinner party at Lulling Vicarage a few years earlier that Robert Wilberforce had first met Dulcie Mulloy. Robert had contacted Charles Henstock about some letters he had come across from Nathaniel Patten to the then rector of St Andrew's at Thrush Green. When he said he was coming south from where he lived in the Lake District, Harold and Charles had tracked down the young woman who was the great-granddaughter of the Victorian missionary and arranged the dinner party.

It was as though the couple were made for each other, and when they announced their engagement a few months later, on the day Thrush Green celebrated the centenary of Nathaniel Patten's birth, the village rejoiced. The young couple now lived and worked in London, and were sublimely happy.

'I suggest,' Harold now said, 'that we ask Charles and Dimity tomorrow, when they come to lunch, if it would be possible for Robert and Dulcie to stay there. I agree there is plenty of room, and we'd be like sardines here.'

'But what if they're full up after all – some of Charles's far-flung cousins descending on them, for instance?' asked Isobel.

'Then we shall just have to be sardines,' replied Harold and picked up his crossword again.

'I thought you were going to light the fire,' said Dimity, coming into Charles's study, startling him. 'Oh, sorry, were you asleep?' she added when she saw the surprised look on his face.

'No, no, I wasn't asleep. I've been thinking. About Ella.'

Dimity sat herself down in the pretty upholstered tub chair facing Charles's handsome mahogany desk. 'Yes, I've been thinking about Ella, too. What are we going to do?'

'Well, we shall obviously have to wait to see what decisions she's come to while at the cottage. If she's determined that she's going to stay there, then I don't honestly think we can stop her. It's her life. All we can do is give her as much support as possible.'

'And what if she's decided she can't stay there? What then? Rectory Cottages when there's a vacancy?'

'Well, it's a possibility. John Enderby will be the first to go, I'm afraid to say, but I happen to know there's quite a waiting list. We can't let Ella leapfrog the queue.'

'Not even if you, as chairman of the Trustees, request it?' asked Dimity.

'Especially because I'm the chairman. It would be quite out of order.'

Dimity knew Charles was right. It would cause bad feeling all round.

'So what then? Go into a home specially for blind people?'

'It's a possibility, of course, but she'd hate that,' responded Charles, steepling his fingers in front of him.

Neither spoke for a moment. The sound of sparrows squabbling on the bird table outside the study window was the only noise.

'We could—' They both spoke at the same time.

'Sorry, you were about to say?' said Charles.

'No, no, you go. I was only thinking aloud,' replied Dimity.

'Well, what about having her here – to live with us here? Or would you hate that?' said Charles, all the words coming out in a rush.

'I was about to suggest the same thing!' cried Dimity. 'Of course I wouldn't mind. But what about you? After all, she's more my friend than yours. Could you cope with her brusqueness, her forthrightness, her . . .' Dimity's voice trailed away.

'Her downright rudeness?' Charles asked, and smiled. 'I'm used to it. It's like water off a duck's back so far as I'm concerned.'

'Oh, Charles – do you think she'd agree?'

'She'd be mad not to,' replied the vicar. 'But I suggest we don't say anything to her until she's told us what conclusions she's reached on her own. If she accepts, then we shall have to sit down and work out the details. It will be a big step – for all of us. And now,' said Charles, 'I *must* finish this sermon.'

Dimity got up and smoothed down the folds of her skirt. 'Lunch at one o'clock suit you? Smoked haddock and poached egg?'

'Perfect, my dear, quite perfect.'

It was dark when Paul finally returned home. He and Jeremy had had the sort of day that all lads of their age enjoyed. They had bicycled up and down the nearby lanes, they had called in to see Dotty Harmer's goats, but had resisted her offer of a 'nice hot blackberry and nettle drink'. After a lunch of cold turkey and huge baked potatoes, they'd gone to Paul's den in old Mrs Curdle's caravan. Jeremy carried Alfie across in an old wicker shopping basket of Phil's, and they'd taken him in to show to Edward and Joan.

Paul was interested to see his father's reaction to the dog, and was desperately disappointed when Edward merely said, 'Yes, nice, very nice,' but did not even put out a hand to touch the dog. They'd had conversations about dogs before, and Paul knew he was on a losing wicket.

When it became too dark to see in the caravan, they returned to Jeremy's room in Tullivers and listened to pop music. In due course, Paul stuck his head round the sitting-room door to say he was going home now, and thanked Phil and Frank for lunch.

'He's such a nice boy,' said Phil after the front door slammed. 'And they're so lucky to have each other.'

Frank nodded his head. 'And let's hope they both stay nice!'

Dimity looked out of the drawing-room windows and then got up to draw the curtains against the winter gloom. 'Do you think we should ring Ella?' she asked.

Charles looked at his watch. 'Four-fifteen. Um . . . I think probably leave it until five o'clock and then ring.'

However, the telephone rang just ten minutes later and Dimity went to answer it.

'Ella, yes.' She listened, then said, 'Of course, I'll see you in about half an hour. We'll have tea when we get back.'

Charles looked at her enquiringly after she'd put down the receiver.

'Don't ask me,' said Dimity, shrugging. 'She said nothing, merely that could one of us collect her in half an hour.'

'Why don't I go?' asked Charles.

'No, I'm happy to go. I can drop off my thank-you letter to Winnie at the same time.'

So it was that half an hour later, Dimity drew up outside Ella's cottage. The lights in the little sitting-room in the front were on, and Dimity could see the large figure of Ella standing in the window. She turned away as Dimity got out of the car, and was standing at the open front door when Dimity reached it.

'Thanks, Dim, for turning out again. Come in,' and she stood aside to let Dimity walk through. 'Go into the kitchen, it's warmer there.'

The kitchen seemed neat and tidy. Dimity had dreaded finding burned saucepans, broken plates.

'See,' said Ella, reading her thoughts, 'nothing burnt or broken. I can cope so long as I don't lose my temper. But I get so frustrated, it's very difficult not to get cross.'

Dimity leaned on the back of one of the kitchen chairs. 'How's the day gone?'

Ella turned to face her. 'I haven't reached any sort of conclusion,' she said. 'It doesn't help having this damned wrist in plaster – makes everything twice as difficult. My appointment with Mr Cobbold, the ophthalmologist, is on Monday in Oxford. He's the chap who I saw before and I expect he'll advise me what happens next. Can I stay with you until then?'

'Of course you can. And I'll take you into Oxford for your appointment.'

'Don't bother, I can take the bus,' Ella said shortly. 'Or get Bert Nobbs to take me.'

Dimity put her hand onto Ella's arm and repeated gently, 'I will take you into Oxford for your appointment, Ella. It's no bother. In fact, I could be very brave and put my nose into one or two of the sales which will have started.'

'Rather you than me!' Ella said, and suddenly flung her good arm round Dimity and gave her a bear hug. 'Thank you, dearest Dimity, for everything. Now,' she said, standing back, 'it's time you got back to Charles. My re-packed case is all ready upstairs. You fetch that, and I'll lock up here.'

'You're incorrigible!' laughed Dimity, and made her way upstairs.

When they arrived back at the vicarage, Ella took the case from Dimity and plodded up the stairs to her room. Dimity took advantage of her absence to tell Charles what had happened. He was in his study, still working on his sermons.

'We're back,' she said quietly. 'I didn't mention our plan.' And she told Charles about the imminent appointment with the eye specialist in Oxford, and they agreed that it would be best to say nothing until after that.

'I'll go and get some tea,' Dimity said. 'Will you join us for it, or shall I bring it in here for you?'

'I'd like to finish this before supper, so in here, please.'

While Charles worked in his study, Dimity and Ella sat in front of the fire in the drawing-room with their tea and slices of Christmas cake, and chatted as though Ella had not a care in the world.

'Heavens, is that the time!' exclaimed Dimity when the little carriage clock on the mantelpiece struck seven, 'I must go and start getting some supper together.'

'Is there anything I can do to help, Dim?' Ella asked.

'No, it's all straightforward. You sit there and keep warm.'

However, Ella heaved herself to her feet. 'If you're in the kitchen and Charles in his study, I wouldn't be disturbing anyone, would I, if I fetched that bally cassette thingy and listened to one of the tapes?'

'No, of course not,' replied Dimity, delighted that Ella was obviously making an effort. 'Shall I fetch it for you?'

'No, thanks, I can manage. Not yet a cripple.'

Dimity ignored the remark, and pointed to a plug in the wall behind the armchair where Ella had been sitting. 'You can plug it in there, and put the machine on this table,' and she moved a small table to beside the chair. 'Give a shout if you need help setting up the machine.'

But she might have been talking to herself. Without a further word, Ella turned and lumbered from the room. Dimity shook her head in exasperation and went to start on the supper.

Jean Burwell, drawing the upstairs curtains at Blenheim Lodge that evening, noticed that the wreaths round the necks of the lion and unicorn on the gateposts were not twinkling as they should have been. She mentioned it to her husband who was reading a magazine about boats in the sitting-room.

'Probably a bulb has blown. Could you check it tomorrow? We want the place to look nice for when the Jervises come to play bridge.'

'I'll do it now,' Derek said, putting the magazine to one side.

But a bulb hadn't blown.

'Wanton vandalism, that's what it is,' he shouted, as he stormed back into the house. 'The lion's wreath has been ripped off and I suspect *trampled* on! Two bulbs have been smashed on the other wreath. *And*,' he said, quite purple in the face and spittle glistening on his lower lip, '*and* the uplighters have been kicked aside again. I'll kill those Cooke boys, I swear I will!'

Jean looked quite alarmed at this outburst. 'Calm down, Derek, for heaven's sake. They're only Christmas decorations.'

'The uplighters aren't. Those bulbs are damned expensive and I shouldn't wonder if the bracket hasn't been broken as well. I'll have to wait to see the damage in the morning, but what won't wait now is my phone call to the so-called chairman of the PCC.'

Jean tried to stop him. 'It's still Boxing Day, dear. You can't go ringing him on a Bank Holiday.'

'I don't care a hoot if it is Boxing Day or Easter Day, I'm going to ring him now!'

But the telephone rang and rang in the Shoosmith household; the chairman of the Parochial Church Council was not at home.

CHAPTER SEVENTEEN

A Vandal is Apprehended

On the Saturday morning, Harold Shoosmith took his second cup of coffee through to the sitting-room. He knew he would have to help Isobel shortly but decided there was time to have a quick look at the crossword. It was one of the jumbo crosswords that newspapers tend to publish at this time of year, and he licked his lips in anticipation. He settled himself in his armchair, adjusted the cushion behind him, smoothed the newspaper out on his knee, and took a pen from his inside jacket pocket.

' "Fall of gentleman in Burgundian town"?' Harold murmured to himself. 'Hum . . . "fall" could be "autumn". That fits but why "Burgundian town"?'

However, any further thought was rudely interrupted by the front door knocker crashing down three or four times. Harold put the paper aside reluctantly and went to see who had knocked so imperiously. His heart sank when he opened the door and saw Derek Burwell standing there.

'Derek, good morning. What can I do for you?'

'My lights have been vandalized again, and I want to know what you're going to do about it?' the weaselly man demanded.

'Come in,' said Harold wearily. He didn't want a public spat on his doorstep.

'Jean and I moved to Thrush Green because we thought it was a nice place, a decent neighbourhood but this . . . this wanton vandalism is outrageous.' At his favourite phrase 'wanton vandalism', Derek flung his arms out wide, almost hitting Harold who had to step back quickly.

'Calm down, man, for heaven's sake,' he said.

Derek was breathing heavily. 'I want to know what you're going to do about it.'

'I don't think there's a lot I can do. Have you talked to the police?'

'What's the point involving the police when we all know who's done it?' Derek said nastily.

'But do you?' replied Harold, careful to distance himself from accusing anyone.

'Course, we do! It's those Cooke kids. I saw them in the road before Christmas, whizzing about on their bikes, doing those dangerous turns in the middle of the road.'

'I think they're called "wheelies",' said Harold.

'Wheelies, whatever, they've wrecked my Christmas decorations *and* my uplighters. As chairman of the

Parochial Church Council, what are you going to do about it?'

'I don't think I'm going to do anything,' responded Harold quietly. 'I don't believe it's part of my remit as chairman to ensure that law and order is upheld within the parish.' Harold realized he was sounding rather pompous, but what else could he do with this terrible little man? 'I suggest you take it up with the police. They are very helpful in Lulling.'

'What? And go and get my name on the police records? Once they've got your details on their records, goodness knows what they might do with them.'

'Well, it's entirely up to you, of course. But I'm not in a position to accuse anyone without actual proof. Why don't you go and see the Cookes if you are sure it's them?'

'Pah!' Derek spat out. 'Waste of time.'

Harold moved round him and opened the front door. 'I'm sorry I can't help you more,' he said politely, and waited until his unwelcome guest spun on his heel and left his house.

The chairman of the PCC stood for a moment. He needed to see Bobby Cooke some time over the weekend, so he thought he would mention the lights. While he didn't care a fig for the Burwells, vandalism should be frowned on.

At that moment Isobel came down the stairs. 'When I heard who was at the door, I'm afraid I decided to stay well out of the way. But I think you are quite right not to get involved. Now, I suggest you light the fire so the sitting-room will be nice and warm. Then can you lay the table – dining-room not kitchen today. The Henstocks and Ella will be here at twelve-thirty.'

It was Albert Piggott who saw Bobby Cooke first. He was taking the run-down to his retirement surprisingly seriously.

'Goin' up to see young Cooke,' he announced to Nelly after they'd finished their Saturday midday meal.

Nelly never went into The Fuchsia Bush on Saturdays. They didn't do lunches that day and Rosa enjoyed being in charge. Nelly had made a warming casserole using the meat from the legs of the turkey they'd had on Christmas Day. She had added onion and celery and made a thick gravy in which the meat and vegetables had bubbled gently, giving off aromas that were enough to keep Albert from The Two Pheasants.

'Goin' to the pub, more like,' said Nelly, stacking the pudding plates together.

'Well, an' that, too. But I've got to see the boy today. I needs to 'ave him in church tomorrer, since it's me last Sunday an' I wants to give 'im one last run-through.'

'I can't get used to you retirin',' said Nelly. 'But it's come at a good time. This place needs decoratin' and you can start at the top.'

Albert didn't bother to answer. He wasn't going to spend his well-earned retirement doing any decorating. If his missus wanted the place sprucing up, then she could well afford to get someone in. He took his grimy cap from the peg behind the back door and left, heading purposefully for the neighbouring pub.

Here Albert was able to kill two birds with one stone since Bobby Cooke and his brother were in the public bar, making a racket at the far end where there were a couple of fruit machines. Albert ordered his pint from Bob Jones, and then walked over to them.

'Now then, Bobby,' the old man said.

'Hey up, it's granddad,' said Cyril cheekily.

Albert glared at him, and turned his attention to Bobby who, to give him his due, muttered, 'Shurrup, Cyril.'

'I wants you down at the church ten o'clock sharp tomorrer,' said Albert. 'Service is at ten-thirty. Don't be late. I'll go across an' turn the heatin' on early. From next week, remember, it'll be you what's in charge.'

'OK, I'll be there,' said Bobby and, satisfied, Albert went to claim his pint.

Bobby was as good as his word. Just before ten o'clock the following morning, he propped his bicycle inside the church wall, and made his way into St Andrew's.

Albert was wearing his suit. He'd decided to put it on since it was going to be his last service in charge as sexton. He looked the Cooke boy up and down. 'If you're not goin' to wear a tie, which you oughter, then at least straighten your collar.'

Bobby did as he was told, then asked, 'What do you want me to do?'

'You stand there, an' open the door when you sees the 'andle turnin'. An' make sure the door is kept shut – quiet, mind – to keep the warm in. I didn't get out of me bed this mornin' before it were light just to see all the 'eat disappear.'

'Do I 'ave to do this for every service?' the boy asked.

'No, you don't 'ave to be 'ere, so long as 'eatin's bin turned on. 'Cept for big services, of course, like Christmas an' Easter an' the like. 'Ave you got yer suit yet?'

'Nah,' Bobby replied, scratching an ear.

'I'll 'ave a word with Mr Shoosmith. Ah, that's 'im comin' in now.'

In answer to Albert's question, Harold said, 'My wife has found a suit that should fit you. It's at the cleaners and I believe she's collecting it this week. We'll let you know when you can come and pick it up. Now, I want a private word with you, Bobby. Can you do the door for a moment, Albert?'

Albert obviously would have liked to hear what Mr Shoosmith had to say to the boy, but Harold manoeuvred Bobby away into the side aisle, and the old curmudgeon went grumbling back to man the church door.

'Now then, Bobby, have you been up to mischief?' Harold asked him.

'Mischief, mister, what sort of mischief?'

It was a fair question because the Cooke boys got up to all kinds of mischief.

'Well, apart from kicking the litter bin halfway across the green the other day' – and Bobby had the grace to look at his feet – 'what have you been getting up to along the Woodstock Road?'

Bobby looked up at that. 'Woodstock Road? What about it?'

'You've been seen up there causing a disturbance.'

'What?'

'Well, apart from anything, doing wheelies in the middle of the road.'

'Yeah, well, there's no law against that,' Bobby said grouchily.

'No, you're right, there's not – at least, not until you cause an accident.'

'Was that it, then?' Bobby asked, beginning to shuffle away.

'What else did you do up there?' countered Harold.

'Nothin'. You can't be goin' accusin' me of doin' nothin' when you ain't got nothin' particular on me.'

Harold flinched at the dropped 'g's. 'So you know nothing about damaged lights at Blenheim Lodge – that's on the right-hand side as you go towards Woodstock?'

'Blenheim Lodge? That the place with the lion and thingy on the columns?'

'Yes, the lion and the unicorn,' said Harold patiently.

'Yup, I know the ones. An' no, I didn't damage no lights. I think they're good.'

'And Cyril? What about your brother?' Harold asked.

'Ah, can't speak for Cyril, now can I?' Bobby jiggled from one foot to another. 'Shouldn't I be gettin' back to me duties, mister? Ol' Albert will be giving me what-for otherwise.'

Harold stood aside and let the boy go. He was glad that the culprit was not, apparently, Bobby. He followed him towards the back of the church and was relieved to see that the Burwells had come in while he'd been talking to Bobby.

He crossed quickly to where they were standing in the nave. 'A word, if I may, Derek,' he said. When he'd told them that it didn't appear to be Bobby who was damaging their lights, he added, 'And please do not discuss it with Bobby. He's said he wasn't to blame, and that's where it should end. If you want to take it further, then talk to PC Darwin.'

'I've spent another fortune on replacing the uplighters,' Derek said sourly. 'We decided not to buy replacement lights for the wreaths since it's past Christmas.'

'Such a shame,' burbled Jean Burwell. 'They were so pretty. Quite the prettiest in the road, we thought.'

'Can I suggest you go and sit down,' said Harold, tired of the subject. 'The rector has arrived and the service will start in a minute.' He sincerely hoped that would be the last he heard about the matter.

On Sunday afternoon, Dimity telephoned John Lovell. 'I'm not disturbing you, am I?' she asked.

'I'm delighted to be disturbed,' John replied. 'I'm beginning to suffer from Excess of Family. What can I do for you? How's Ella?'

And Dimity told him about how Ella had walked out on Boxing Day. 'But it's not her wrist that's troubling her,' she said, 'it's her eyes.'

'Ah, yes,' the doctor replied. 'Ella told me all about that when we were at Dickie's, waiting for her wrist to be plastered. Macular degeneration.'

'Do you know much about it?' Dimity asked.

'Only a little, I'm afraid. It's a very tricky complaint and I tend to refer anyone who comes to me with symptoms to a good optician, and they generally pass them on to a specialist. As you probably know, while it isn't life-threatening, there isn't a cure. Ella will need to learn to adapt to it which, knowing Ella, isn't going to be easy.'

Dimity then told him of the plan she and Charles had hatched the day before.

'Well, I think you are both saints,' John Lovell said. 'It would be wonderful if Ella could live with friends who can keep an eye on her. As she gets used to her sight deteriorating, she'll adapt, of course, and you'll find she'll be able to do plenty for herself, especially when the wrist has mended. And I will help all I can.'

Dimity thanked him, and asked him not to mention anything to Ella. 'We need to choose our moment, and certainly after she's seen Mr Cobbold tomorrow.'

The following morning, Dimity drove Ella into Oxford for her appointment with the ophthalmologist.

'Would you like me to come in with you?' she asked when they arrived at the hospital.

'Why?' said Ella, scrabbling in the foot-well for her vast handbag.

'Well, I sometimes think that a second person listening to what the specialist is saying is helpful,' Dimity replied.

'Dimity,' said Ella firmly, 'I'm going blind, not deaf!' And with that she heaved herself out of the car, slammed the door shut and marched through the hospital's big front entrance.

Instead of driving into the middle of Oxford in order to get exhausted going round the sales, Dimity decided to park the car and then go and wait for Ella in the hospital. After circling the large car park several times, she got a space at last as someone left. She got directions to Mr Cobbold's consulting-room, and sat for nearly half an hour in a nearby reception area, idly turning the pages of magazines.

'Mr Cobbold is running a little late,' she'd been told when she arrived, 'but Miss Bembridge is being seen now.'

Dimity didn't like hospitals. But then who did? She admired Charles so much when he dutifully made hospital visits to his parishioners. The consulting-rooms were in a quiet part of the hospital, away from trolleys and nurses, and clanging bells. But most people who came and went from the sitting area seemed to have worried faces, or worse, scared faces.

'Ella, I'm here!' Dimity cried, when Ella at last appeared through a set of swing doors.

Ella turned towards her, and immediately bumped into the back of a chair. She stood still and let Dimity come up to her.

'Come on, my dear, let's get you home,' she said kindly, and took Ella's arm. 'You can tell me all about it in the car.'

'Nothing much to tell,' said Ella, allowing herself to be propelled out of the reception area.

Once they were in the car, and seat belts fastened, Dimity turned to her old friend. 'Now tell me, what did he say?'

'Bloody awful.' Ella sat slumped back in the seat, staring out of the side window. Then she gave a huge sigh, and said in a small voice, 'He said there has been a rapid deterioration' – she paused, and gave one of her short laughs – 'I could have told him that for free. Possibly there's been a bleed – a haemorrhage which won't have helped . . .' Her voice trailed away.

'Oh, Ella, I'm so sorry,' Dimity said, touching her friend's arm. 'What happens next?'

'You mean, what does the future hold for me?' said Ella bluntly, turning to face her.

Dimity nodded.

'Mr Cobbold said the good news is that it won't be painful, and I won't go totally blind.'

'Well, that's something!' exclaimed Dimity.

'I should have enough peripheral vision to get around, and most people can keep their independence.' Dimity began to say something, but Ella raised her hand, stalling her. 'That is, if they've got someone else living with them – a husband or daughter, that sort of thing. I *could* continue to live at the cottage on my own, but he says not for long. Not safe, apparently. I'll probably start hallucinating soon.'

'Hallucinating!' exclaimed Dimity.

'Yes, seeing things. I've already seen patterns on the walls that I am pretty sure aren't there, but apparently this could get worse. Gargoyles and monsters, that sort of thing.'

'Ella, that's awful,' said Dimity.

'If I'm lucky, he said I might see flowers out of the corner of my eye rather than monsters. And I'll probably lose all sense of colour.'

Dimity didn't know what to say. Ella's future seemed dire.

'And there's worse,' Ella said.

Dimity turned in her seat to face Ella. 'What?' she said in a tiny voice.

'Mr Cobbold has said that I should . . .' she paused, and then said, 'You'll be pleased about this, Dim.'

'Pleased?' said Dimity faintly. 'I don't think that's possible. What else?'

'He says I should give up smoking. He doesn't think it helps.' And as if to confirm the specialist's advice, she went into a paroxysm of coughing. When she had spluttered to a stop, she fumbled in her jacket pocket, wound down the car window and tossed the battered old baccy tin out onto the concrete forecourt. 'Bye-bye, ciggies. Nice knowing you,' and then she burst into tears, drumming her good hand on the dashboard in frustration.

Dimity touched Ella's knee. 'Let's get you home. We can talk there,' and she started the car. For once, Ella didn't argue about whose home.

On both the Saturday and Sunday evenings, Derek Burwell had insisted on leaving the sitting-room curtains ajar. The room – which was both over-cluttered with knick-knacks and over-heated – looked out over the front garden and the drive. Even when they were playing bridge with their friends the Jervises on Saturday, he had insisted on always sitting so he faced the windows and could keep a beady eye on the gap in the curtains. So long as he could see the continuous glow from the uplighters, he knew they weren't under attack.

When the Burwells waved their guests goodbye at the end of the evening, the uplighters with their new bulbs were still shining in the dark, and they were, too, on the following evening.

'I think it probably *was* the Cooke boys, and that Shoosmith has put the fear of God into them,' Derek said as he locked up on Sunday night.

'I expect they're busy damaging someone else's property,' said his wife.

On the Monday afternoon, Derek spent some time in his workshop attached to the garage. He was one of those people who liked to boast about 'my workshop', where expensive tools and gadgets were hung in rows, all neatly labelled and mostly unused. He did occasionally take down a drill or a hammer, but if there was anything awkward to be mended, he'd invariably call in the local handyman.

It was just after four and was almost dark. It had been a cloudy, overcast day and lights had been on in his and neighbouring houses for some time. Despite the weather, a thrush was singing his final evening tune from some-where near. Derek went to the door of his workshop and looked around to see if he could locate the sweet songster.

He walked a little way into his drive and then looked back at his house but the bird wasn't on the chimney or the roof ridge. The song had temporarily ceased, and Derek was just going back into his workshop, ready to pack up, when the bird began to sing again, repeating its flute-like phrase again, and then again.

Derek turned and this time located the bird – perched on top of his lion's head.

'Hey, bird, shoo!' he said, marching towards the gateway. He knew what birds did just before taking off from a perch, and he didn't want his lion sullied. The thrush didn't wait to be told twice, and took off quickly, flying into the neighbouring garden.

As he reached the gateway, Derek heard a shout of laughter from the road, and then a cacophony of hooters. Three figures on bicycles roared past. Two were definitely the Cooke boys. Attached to their bikes were klaxons emitting the most awful noise – one sounded like the New York police in full cry after a Mafia mob, another resembled a demented donkey, while the third cyclist, a little in the rear, had a hooter that rang out with a discordant wolf whistle. Derek shook his fist after the retreating cavalcade and shouted, 'You ruffians! You'll pay for this,' but his words were lost to the wind that was rustling in the nearby trees.

He saw red lights shining a hundred or so yards down the road then the flickering lights returned towards him. He stepped out into the road to try to stop the noisy youths and reprimand them, but they swerved either side of him with jeering laughs.

Derek Burwell was furious. He marched back to his workshop, grabbed his jacket that he'd discarded, turned off the light and then returned to the gate. He was absolutely certain that the Cooke boys were responsible for vandalizing his uplighters and Christmas wreaths, and he was determined to catch them at it should they dare try again.

He walked up the dark drive to just short of the gateway, then crossed onto the grass, and turned his back so the wall and a beech hedge were between him and the road. He was willing to stay there and guard his property

– or, better still, catch the culprits red-handed – for as long as necessary. He pulled his jacket closer round him and stamped his feet up and down. It was damp and it was cold.

A car passed in the road, followed by another. For a while, all was quiet. A motorbike was approaching, but it throttled down and Derek assumed it had turned off into a drive. Silence again. Suddenly there was some shouting from down the road, followed by the noise of klaxons approaching. Derek stepped back into the beech hedge but the crackling of the dried leaves still on the twigs made him hastily step forward again. He tensed, listening as the noisy gang of youths grew closer, but they didn't stop, just seemed to give their klaxons an extra squeeze as they roared past. The hidden man stood stock-still to see what would happen next. The klaxons faded away down the road. Silence. Derek was about to move when a wolf whistle pierced the night air. More laughter then it faded away, and all was quiet once more.

The secret watcher remained where he was. Having stood out here this long, he didn't now want to reveal himself should one of the raucous gang return, intent on damaging the lights yet again. Three minutes, four minutes passed. A few cars drove by but it appeared the Cooke boys had gone.

Derek was about to move when he heard a different sound out on the road – the sound of a slightly squeaky set of brakes. He tensed, stood absolutely still. Then he heard what he was sure was a bicycle being leaned against the curved wall of the gateway. Suddenly there was the noise of a boot kicking hard against what Derek assumed was one of his uplighters. Yes! The light onto the drive changed as the assailant once more kicked in the light.

After a pause, there were more sounds of boot against uplighter and Derek quickly made his move. With surprising agility, he ran quietly across the few yards of grass, onto the drive and had pounced on the figure before his quarry had time to register there was someone there.

'Got you, you scoundrel!' Derek shouted, getting a firm grip on the collar of the person who was squirming and wriggling in an attempt to get away. 'No, you don't! You're coming with me, and then we will ring the police.'

'No, please,' quavered a voice.

'Yes, yes,' responded Derek Burwell and marched his trophy down the drive towards the house and light.

CHAPTER EIGHTEEN

The Culprit Unmasked

Joan Young was sitting at the table in her kitchen, going through the shopping list she would take into Lulling in the morning, when the front door bell rang. She listened for a moment to see if Edward would answer it and when she heard the study door open and his footsteps cross the hall, she continued checking the list. However, raised voices soon made her lay down both list and pencil and she went to see what all the noise was about.

In the hall, with a firm grip on her son's shoulder, was Derek Burwell.

'He's a wanton criminal,' he spluttered. 'He's cost me nearly thirty pounds in new lights, not to speak of what it's done to the wife's nerves!'

'What's happened?' Joan cried in alarm.

The man swung round to her. 'He's the one who's been kicking in my lights. He's the one who's been wrecking our Christmas decorations. He's just a common criminal!'

Joan put her hand up to her mouth in horror. Her son – a criminal?

Edward was torn between admiration for his son, and fury that he had been caught doing something he would dearly have liked to do himself. However, he knew he had to take a strong parental line.

'Paul,' he demanded fiercely, 'is this true? That you've damaged Mr Burwell's lights?'

The boy shuffled his feet a bit then looked up at his father with pleading eyes. 'Yes, Dad, but—'

'But nothing,' cut in Edward quickly. He didn't want Paul to have to explain why he had done such a thing because he had a pretty good idea what lay behind the boy's actions. 'You must apologize to Mr Burwell this instant, and of course repay the cost, the full cost, of the damage.'

'Apologies aren't good enough,' Derek Burwell shouted. 'Nor the cost of replacing the lights. The boy's a dissolute lout, and needs disciplining – and since he obviously doesn't get it in this house, then we'll see what the police have to say.'

Joan gasped and cried out, 'Surely—' but Edward flapped a hand at her to be quiet, and she stopped.

Edward realized with dismay that he was going to have to crawl to this odious man. He took a deep breath. 'Paul, will you please apologize to Mr Burwell, and then go to your room. I will deal with you later. I would like to speak to Mr Burwell alone.'

Paul mumbled, 'Sorry, Mr Burwell.'

'That's not good enough!' snapped his father. 'Say you're sorry properly.'

'I am sorry, Mr Burwell, that I damaged your lights,' said Paul, and then through gritted teeth added, 'I won't do it again.'

Derek Burwell harrumphed, which Paul took as acceptance of his apology and scurried up the stairs.

'Let us go into my study, Derek,' Edward said, 'and talk about this.'

As he shepherded the man through the door into his study, Edward threw a look over his shoulder at Joan, who was twisting her hands in her apron in agitation. The look said quite clearly, 'Heaven help us from little men!'

'Do have a seat,' Edward said, indicating a chair, and then swivelled his own office chair round so it was facing his visitor.

'Don't think you can sweet-talk me out of this,' said Derek, still purple in the face. 'The boy's no better than the estate kids that break windows and pull old folk's plants out of their window-boxes. In fact,' he said triumphantly, 'he's no better than the Cooke gang.'

That stung Edward. To have his son compared to the Cooke boys was appalling. Somehow, he thought, he had to find a reason for Paul to have done this without revealing what he was sure was the truth.

'Paul is an adolescent, Derek, and all lads of that age have growing pains. I don't for a moment condone what he has done, but I would ask you to reconsider your threat to report him to the police.'

'It is not a threat, Edward,' Derek replied. He was rubbing his hands together almost as though he were really enjoying making Edward squirm. 'It is exactly what I'm going to do. Wouldn't you do the same if someone had hurled a brick through your window?'

'Yes, but it isn't quite the same. A brick hurled through a window could hurt someone walking past that window at just that time. While what Paul did was undeniably wrong, he wasn't causing any danger to anyone else. You see, it is different.'

'All right, but that doesn't change the fact that what he did was' – Derek paused, and leaned forward for effect – 'wanton criminality!'

'Derek, remind me,' said Edward, 'do you have children?'

'No,' Derek said shortly. 'My wife and I married late in life.'

When no one else would have them, thought Edward, and then hurriedly continued: 'It is difficult for anyone without children to understand them properly. When they get to Paul's age, their bodies are changing. They seem to grow faster than their brains. They have energy that needs to be released. In the summer, they can use up that energy by being outdoors, walking, cycling, playing cricket. But in the winter, in the sort of bad weather we've been having, it's much more difficult. They sort of boil over.'

'Well, I don't want anyone boiling over at my expense,' Derek retorted. 'The boy's got to be taught a smart lesson.'

'I don't deny that,' said Edward. 'But I believe I can deal with him more competently than the police. I know the boy. I know what punishment will hurt most. That is much better than involving the police – and, I have to be honest with you, Derek, it would do the boy no good at all to have his details placed on police record. Had you had children, I'm sure you would feel the same.'

'Yes, well, maybe.' Derek looked round the book-lined room, and Edward sensed the tide was just beginning to turn. 'What punishment would you give him then?' he asked.

Edward had to think quickly. 'Again, it is difficult to impose much punishment at this time of year. In the summer I could have stopped him going to watch cricket – he loves cricket, and often goes into Oxford to watch the games at The Parks.' Then he had an idea. 'What about at Blenheim Lodge? Is there any work he could do there for you, in the garden perhaps?'

Derek Burwell thought for a moment then said, 'I have to admit that would be a good idea. My gardener chappie has gone to Canada to see his son and family for a month, and there are things young Paul could do.'

'And perhaps clean the car, the windows?' Edward said. 'In other words, be at your beck and call for the last fortnight of the holidays.' When he sensed Derek Burwell was hesitating, he added, 'If that would persuade you not to make this a police matter, my wife and I would be *so* grateful.'

Derek was disappointed at the fading image of marching the boy into Lulling police station but it would keep his own name from the police records, too, and he did like the idea of having all sorts of odd jobs done at Blenheim Lodge.

'Very well, then. I agree. Exuberant youth is difficult to cope with, I can see that. Shall we say ten o'clock tomorrow morning?'

'Yes, yes, of course. I will see he's with you on time. Perhaps two hours a day until the end of the holidays?'

'Yes, I agree to that.'

Both men stood up, and Edward showed his visitor to the front door.

'Thank you, Derek,' he said, offering his hand, 'thank you for understanding.'

Derek gave another of his harrumphs, but took Edward's hand and shook it before strutting off down the garden path.

Edward heaved a huge sigh of relief, and shut the door behind his unwelcome guest. He stood in the hall and bellowed up the stairs, 'Paul! Down here! Now!'

The kitchen door opened, and Joan stood there. 'Be gentle with him, dear,' she said.

Paul came down the stairs slowly. He reminded Edward of a puppy crawling on its tummy to its owner, knowing that it had done something wrong. Edward stood and waited.

When he was on the bottom step, Paul stopped. 'I'm really sorry, Dad. I didn't mean to cause so much trouble. But I did it for you. I knew how much you hated those awful lights.'

Edward knew this was the truth. But he also knew he couldn't let the boy go without a serious ticking off, and he pointed to the study door. As the door shut behind father and son, Joan sighed deeply and returned to the kitchen.

The following morning, at ten to ten, Paul was ready to leave for Blenheim Lodge. He was going to have to walk because, of course, his bicycle was still against the wall. He just hoped that no one had stolen it overnight.

In his jacket pocket were two envelopes. In one were three ten-pound notes to repay Derek Burwell for the cost of the replacement lights. Paul had produced twenty pounds himself – money he had received at Christmas from Granny Young and his godfather; the new bike he was saving for seemed to be much further away now. The other ten pounds had come from his mother's purse – strictly a loan.

The other envelope, marked 'Jean and Derek Burwell', held an invitation.

After Ella's outburst of frustration in the car, having seen the specialist, she and Dimity had driven back to Lulling in silence. Dimity had made a couple of efforts to talk but when Ella said, 'Leave me, Dim, I've got to sort this out for myself,' Dimity stayed silent.

Once back at the vicarage, Ella asked Dimity to make her two large turkey sandwiches and then went to her room. Dimity didn't disturb her. Once, passing outside the spare-room, she heard the cassette machine playing one of the tapes.

Before supper, Charles went upstairs and knocked on Ella's door. 'Supper's ready.'

'I don't want any supper.'

'Come on, Ella, you've got to eat,' Charles called gently.

'Just let me be, will you? I'm thinking.'

So they left her, but downstairs they talked through the plan once more.

'You must be sure, my dear,' Charles had said, 'that you're not just doing this because you feel sorry for Ella. If that were the case, it would be bound to show after a time, and make Ella very unhappy. And probably you, too.'

'I'm absolutely certain it's the right thing to do. After all, Ella and I shared her cottage for many years. We know we get on with each other. But what about you? Can you cope with two women nagging you?'

Dimity was smiling, and Charles knew she was joking. 'I'm sure, too. All I ask is that my study remains my sanctuary.'

The next morning, Dimity took up a tray of tea and toast and marmalade. 'Ella, I'll leave this tray with breakfast outside. Do have something. It's not good for you not to eat.'

There was silence and, worried that Ella might have done something extremely silly, Dimity persisted. 'Ella, are you all right? Just answer and then I'll leave you alone.'

'I'm fine,' came Ella's voice and, much relieved, Dimity left the tray and returned downstairs. She was very worried about her old friend, but felt it was better that she should sort out her mind in her own way.

Ella emerged from her room at about twelve-thirty. She appeared in the kitchen just as Dimity was wondering whether to make lunch for one or two; Charles was out and about in the parish and said he'd be back around teatime.

'Hello, it's me,' said Ella from the doorway, making Dimity jump. 'Any chance of some lunch?'

Dimity crossed the kitchen and gave Ella a great big hug. 'Of course, my dear. You must be starving. Would some of Sunday's lamb be all right, with salad? I put in two baked potatoes and they'll be ready in five minutes.'

'That sounds just what the doctor ordered,' said Ella, and then laughed. 'Or, anyway, Mr Cobbold.'

Ella seemed ready to talk once the two women were sitting companionably at the kitchen table, Dimity having cut up the lamb on Ella's plate into small pieces.

'Much as I *hate* the idea,' Ella said, 'Mr Cobbold advised me that it would be sensible for me to leave the cottage sooner rather than later.' She paused, then took a deep breath and continued: 'And in that case I've decided it may as well be now. I know that if I go back, once my wrist is mended, I'd find it impossible to leave. Also, I'll still be able to see enough to choose what to take with me – wherever that might be.'

'You must do what you think best,' Dimity said. 'Go where your heart leads you.'

Ella gave her bark of a laugh. 'Heart doesn't come into it, I'm afraid. It's got to be my head, my brains.' She paused while she speared another piece of meat then continued: 'Mr Cobbold is going to put me in touch with a help group, but that won't be until the New Year.'

'And in the long term?' Dimity ventured gently.

'Ah, the long term. Well, I suppose it will be a home of some sort. Mr Cobbold said there are places that aren't just full of senile people, dozing and dribbling their days away. He'll let me have a list.'

Ella's voice trailed away, and Dimity knew just how

much effort she was making to be positive. She almost, then and there, asked Ella if she would move into the vicarage with them, but stopped herself in time. She and Charles had agreed to speak to her together.

Instead she said, 'If you like, when you get the list, we could go and look at the places together.'

'Thanks, Dim, I'd like that. Now, is there any of that delicious Stilton left?'

That evening, Tuesday, 30 December, was no different from any other for Albert Piggott. Nelly had returned from The Fuchsia Bush at the usual time, and had given her surly husband a plate of cottage pie and carrots.

'What, no puddin'?' he'd grumbled.

'You know it's me Bingo night,' replied Nelly, peering at her face in the little mirror propped on the dresser shelf. 'There's some Cheddar in the fridge you can fill up on. Or have some crisps with your beer when you goes over to the pub.'

'I'm not minded to go over tonight,' Albert said, rummaging in the fridge. 'It's me last day tomorrer and I think I'd best 'ave an early night.'

'You must be ill, Albert Piggott!' Nelly exclaimed. 'Not goin' to the pub indeed!'

'Well, perhaps a swift 'alf then, when I've finished me supper.'

'I'll be off,' Nelly said. 'I'll be back about ten, so don't lock me out.'

Albert didn't answer. He was carving himself a great chunk of cheese as Nelly left. But instead of crossing the

green to walk down the hill to Lulling, Nelly turned in the
opposite direction and headed for The Two Pheasants.

Twenty minutes later, Albert pushed open the door of
his home-from-home and, as his ancient arthriticky body
came into the bar, there were cries of 'Happy Retirement'.
He stood there, swaying gently, looking at the scene in
front of him.

'Hello, Dad,' said Molly, and came forward to give his
bristly cheek a peck of a kiss.

'What you doin' 'ere, gal?' Albert gazed round. There
was Nelly, not at Bingo but perched on a bar stool with
what looked like a large gin and tonic in her hand. There

were the Hodges, Percy grinning inanely. His other drinking cronies were all gathering round – Joe, George Bell with his wife, Betty, and half a dozen others.

'Blimey, what a surprise!' he said, pushing back his cap and scratching at his thinning grey hair. 'Is this for me?'

'Yes, all for you!' they chorused back.

'But what about the party I arranged for Thursday evenin'? You, Bob,' he said, shaking a fist at the landlord, 'you said the room were already taken tonight.'

'That was no lie,' said Bob Jones. 'It had already been booked by Mr Shoosmith for this party.'

'Well I never!' said Albert, shaking his head.

Then Harold, who had been standing to one side, came forward and shook Albert's hand. 'We couldn't let you retire without giving you a party. Now, what are you having?'

'Ah well, now you're talkin',' said Albert, moving towards the bar. 'A pint of me usual, Bob – and make it a big pint!' He turned to Cyril Cooke perched on a bar stool next to Nelly. 'Off with you, that's my seat!' and the lad slid off without a word.

Bob Jones pushed a pint of frothing ale across the counter. They all watched as Albert picked it up, toasted the air, 'To me retirement!' and then drank long and deep. When he banged the tankard down on the counter, half the pint had been consumed and Albert was left with a frothy moustache across his upper lip. This he wiped with the back of his hand that he then wiped down the side of his trousers.

'Albert!' chided Nelly. 'Manners!'

'A drink for everyone, please, Mr Jones,' called Harold, 'I'm paying for this round.'

There was a flurry as those with already full glasses quickly downed the contents. From somewhere behind Percy Hodge came a rather loud hiccup. It was Mrs Gibbons, one of the members of the PCC, who had turned out to wish Albert a happy retirement. 'Dear me, dear me,' she spluttered genteelly into a lace hand-kerchief, but then put her empty glass on the bar with the rest.

When everyone had a full glass, Harold made a short speech and presented Albert with a little carriage clock. 'From the PCC, for everything you've done for St Andrew's over the past heaven only knows how many years.'

Albert was totally overcome, so much so that he told the landlord to stand by since the next round would be on him.

'Wonders will never cease,' remarked Percy Hodge to Betty Bell. 'That'll be the first time the ol' booger 'as ever dipped 'is 'and in 'is pocket for so many people.'

'I 'eard that, Percy 'Odge. Enjoy it while you can cos it'll be the last time an' all.'

Charles Henstock had telephoned Harold during the afternoon, and briefly told him about Ella and what the specialist had said. He hadn't mentioned anything about his and Dimity's plan, but he excused himself from Albert's party, saying that things were a bit difficult at home, and he thought he should stay to support Dimity.

'I quite understand, old chap. We'll manage without you. Give my love to Dimity.'

After supper that evening, Charles stoked the fire so it blazed in the grate, and then got some port glasses from the dining-room, along with the bottle of port Ella had given him for Christmas.

'This really is a most excellent bottle, Ella. I can't tell you how much I'm enjoying it. Can I give you a glass?'

'Thanks, Charles, I most certainly will.'

Charles poured out three glasses, and put one by Dimity's chair, and handed one to Ella. Then he sat himself in his armchair on one side of the fire but didn't pick up his book to read as he usually did.

Dimity came in with a tray of coffee cups, and handed them round.

'Where's that box of chocolate-covered ginger?' asked Ella. 'The one that Harold and Isobel gave me.'

Dimity found it and handed it round before she, too, sat down on the other side of the fire.

Ella gave a long, contented sigh. 'If it weren't for this wretched wrist, this would be nearly perfect.' She stretched out her large legs towards the fire.

'Nearly perfect?' asked Charles.

'Perfection would be a ciggy, of course! Do you know, it's thirty-six hours since I had my last one. And so far, touch wood, I haven't really missed them. That damn specialist gave me such a rollicking about smoking that it really does seem that I mustn't smoke again.'

'Poor Ella,' said Dimity with feeling. She had lived with

Ella long enough to know how much those pungent cigarettes had meant to her.

'I'll have to find something else to do to compensate,' said Ella, scrabbling in the box for another chocolate and then leaning forward to pass them to Charles. 'Singing, perhaps.'

'Singing?' Dimity said, horrified. 'But you can't sing a note. Totally out of tune.'

'Well, perhaps I should learn.'

'Don't you think you're a bit too old to have singing lessons, my dear?' asked Charles.

'Well, if not singing, then something else. What do blind people do all day in those old folk's homes?'

Neither Charles nor Dimity answered that, and there was silence for a few moments. Then Charles cleared his throat.

'Ella, my dear . . .'

Ella slanted her head towards him, presumably so she could see him with her peripheral vision.

'Charles.'

'Ella, my dear,' Charles repeated, 'Dim and I have been talking.'

'Well done!' Ella quipped.

'Shush, listen,' said Dimity. 'Listen to Charles for a moment.'

'Dim and I would very much like you to come and live with us here at the vicarage. Full-time, not just for now. We've plenty of space here. It will just mean changing the rooms round a bit. You can have all the independence you want, but we suggest you eat with us.'

'And it would be so easy for you here, almost in the middle of Lulling. Quiet, yet just five minutes from the High Street,' added Dimity.

'What?' spluttered Ella, unable to take this in. 'Here? Permanently? Not go into a home?'

'Yes,' Dimity and Charles both said together, then Dimity added, 'We'd love to have you here with us.'

For a moment, no one spoke. The clock ticking on the mantelpiece was the only sound.

Then into the silence, Ella said one word. 'Yes.'

Dimity leaned forward. 'Yes? Yes, you'll come?'

'Yes, if you're both sure.'

Dimity immediately went across to her friend and gave her a big hug. 'Oh, my dear, I am so pleased.'

'What you mean,' Ella said, 'is relieved that you won't have to trail round all those bins with me.'

'No,' said Charles, 'but I think all those homes will be thankful that Miss Bembridge isn't going to be one of their residents. I think this calls for another glass of port, don't you?'

And both women held out their glasses to be filled up.

It was agreed to leave further discussion about the Grand Plan until the next morning. Charles picked up his book, Dimity her knitting and the two women talked quietly together, mostly about the old days at Ella's cottage.

'It's come full circle, Dim,' Ella said when she rose to go to bed some time later. 'My coming to live with you here. I can't thank you enough.'

'It's going to be fun for us all. Now sleep well, and we'll talk in the morning.'

CHAPTER NINETEEN

Ella Makes Plans

Ella woke early the next morning; it was only six-thirty and much too soon to be thinking of getting up. She switched on the bedside light and took her book from the table beside the bed. A folded sheet of paper marked her place but instead of continuing to read from where she had last reached, she unfolded the bit of paper and read out loud the words she had written on it in bold capital letters.

' "Lord, thou knowest, better than I know myself, that I am growing older and will some day be old. Keep me from being talkative and particularly from the fatal habit of thinking I must say something on every subject and every occasion." ' Ella paused. 'Hmm . . .' she said, 'no one could accuse me of being talkative – unless you count talking to myself.' She continued to read the words she knew so well. ' "Release me from craving to try to straighten out everybody's affairs." ' Ella snorted. 'It would be nice if everyone else stopped trying to sort out *my* affairs,' she said, and then immediately felt guilty. Dimity and Charles were being so kind.

Ella resumed reading from the prayer that had been written by a seventeenth-century nun. ' "Teach me the glorious lesson that occasionally it is possible that I may be mistaken." Very very occasionally,' she added, and then laughed at herself. ' "Keep me reasonably sweet." '

Ella put down the sheet of paper, and gazed round the room. Dimity had done so much to make her comfortable. There was a vase of sweet-smelling freesias on the dressing-table, and on the bedside table beside her was a little round tray that held a glass, a carafe of water and a tin that she knew contained digestive biscuits. 'Dear Lord,' she said, 'give me strength to be sweet. I must show my appreciation of all they are doing for me.'

Then, satisfied, Ella found her place in the large-print book and settled down to read until it was time to get up. She had brought some loose-fitting garments with her from the cottage, which she could manage to put on herself, and she presented herself, brushed and dressed downstairs for breakfast.

'Good morning, good morning,' she said, coming into the kitchen.

After exchanging the usual pleasantries about sleeping well, Dimity sat Ella at the kitchen table and passed her the cereal.

'I've got morning prayers in St John's at ten,' Charles said, 'but I'm free after that. I suggest we sit down together then and talk. What time are Robert and Dulcie arriving, Dimity?'

'They said they would leave London soon after lunch. So about mid-afternoon here. The traffic shouldn't be bad coming this way. Most people will be heading back into London after the long Christmas break.'

'Splendid,' said Charles, beaming behind his round spectacles. 'That'll give us plenty of time.'

While Charles was out, Dimity and Ella made preparations for the Wilberforces' arrival. When Isobel had asked if there would be room for them at the vicarage, Dimity had agreed eagerly. She and Charles were very fond of the young couple and she had been thrilled to hear that a baby was on the way.

Dimity had already made up the beds in the second guest room but Ella now flicked a duster round and put a carafe of fresh water on the tray with two glasses that sat on the chest of drawers.

They were asked for eight o'clock at the Youngs' party so Dimity made some drop scones and flapjacks for tea. 'We'd better line our stomachs well before the evening's celebrations,' she said.

When Charles returned to the vicarage shortly after eleven, he found an empty kitchen and a cooling tray of drop scones. It was no surprise to Dimity to find one missing when she walked in a moment later.

'Just testing they're up to scratch,' said Charles, looking a little guilty.

'I thought you might, which is why I made one extra,' Dimity replied. 'I'll make some coffee, then I suggest we sit down and talk. Will you call Ella? I think she went up to her room.'

So the three friends settled down at the kitchen table, with mugs of coffee at their elbows and a plate of biscuits between them. Dimity and Charles had decided that Dimity would outline their proposal since she was the practical one of the pair, and knew Ella backwards.

'What we suggest is that we make you a sort of apartment upstairs. We would like to retain our two spare-rooms for ourselves, but it seems to us that the rooms in the Victorian extension – those that are above us now – would be ideal for you. They would give you all the privacy that you wanted – although, of course,' Dimity hastily added, 'we're not expecting you to stay a prisoner up there. The whole house will be your home, and you must spend as much time with us as you want.'

'Is that where the back stairs lead to?' Ella asked, pointing to a door set in one of the kitchen walls.

'Indeed, it is,' said Charles, 'but they are rather steep and we think it would be much better, safer, for you to use the main staircase. The main part of the vicarage is a classical Queen Anne house,' he explained, 'then around the mid-nineteenth century they built an extra chunk onto the back. I suppose it was to house the huge families that the Victorian clergy were so fond of.'

'Poor wives,' muttered Ella.

'Indeed. But at some point between the two world wars, the Victorian wing was demolished. Not all of it, but most of it. Thus we are left with the original house plus a much smaller extension and that is where we are now. This big kitchen, and the larder, boot-room and so on. The rooms above have never really been used while we've been here.'

'We've used them just a couple of times,' said Dimity. 'Once when that choir from Sweden came to perform in St John's, and we had to put up seven or eight of them, and . . .' she paused, frowning to remember.

'We had that family from France when that ecumenical conference was held in Oxford,' added Charles.

'Could we go upstairs and have a look?' Ella asked.

'Of course.'

And so the three of them made their way across the big hall and up the wide curving staircase.

'We've seen from the time you've been here,' Dimity said, from behind Ella, 'that these stairs don't seem to give you any problems.'

'Those eighteenth-century chaps always built good staircases,' said Ella, puffing a bit. 'None of the uneven risers that I've got in the cottage.'

Charles opened a door off the landing that led into a passage with a window at the end.

'Being at the back of the house, these rooms get the morning sun but otherwise, I'm afraid, are a little dark.'

Ella barked her laugh. 'That won't worry me, will it?'

Charles opened a door on the left onto a not very large square room into which the pale winter sunlight was filtering. The walls were simply white-washed and in one corner the staircase from the kitchen below arrived. It wasn't furnished in the proper sense, but there were two divan beds, a small scrubbed pine table and a couple of bentwood chairs. Standing in a row against the nearest bed were several suitcases and some cardboard boxes.

'This is the closest we got to decorating when the choir came. Otherwise, as you can see,' said Dimity, 'the room is used as a sort of dumping ground. But it's a very useful place to keep the cases. Saves climbing up into the attic.'

Charles led the way back into the passage and showed Ella a slightly larger room next door to the first; it was similarly furnished although it had the luxury of a rag mat between the two beds.

'There are three rooms on the other side of the passage, two quite small,' said Charles, opening doors. 'The bathroom's in this one, but I suggest it would be better to take it out and start again.'

He was probably right. There was a very stained narrow bath on legs, a large washbasin set in a wooden surround, and a lavatory with a cistern mounted high above on the wall.

The three stood silently, surveying the dismal room.

Then Ella broke the silence. 'Could you leave me here for a moment?' she asked. 'I'd like to look around on my own.'

Obediently, Charles and Dimity went back into the main house. 'I'd forgotten how awful it is,' said Dimity as Charles shut the connecting door.

'It's not that bad,' said Charles, sitting down on a chair on the landing. 'It's suffering from neglect, that's all. A lick of paint and a few open windows would make all the difference.'

'Yes, I realize that,' replied Dimity, running her finger

along the top of a picture, and tut-tutting at the ridge of dust collected on her finger. 'I must remember to get Mrs Allen to do these pictures next week.'

'Talking of Mrs Allen, would she have time to do for Ella, too?' asked Charles.

'I hadn't thought of that, but in fact I think it would work very well. Mrs Allen told me only the other day that one of the people she cleans for is moving in the spring. Perhaps she would like to put in more time here instead. I'll ask her.'

'Once we know what Ella thinks,' said Charles. He got up and walked along the landing, then stood and looked down into his much-loved garden. It was asleep now, of course, but soon things would be stirring. The first snow-drops wouldn't be far away.

And Charles was moved to quote one of his favourite poems.

> *And in that Garden, black and white,*
> *Creep whispers through the grass all night.*
> *And spectral dance, before the dawn,*
> *A hundred Vicars down the lawn;*
> *Curates, long dust, will come and go*
> *On lissom, clerical, printless toe;*
> *And oft between the boughs is seen*
> *The sly shade of a Rural Dean.*

Dimity laughed. 'I don't think Rupert Brooke wrote that for you, my dear. No one could say you were "lissom"! Nor "sly" for that matter.'

'I'm glad about that,' said Charles. 'Look, the sun is just touching the golden weathercock on St John's. It's turning out to be a nice day.'

He returned to his chair and hummed to himself for a moment or two, then polished his spectacles vigorously on a large white handkerchief. 'The thing is, Dim,' he said at length, 'I'm not sure Ella wouldn't be better—' but he broke off when the connecting door opened and revealed Ella's large frame.

'If I can do what I'd like to do then I think this would suit me very well,' she said, almost as though she were talking to a shop assistant about a new dress she was trying on. 'Let me show you.'

Charles and Dimity exchanged glances and then followed Ella through the door.

'I would like to make this room,' she said, indicating the first square room on the left, 'my bedroom. Then' – and she moved on down the passage – 'if I was allowed to knock down these walls,' and she indicated the walls of the rooms at either side at the end of the passage, 'and build a new wall here,' and she waved her good arm across the passage, 'that would make a bigger room for my sitting-room by taking in this end of the passage and the rooms on either side. The two extra windows would make it much lighter, and it's lovely looking out over the garden below.'

Charles knocked on the passage walls. 'I think they're only partition walls, easy enough to take down.'

'But if you blocked off the passage, it would be as dark

as night here without the light that the end window now gives,' Dimity said.

'I've thought of that. If the door leading into the sitting room was a half-glass door, then the passage would be perfectly light enough – for me, anyway. Then,' said Ella, indicating the middle room on the other side of the passage, 'this would make a perfect little kitchen.'

'But I thought you'd agreed to eat with us?' said Dimity, immediately worried about Ella's safety.

'And so I shall, for the main meals. But I don't see why I can't have a small kitchenette – dreadful word! – so I can make my own breakfast, a snack if I want one when you are out, or even supper if you are entertaining and don't want me hanging around. I could get one of those microwave things. I wouldn't want an oven or anything like that.'

Much relieved, Dimity said, 'It all sounds an excellent idea.'

'And then the bathroom. I agree with you, Charles, that it would probably be better pulled out and started again.' Ella turned to face her friends, hands on hips. 'Now, what do you think?'

'It sounds as though you have it all mapped out,' said Dimity. 'I should have known that your talent for design would see a way of turning these dark rooms into something liveable in.'

Charles raised a hand. 'If I may come in here? I must point out that all this will need to go in front of the Church Commissioners. This vicarage is, after all, their property.'

Ella turned to Charles. 'Oh, Lord! I had quite forgotten the Church Commissioners. Will they allow this?'

'I took the liberty of doing a little telephoning yesterday. The agents for the Church Commissioners with whom we shall have to deal were, of course, not yet back from the Christmas break. So I talked to Anthony Bull.'

'Dear Anthony . . .' murmured Dimity, which seemed to be the stock phrase whenever the name of Lulling's previous incumbent was mentioned.

'Anthony didn't think there would be much difficulty. In fact, he reminded me that the Commissioners are selling quite a bit of their property, moving the clergy into smaller, newer houses, and selling off the larger properties for huge sums of money. He thinks it would find favour if we had someone else living here with us.'

'Is there any chance that the vicarage will be sold off?' Ella asked.

'Anthony doesn't think so. After all, we have the church fête here every year, and use the dining room for parish and endless other meetings. He has given me the name of a friend in Hampshire who apparently did just what we are planning to do. I shall ring him later this week.'

'Thank you, Charles,' said Ella. She had assumed a rather business-like manner which made Dimity smile. 'Now, before we go any further, I want to make one thing absolutely clear. I will pay for all the work that needs to be done – after all, I shall have plenty of money once the cottage is sold. And I will come here on a trial period. If it doesn't work out, and we end up fighting—'

'Ella,' protested Dimity, 'I'm sure that won't happen.'

'I'm sure, too, but we must make plans in case it were to. If it doesn't work out, then I'll find a place in one of those homes, but if I get to the end of the trial period with marks for good behaviour, then I think there should be a proper agreement setting out the terms of my rent and all that that encompasses. And there must be a clause whereby either of us can get out of the arrangement, say three months' notice. So, assuming we get the OK from the Church Commissioners to go ahead, will you both agree to my terms?'

'We agree,' Charles and Dimity said in unison.

'Wonderful!' cried Ella. 'I know I'd be very happy here, and although I'll be heartbroken leaving my cottage, this will be a haven. And I shall be eternally grateful to you both for re-housing this broken-down old thing.'

'What rubbish!' said Dimity, mightily relieved that it looked as though – the Commissioners apart – Ella was prepared to give up her independence and live with them.

'Now the garden,' said Charles. 'Like the house, you must treat that as your own.'

'Thanks, Charles, that means a lot, especially since your garden is such a fine one.'

'Excellent, excellent,' said the vicar, rubbing his hands together. 'Now, I suggest we go downstairs and have a celebratory glass of sherry. We can talk some more in the comfort of the drawing-room.'

On the way down the main staircase, Charles suddenly stopped and turned to look back up at Ella who was following behind Dimity.

'On the subject of the garden, Ella, what are you like at weeding?'

The Youngs' house on Thrush Green was a hive of activity. It was a case of all hands to the pump. Paul helped his father move small items of furniture out from the hall and drawing-room, making the two rooms look strangely empty.

'I've got to go now, Dad,' Paul said, looking at his watch. 'Time to dance attendance on the Burwells.'

'Don't worry,' Edward said as his son pulled on a warm jacket and woolly hat, 'we'll leave plenty for you to do when you get home. Work hard!'

'Have fun!' called his mother.

Whatever Paul replied was lost as he slammed the front door behind him.

He and Jeremy had spent the previous afternoon in Mrs Curdle's old caravan in the orchard, Alfie curled up on an old cushion on the floor, and Jeremy had listened wide-eyed at the details of Paul's escapade.

'Gosh!' he'd said. 'You were brave.'

'Well, those lights were truly awful. Dad was quite right to go demented about them.'

'What did you have to do this morning?' Jeremy had asked.

'Clean old Burwell's car – and I've got to do Ma Burwell's tomorrow. I did it really slowly so I wouldn't have to do anything else, but they cottoned on and hurried me up. Then I had to sweep out the garage and his workshop. I don't know what they're going to find for me to do right up to the end of the hols.'

After Paul had set off for his two hours of hard labour, Edward went into the kitchen where Joan was stirring soup on the stove.

'How many did you say we were going to be? I'll need to check we've got enough chairs.'

'With the Wilberforces, it's twenty,' said Joan. 'I had hoped that either Kit or Connie would come but they've both decided to stay in with Dotty.'

'Have we got twenty chairs?' Edward asked.

Joan paused, spoon in mid-air. She then conducted the spoon round the house. 'You add up as I go. Eight in the dining-room, three in the drawing-room, two in the hall, two from your study—'

'Forget those,' said Edward. 'We should have taken them out before we filled the room with furniture. It's too late now.'

'All right. I'd rather not use the chairs from in here. They're not very comfortable. Where was I? Ah yes, upstairs.' And so she counted on round the house. 'How many is that?'

'I make it eighteen. We need to get two from somewhere.'

'You can have two of ours,' said Molly, who was peeling oranges at the sink. 'I'll get Ben to bring 'em over when he gets home.'

'Ah, thanks,' Edward said. 'And Ben is sure he's happy to help us tonight?'

'Course. We both are.'

'Who's looking after the children?' Joan asked.

'Well, you'll never guess. Nelly's coming over! There's a turn-up for the books. She never done that before. Offered, too. I didn't ask.'

'So she's not cooking a grand meal for your dad, then?'

'No. He'll be with his cronies down the pub, celebrating his retirement all over again. Ben an' me will enjoy being here this evening. I'm looking forward to seeing Miss Watson an' Miss Fogerty again. Seems ages since they was here.'

'I think everyone will be glad to see them,' replied Joan. She tasted the soup. 'There! I think that's just right. All it will need is heating through, and the cream adding at the end.'

Wiping her hands on her apron, she peered at a large list that was attached to the fridge door with a magnet. 'What's next?'

'I'll go and collect the trestle for the hall, so if we could decide who's sitting where, then I can get the chairs in the right place so the lightest people sit on the more delicate chairs.'

'Good idea,' said Joan. 'We'll need a good stout one for Ella. That chair she sat on last Christmas has never been the same. And we'd better place her at the end of a table so her poor arm won't get knocked. Oh, what fun this all is!'

'I hope you'll be thinking the same in twelve hours' time,' laughed Edward, pulling a pad of paper towards him. 'Who on earth are we going to put next to the burbling Burwells?'

'Whatever you do, don't put them anywhere near Winnie or Ella. They haven't forgiven Jean for interfering with the crib in St Andrew's.'

'Now there's a temptation,' mused Edward, and in his neat hand drew two large rectangles on the sheet of paper. 'That would really put the cat among the pigeons.'

At the time that Albert Piggott would normally go into The Two Pheasants for his dinnertime pint, he set off along the little alleyway next to his cottage that led to the path to Lulling Woods. If such a thing were possible, there was a spring in the bent old man's step. Four more hours, and then he'd be retired! But he was not such a fool that he didn't realize that even he couldn't spend all day in the pub, and he'd get bored with nothing to do. Which was why he wanted to have a word with his old friend, Dotty Harmer.

Because it was a nice day, without any wind, Connie had not stopped Dotty going outside and pottering around the garden. It was here that Albert found her, gazing fondly at the ducks on the little pond.

'Still usin' that little landin' stage I made for 'em, I sees,' said Albert, coming through the gate.

Dotty turned to greet him. 'Hello, Albert. Just the person I need. Don't you think that Jemima there' – and she pointed to a large Aylesbury duck preening its feathers on the side of the pond – 'is looking a little peaky?'

'Um . . .' murmured Albert. He wasn't sure he could tell if the duck was under the weather or not.

'I was just wondering if I might add a drop or two of my tincture of iron to her feed.'

'What you make that from? Nettles, is it?'

'No, no! I mean the iron tonic that Dr Lovell insists I take.'

'She looks awright to me,' Albert said hastily, hoping to spare the poor duck from a dose of Dotty's medicine. 'Now, what about a cuppa for your old friend? I've something I wants to discuss with you.'

Over cups of tea in Dotty's kitchen, Albert explained that as he was about to retire he would have time on his hands. 'What about me comin' down 'ere a couple of days a week and doin' any maint'nance work what needs doin' in the garden? An' I could dig you a little patch for some vegetables. What do you think?'

'I think it's a splendid idea!' cried Dotty. 'It would be companionship for us both – and allow Connie and Kit to have some time off. They seem to think that I can't be here on my own.'

'Well, that's fixed then,' said Albert, and a rare thing happened. He actually smiled. 'I'll come down on Friday af'ernoon. I needs to be around in the mornin' to check up that young Cooke has got out of bed and is at work.' He slowly got to his feet, grimacing as arthritic pains shot through his ancient body.

Dotty noticed. 'And I'll get you started on some of my best remedies for your rheumatics,' she said. 'Fair return for the help you'll be giving me.'

As Albert walked back to Thrush Green, he feared he might come off worst in this new arrangement. But he was fond of the old girl and, as she said, it would be companionship. He paused as he stretched out his hand to open the door of The Two Pheasants. There was a familiar car driving slowly along the side of the green.

'That's Miss Watson's car!' he declared to himself and then hobbled into the pub to be the first with the news that 'the schoolteachers is back'.

*

Isobel had positioned herself in the window of the sitting-room so she could watch for their guests' arrival. They had said they planned to arrive in time for lunch and here they were, right on time.

'They're here!' she called to Harold. 'Can you come and help with the luggage?'

Isobel opened the front door and flew down the garden path in order to greet Dorothy Watson and especially Agnes Fogerty.

'Why, Agnes,' she cried, having given her old college friend a huge hug, 'I do declare you're even smaller than ever. Have you shrunk?'

'Certainly not!' beamed little Agnes Fogerty. 'Oh, Isobel, it's so lovely to see you. And to be here in Thrush Green again.' She stepped back across the little road and looked at the school house next door. It was bigger now, of course. Alan Lester had built on to it but the front was just the same. Memories of the years she had spent there with Dorothy came flooding back, but Isobel would not let her linger with them for long.

'Come on in!' she cried. 'Here's Harold to take your cases. And Dorothy,' she exclaimed, giving the larger woman a big kiss on the cheek, 'how are you? You look wonderful. And I love your hair. You've had it cut differently.'

'We have a very good hairdresser in Barton,' said Dorothy, patting her hair. And so the old friends, chattering nineteen to the dozen about the journey up from Hampshire, the benefit of a really good haircut, and how their Christmases had been, went into the house.

CHAPTER TWENTY

A Gathering of Friends

At about four o'clock that afternoon, the tyres of Robert Wilberforce's expensive Jaguar crunched across the gravel drive of Lulling Vicarage. From the kitchen Dimity saw them arrive and hastily took off her apron. She hurried across the hall and popped her head round the drawing-room door.

'They're here!' she cried, and then went to open the front door to greet Robert and Dulcie.

'Hello, hello! Welcome!' Dimity cried. 'Did you have a good journey?'

'Indeed, yes,' replied the handsome dark-haired Robert. 'Sorry we're later than we said. We got stuck with some friends who came for morning coffee and stayed for lunch.'

Dimity gave Dulcie a kiss on both cheeks, and then stood back to look at her. 'You are obviously very well. You look blooming!'

Charles bustled out of the house, and shook Robert warmly by the hand. 'So good to see you, so good,' he said. 'Come along in. We are longing to hear all your news.'

Ella had emerged from the drawing-room and was in the hall waiting to greet the Wilberforces.

'We did meet briefly when you were here for the Nathaniel Patten centenary celebrations,' she said. 'My cottage looks across the green to the statue.'

'Of course, I remember. You had a beautiful late rose climbing up the front,' replied Robert, shaking her hand.

Ella laughed. 'What a memory you have! It's a climbing White Iceberg.'

'Charles, will you take Dulcie and Robert upstairs, and I'll get the kettle on,' said Dimity, ever the good hostess. 'You must be dying for some tea.'

'That would be lovely,' said Dulcie. 'Oh, it's so good to be here again. What memories I have of this house.' For it was, of course, here that she and Robert had first met.

Fifteen minutes later, they were all gathered in the drawing-room. Robert stood with his back to the fire, warming himself. Dimity was pouring cups of tea, and Ella handed round the plate of drop scones that were glowing with deep yellow butter.

While Dimity and Dulcie chatted about matters concerning babies, and Charles and Robert were talking about world affairs, Ella sat quietly in her armchair. It was at times like this, she thought, that she would in future quietly withdraw to her rooms upstairs. She didn't want Charles and Dimity to feel they had to include her in everything. Anyway, she preferred her own company to the chit-chat of others. She looked at the fire burning brightly in the handsome fireplace. The flames were distorted, the top seemingly disconnected with the bottom; she was not worried by this. Mr Cobbold had told her it would happen.

Having exhausted the subject of babies, Dimity suddenly realized that Ella had not joined in the conversation. Not surprising, really: Ella and babies were about as compatible as red wine and chocolate.

'The Church Commissioners and planners permitting, Ella is going to come and live here with us,' she told Dulcie.

'My eyes. Can't see much any more, and Dim thinks I'm not safe in my cottage. Probably true,' Ella said in her forthright way.

'We must show you Ella's plans for upstairs,' Dimity said, stretching for the teapot. 'Anyone for more tea?'

Robert put his cup forward, and then Ella. Dulcie shook her head.

'Charles, more for you?'

'No, thank you. However, is that last drop scone going free? Robert, what about you?' said Charles, holding up the plate with just the one drop scone left. Robert declined. 'Ella, take the last one and find a handsome husband.'

'Chance would be a fine thing,' laughed Ella. 'Go on, Charles, you know you're dying to have it.'

'Well, I must admit,' said Charles, helping himself,

'Dimity does make the best drop scones in the whole world.'

Shortly after eight o'clock, the Youngs' front door bell rang. Opening it, Edward found the Burwells standing there. Oh, God, they would be the first to arrive, he thought, then forced a bright smile on his face. 'Derek and Jean, how lovely to see you. Do come in.'

'Thank you,' trilled Jean Burwell.

Edward stepped aside, and let the couple cross the doorstep into the hall. 'I think you know my son, Paul. He'll take your coats for you.'

Derek Burwell sniggered.

'Good evening Mrs Burwell, Mr Burwell,' said Paul. He would be as polite to them as his father demanded, but he was not prepared to toady to them. He took their coats. It was then his turn to snigger.

Jean Burwell was mutton dressed as lamb: her mauve chiffon confection had a swooping neckline, and she was tottering on very high strapless shoes. At least, Paul thought, turning away to hide his grin, the colour matched her hair.

'Now come into the drawing-room and we'll get you a drink. Joan will be here in a moment. She's just finishing off in the kitchen. Watch out for the table as you go in.'

With twenty for dinner, the Youngs had laid two tables. The main table in the dining-room sat ten people and Edward had borrowed a large trestle table from the village hall, and this would seat another ten. It was in the hall, now pushed back against the wall, and just before dinner it would be pulled out into the middle of the room. Covered with a bright white damask tablecloth, and beautifully laid, no one would have known just a trestle table lay beneath.

Edward and the Burwells were followed into the drawing-room by Ben Curdle who had emerged from the kitchen. He was wearing his one and only suit, and his mop of curly brown hair had been brushed into some sort of submission.

'Good evening,' he said politely, and offered a tray of glasses. 'Would you like a drink? There is champagne, or would you prefer something soft?'

'Champers would do just fine,' said Derek and, without bothering to see what his wife wanted, took a glass from the tray.

Jean hesitated. 'I don't want to get tiddly,' she squeaked. 'There's a long night ahead of us.'

'Go on, girl,' her husband urged. 'Got to get into the party spirit.'

God protect me from the burbles, thought Edward, smiling through gritted teeth. Luckily the front door bell went again, and he made his escape.

It was Winnie Bailey, well wrapped up in her tweed coat with a scarf looped round her neck.

'Come in, come in from the cold, my dear,' cried Edward. 'Joan's in the kitchen, she'd love to see you.' He leaned down and gave Winnie a resounding kiss, at the same time whispering, 'The Burwells are here, best to avoid them until more people arrive to dilute them.'

Winnie looked a little startled but, having let Edward

take her coat and scarf, she went obediently into the kitchen.

'Hello, Winnie,' called Joan, looking up from adding some blobs of thick cream to the top of a huge cut-glass bowl of chocolate soufflé. 'Don't tell me Edward has sent you in here to help.'

'No, I don't think so. Something about avoiding the Burwells. What on earth are they doing here?' asked Winnie, and then felt rather guilty at her uncharitable remark.

'Ah, it's a long story. You must ask Paul.'

The front door bell went again, and the sound of noisy greetings floated through to the kitchen. 'That sounds like the Shoosmiths with Dorothy and Agnes. That will make things easier for you. I'm just about finished in here. Molly, it's all over to you.'

Pretty Molly Curdle smiled. 'Good evening, Mrs Bailey. From the looks of all the food what Mrs Young's prepared, it's going to be a feast. You go now, Mrs Young. Ben an' I'll be all right. As agreed, we'll aim to serve up at nine.'

'I hope that isn't too late for you, Winnie dear,' said Joan, taking off her apron and hanging it on the back of the kitchen door. 'But we thought if we ate any earlier, people would be asleep before twelve o'clock.'

'No, that's fine. I had a late tea on purpose. Jenny will come across at about eleven, and we'll just slip away.'

Joan held open the kitchen door, and the two women went into the hall and were soon enveloped in embraces with Dorothy Watson and Agnes Fogerty. 'How simply wonderful to see you both,' Joan cried. 'And you are both looking so well!'

Dorothy had, as usual, spent hours agitating about what to wear. She was sure that the red dress she wanted to wear had been 'seen' the previous year when they'd been staying in Thrush Green. She had therefore decided on a dark blue dress with white polka-dots that she knew hadn't had a Thrush Green airing since she had only bought it a few months previously.

Agnes never had any trouble in choosing what to wear. Her wardrobe was much more limited than Dorothy's. Although she knew her deep pink velvet skirt had often been seen at Thrush Green parties before, she was wearing a new cream silk blouse with which she was immensely pleased. She had won fifty pounds on the Premium Bonds, and had splashed out some of it on this new blouse.

Paul was kept busy with the coats, but he had help as soon as Jeremy arrived with his mother and Frank.

'Just you two keep off the wine dregs,' warned Edward, smiling, and the boys grinned sheepishly at each other.

There were cries of pleasure when Charles and Dimity arrived, not only with Ella but with Robert and Dulcie. Harold pumped Robert's hand vigorously, while Isobel stood back to inspect Dulcie.

'Oh, look!' she cried. 'A bump!'

Dulcie laughed. 'And fairly energetic, too. I am sure it's a boy and he'll be playing rugby for England.' The two women went arm in arm into the drawing-room.

'Doesn't the room look pretty!' Dulcie cried. 'All those

cards,' she said, indicating the Christmas cards that were pinned to red ribbon and hung from the handsome ceiling cornice. 'What a lot of friends the Youngs must have.'

'And isn't the tree a fine one,' said Isobel. 'I believe Edward always gets his off the Blenheim estate.'

'What? He creeps in and cuts one down under cover of dark?' asked Dulcie.

Isobel laughed. 'No, of course not! From the Blenheim estate, I should have said. They sell them commercially.'

Most of the guests stood around in groups, chatting, but Ella plumped herself down on one of the sofas, and Winnie came to sit next to her.

'What on earth is that woman doing here?' said Ella rather too loudly, nodding towards Jean Burwell who was sitting close to her husband on the opposite sofa.

'Joan has told me. Apparently it was Paul who kicked in those lights on the Burwells' gateposts, and wrecked their Christmas wreaths. They agreed not to go to the police and this is by way of thanking them.'

Ella thumped her knee so hard with delight that a little of her champagne spilled out onto her tartan skirt, which she totally ignored.

'That's the best thing I've heard in a long time!' she chortled. 'I just hope they don't spoil this evening.'

'Shush, dear, keep your voice down. Now, tell me about your poor wrist. Is it getting any better?'

Edward was circulating with the bottle of champagne, topping up glasses. He realized the Burwells' glasses were empty for the third time.

'Do let me know if you would like something soft,' he

said hopefully, but they held their glasses out to him nonetheless.

Just after a quarter to nine, the Lovells arrived. Joan went into the hall to greet her sister and brother-in-law.

'We're so sorry to be late,' said John. 'I was called out to a difficult home birth. I think the mother was trying to hang on so the baby was born at midnight, and I was trying to hurry things along so I could get here.'

'Never mind, you're here now. Go on through and catch up.' She took their coats and was pleased to find Paul had followed her into the hall so handed them to him to take upstairs.

'Tell Dad that I'm going into the kitchen to help Molly. I think the table here could be pulled into position now everyone's here. We'll eat in ten minutes.'

As the grandfather clock standing in the hall struck nine, Edward clapped his hands together, and called people to go and eat. With a piece of paper in his hand on which the place-sittings were written, he organized everyone to their right place in masterly fashion. He was at the head of the dining-room table, close to the side-board where the wine was. Joan was in the hall, near to the kitchen.

'How attractive the table is,' said Phil, as she sat herself between John Lovell and Robert Wilberforce.

Bright red napkins stood out against the white damask tablecloth, and matching red candles flickered in a row of single silver candlesticks set down the middle of the table.

'Can we pull the crackers now?' asked Paul, who was

seated in the hall – in the same room as the Burwells, but thankfully not next to either.

'Certainly not,' laughed his mother. 'That comes much later.'

Harold, sitting on one side of Ella who was seated at a stout chair at the head of the table, noticed that poor Charles had drawn the short straw and was seated next to Jean Burwell and opposite Derek.

Molly and Ben handed round the bowls of soup, a swirl of cream and a scattering of green on top of each.

Harold bent forward and sniffed appreciatively. 'Goodness, that smells good. What's in it?'

'It's tomato and mascarpone cheese,' said Joan. 'I got it off one of the cooking shows on the television. Do you ever watch them?'

Harold laughed. 'No fear, but Isobel does and I'm more than happy to help test her efforts. I don't think we've had this. What are the green bits?'

'That's basil. There's already some pesto whizzed into the soup. Now, do have some of these,' and she passed a pretty china bowl brimming with little golden croutons.

'Can I give you some, Ella?' asked Harold.

'Yes, lots, please, Harold,' Ella replied. 'I can never be bothered to make the fiddly things, but am always willing to eat other people's.'

Little Agnes Fogerty was sitting between Paul and Derek Burwell. For a while she talked to Paul, who had been one of her pupils at Thrush Green School, asking him about how he was getting on at boarding school, then she turned to her other neighbour.

'Now tell me exactly where you live,' she said. 'You arrived in the village after we had left.'

Joan looked down the table and was relieved that Agnes and the Burwells seemed to have plenty to chat about. Charles and Dulcie were deep in conversation nearby.

In his domain in the dining-room, Edward reckoned everyone was getting on well with their neighbours. He was worried for a moment that Jeremy was a little out of his depth since Dorothy seemed to be grilling him, but he relaxed when he heard Jeremy say quite firmly, 'I'm afraid I have to disagree, Miss Watson. I don't see any point in forcing a person to continue with, say, maths and physics when all they want to do when they are older is to be a journalist.'

'Sorry to break up your conversation,' Edward said a little later. 'Jeremy, could you be very kind and help take the plates out to the kitchen.'

The boy leapt to his feet, and collected the plates as bidden.

Edward picked a couple of bottles of claret off the sideboard and took them into the hall. 'Harold, can I put you in charge of wine in here? Ben will bring some white through in a moment. We're eating chicken.'

And so the party went on. The wine circulated, plates were filled and emptied. Some of the men had more.

After the main course plates were cleared away, Edward suggested people should change places so they were sitting next to someone new, including some moving rooms as well as seats. There was a General Post – that is, apart from the Burwells who refused to budge. Joan saw that Dulcie was struggling with the dreary pair, whose conversation appeared to have dried up, so she indicated the young woman should move into her seat, opposite Robert who had come in from the dining-room. She was confident that Ella, still in her big chair at the top of the table, would keep the young couple well entertained. Frank had come to take Charles's place next to Jean Burwell but Joan didn't see why he should have to suffer the stuttering burbles either, so she moved him up and sat down beside Jean.

After making sure everyone at her table was settled, Joan took a deep breath and turned to Jean Burwell. 'I thought the flowers in St Andrew's over Christmas were lovely. Which arrangement were you responsible for?'

She was rewarded with a glassy stare, and then a hiccup.

Oh, Lord, thought Joan, she's pooped. After a moment, she tried again. 'I believe you often go into Oxford. Don't you find the parking very difficult?'

'Spark-an'-ride,' mumbled Jean, desperately trying to focus on her hostess.

'How interesting,' Joan muttered, and inwardly cursed her son for getting them into this situation.

At that moment, Molly and Ben appeared at her side.

'Ah, pudding,' said Joan, thankful for the diversion. 'Which would you like, Jean? Chocolate soufflé or caramelized oranges – or, perhaps a bit of both?'

Jean swung her head unsteadily towards Molly. 'Shlots of shocolate.'

Derek Burwell stared at his wife. Then he waved Molly and the food away and leaned across the corner of the table to whisper in Jean's ear. A moment later, he pushed back his chair and said rather loudly, 'Sorry to break things up. Got to get Jean home. She's not well.'

He pulled Jean out of her chair and pointed her towards the front door.

Joan quickly got to her feet, and put a hand onto Derek's arm. 'Hang on a moment, and I'll get your coats.'

The Burwells just stood there, seemingly oblivious to the spectacle they were creating. Jeremy's young eyes were as big as saucers as he gazed at the apparition in mauve who was being firmly gripped by her husband. Those at the hall table were now totally silent and Edward, sensing from the dining-room that something was amiss, appeared in the doorway in time to witness the Burwells' stumbling exit. Joan shut the front door behind them, leaned against it and said, 'I'm so sorry about that, everyone. I think it's time to pull the crackers. Let battle commence!'

It was just what was needed to get everyone back into the swing of the party, and after bangs and oohs and aahs, and 'oh, it's not fair, you've won again,' all the guests seemed to sport a splendid paper hat on their heads and were soon tucking into the puddings.

It was when the cheese was on the table, and the decanters of port were being passed round, that Robert moved his chair a little closer to Ella.

She stayed her hand that was halfway to her mouth

with a piece of cheese carefully balanced on a biscuit. 'I'm a bit blind, Robert, not deaf!'

'I know, Ella, forgive me, but I didn't want to shout this out.'

'Shout what out?' asked Ella, crunching on the biscuit.

'I just wondered . . . Dulcie and I wondered . . .'

Ella turned her head towards him. 'What did you wonder?'

'If you get all the necessary permissions from the planning department and the Church Commissioners to turn those rooms at the vicarage into an apartment so you live permanently with Charles and Dimity, we, er, wondered . . . would you then be selling your cottage?'

'Have to, wouldn't I? Got to have the cash to pay for the alterations and to pay my rent to Charles and Dim. Why?' But before either Robert or Dulcie could answer,

Ella continued, 'Ah, is it because you two would like to buy it?'

They both nodded intensely.

'Why?' Ella repeated in her forthright manner.

'As you may know, we sold my house in the Lake District a couple of years ago but I have to admit that I miss the country more than I thought I would. Then, with junior on the way, we would very much like to have a foot in the country again. That's one of the reasons why we came down here now – to have a drive and look round. The estate agents won't be open tomorrow, of course, but we might see a board or two. But nothing, nothing,' Robert repeated vehemently, 'would give us more pleasure than to bring our child up in the village where his or her great-great-grandfather was born.'

Ella gazed from one to the other. For once her vision was quite clear, and she could see the passion shining in their eyes.

'Well, I have to say that it would please me, too, to know that someone I liked was going to live in the cottage that has meant so much to me all these years. I was only thinking earlier this evening how awful it would be if those excruciating Burwells, or someone like them, bought the place.'

'So do you think it would be possible?' asked Dulcie, leaning forward excitedly.

But before Ella could answer, Edward appeared in the doorway of the dining-room, calling out, 'It's very close to midnight. Come on, everyone into the hall. Molly, can you turn the kitchen radio to full volume so we can hear the chimes of Big Ben.'

With a great deal of chatter and laughter, the eighteen good friends gathered round the table in the hall and crossed hands. Seeing not only Molly and Ben standing near the door into the kitchen, but Winnie's Jenny as well, Joan broke the circle of hands and called to them to join in. As the chimes of Big Ben echoed through the hall from the kitchen and then the first of twelve booms to indicate the New Year, Frank, in his fine voice, started everyone off on 'Auld Lang Syne'.

> *Should auld acquaintance be forgot,*
> *And never brought to mind?*
> *Should auld acquaintance be forgot,*
> *And auld lang syne!*
>
> *For auld lang syne, my dear,*
> *For auld lang syne,*
> *We'll tak a cup o' kindness yet,*
> *For auld lang syne.*

And as they rather raggedly reached this point, the circle broke up and in a moment everyone was hugging their neighbour. 'Happy New Year!' they called out. Husbands kissed wives and mothers kissed their sons, the men shook each other by the hand. Winnie embraced Jenny saying, 'I had quite forgotten that I was supposed to be going home early. We've been having such a good time.'

Robert took Dulcie's face in his hands. 'Happy New

Year, darling. It's hard to think that this time next year we'll be three. You're going to make a wonderful mother.' He kissed her gently on the lips.

The two of them then turned towards Ella. The large woman held out her good arm towards them. 'Yes,' she said, 'if everything goes to plan, I think my little cottage would like to have you living there.'

'Oh, Ella, how simply wonderful,' Dulcie cried, and flung her arms round Robert. Over her shoulder, he mouthed those simple but such important words to Ella, 'Thank you.'

When the two disentangled themselves, they both embraced Ella, being careful not to squash her bad arm.

It had been agreed at Lulling Vicarage before the start of the evening that it would be wise not to discuss the Grand Plan and Ella had parried enquiries about her future all evening, as had Charles and Dimity.

'Remember,' Ella now said, shaking herself like an old spaniel, 'not a word about this to anyone. There will be plenty of time in due course.'

The party continued unabated. The port decanter circulated, plates of walnuts and tangerines were placed on the table, and those who had been in the dining-room brought their chairs through to the hall. But, as always, good things have to come to an end.

The first to leave were John and Ruth Lovell since John was on call the following morning.

'I'll come round after breakfast,' Ruth said to her sister, 'and help you clear up. Thanks for a wonderful evening.'

Winnie was the next to leave, walking the short distance home with Jenny, her friend and companion. She stood for a moment outside the house where she had lived for so many years, and lifted her face to the almost full moon above. 'It smells to me as though it's going to be a very good new year,' she said, her breath pluming out into the cold air.

An owl, flitting through the chestnut trees on the green, hooted in response.

'Come along in,' said Jenny. 'I think a mug of warm cocoa will settle you nicely for the night.'

Harold and Isobel, with Dorothy Watson and little Agnes Fogerty, made their farewells shortly afterwards.

'It's at times like this that I really miss Thrush Green,' said Dorothy, pulling her coat tightly round her as they set off across the green to the Shoosmiths' house.

'But we're very happy in Barton,' chimed in Agnes.

A voice called out through the dim light round the green. 'Goodnight. An' a very happy New Year to you all.' It was Nelly Piggott, making her way home, having been relieved from baby-sitting duties by Ben and Molly.

'Goodnight, Nelly,' they all chorused. 'And a happy New Year to you, too.'

As Harold closed the garden gate, he turned and leaned on it for a moment. Moonlight was shining down directly onto the statue of Nathaniel Patten a few yards away on the green.

'And you, too, old chap. A happy New Year!' he said, then turned and followed the others into the house.

Phil and Frank walked, arm in arm, the short distance back to Tullivers, the lad running ahead, eager to be re-united with young Alfie. He and Jeremy had made plans to meet the following day.

'That was some evening!' said Phil dreamily, leaning her head on Frank's shoulder.

'Pity about the Burwells,' replied Frank. 'It was a decent idea of Edward and Joan to have them, con-sidering the trouble Paul had caused, but it goes to show that however much you try, you can't get a round peg to fit into a square hole.'

'Shouldn't that be the other way round?' Phil asked.

'I don't know, and I don't care,' answered Frank. 'It's much too late, and I'm ready for my bed.'

The last to leave the Youngs' house was the party heading for Lulling. They had come in Robert's big car and Dulcie, who because of her expectant state had not drunk all evening, drove them home. As had been agreed, nothing was mentioned about Ella's cottage but Ella noticed both turned their heads towards it as the car drove quietly past. She sensed the young couple were very excited.

When they got back to the vicarage, Robert and Dulcie said their goodnights. 'It's been a very long day for junior and his mother,' said Robert. 'It's straight to bed for us.'

'We'll talk in the morning,' was all Ella said, some-what enigmatically as far as Charles and Dimity were concerned.

'What a lovely evening,' said Dimity and, sitting on the hall chair, she took off her shoes. She wriggled her toes in bliss. 'Oooh, that's much better.'

'The best part of every good evening out,' said Ella, 'is coming home.'

'Home?' repeated Dimity, looking up at her old friend. 'I can't tell you how good it is to hear you say that word.'

'Do you remember, Dim,' Ella asked, 'what you said when you were packing your things at the cottage, before you left to marry Charles?'

'Remind me,' Dimity said.

'We'd been very happy there,' continued Ella quietly, 'but I knew some man would gather you up one day. As we were packing your china, I remember saying to you, "It was good while it lasted." And you said to me . . .' She paused.

Dimity smiled. 'I remember now. I said, "It will go on lasting." And so it has proved.'